Steampunk Carnival

by

Cassandra Leuthold

Steampunk Carnival
Copyright © 2014 Cassandra Leuthold
All rights reserved.

Published by Green Hill Press
South Bend, IN

ISBN-10: 0991131959
ISBN-13: 978-0-9911319-5-2

Cover design by Deranged Doctor Design

for the Cianis, Zurawskis, Howlands, Schwalms,
and all of those who have the courage
to cross great distances to forge a new life
in a new country

Steampunk Carnival

1884

Naperville, Illinois

Chapter One

The journal rose to become my lifeline, the only thing I live for. I guard it as my greatest secret, and it haunts me during the day like nothing else. When sweat drips into my eyes, when my hands smear grease across the legs of my trousers, I envision its pristine pages before me. As I close my eyes against the repetition of the machines and the men I work with, I imagine turning the pages, glancing at what I've written to arrive at the first white sheet. I wish they were there so I could fill them, even if oil and moisture bled the pencil's smooth lead across their surfaces.

If I could, I would carry it with me everywhere – to work at the factory, on my strolls through the memorial park, on my visits to Saints Peter and Paul Church. As it is, I leave it buried in the bottom of the drawer beside my bed, beneath newspaper articles and whatever scraps of paper I can find.

No matter what happens during the day, I focus solely on finishing the journal. When my boss drops my wages into my hand, I rush to buy new pencils. When the weather warms, I want to take it outside and make notes in the shade of the mighty oaks. When I feel abandoned and alone, I long to hold it. When the sunlight finds a clean spot on the grimy factory windows and pierces my eyes, I wish I could picture the way it streams through the boarding house glass and falls across the bed where I scribble in the lamplight every night.

Whatever greets me when I arrive home from the factory, I draw out the journal. While a fight rages in the street or someone whistles in the hall or I'm stuffing a roll from my supper into my mouth, I fish a pencil out of the drawer and set its tip to the page. I don't let myself hesitate, and I don't need to. Whatever ideas grew in my head throughout the day fly across the paper. This stolen hour at night is never wasted sitting and thinking. I write without stopping, sheet after sheet until I worry I will run out of paper before my ideas are done.

If I didn't need sleep, I would write through the night, but I make myself stop. I jot down my final thoughts in a flurry and fold the book closed. I fling the pencil in the drawer, nestling the journal in the bottom and concealing it again. In the turmoil of sleep, I dream about it, finishing it, marking that last blank page with lines of lead. The grey strokes intertwine and thicken and twist into a mass until there is nothing recognizable as paper left.

My heavy boots stomp up the wooden stairs of the boarding house. The journal looms closer with every clomp and creak. I follow the hall to my door and turn the knob. I can feel the pages in my fingers, thick and dry, before I have even touched the book. I ease the door closed behind me. I forget my boots on my screaming feet as I drop to sit on the edge of the bed and reach for the hanging drawer pull. I dig out a pencil and shift the loose pages aside.

No matter what I do or how long I look, there's no mistaking it. I cannot find it. Even when I tear the drawer out of the bedstand and shake its contents all over the floor, growling through gritted teeth, no sign of it announces itself. The journal is gone.

1887

Indianapolis, Indiana

Chapter Two

Katya jumped as the office door slammed open. She stood under the great Warden wheel, helping Heinz make sure all the guests had climbed off and no children were hiding in its many compartments. Katya gave her full attention to William Warden as he stormed out of his office, a small building tucked behind the eastern food stall. He raised his fist, holding up what Katya barely recognized in the hazy lamplight as a twisted piece of paper.

Mr. Warden's dark eyes blazed. He glanced from face to face, from Heinz to the man several yards behind Katya closing up his game stall to the cooks in the food stall cleaning up after another busy night. His voice rang out confident but strained. "I won't be threatened." The words echoed off the metal engines and supports of the nearby rides, and the cooks turned their heads. "I'm not afraid of you, whoever you are." Mr. Warden paused, turning the page in the air. He explained, almost casually, "Another death threat."

Katya stepped back, bumping into Heinz and ignoring the exasperation he huffed out under his breath. She had no wish to stand any closer to Mr. Warden than she had to, as if expecting the threat to be carried out immediately now that he had stepped out into the open. She looked to the food stall to see if Magdalene was watching. Even her industrious friend had stopped moving to stare at Mr. Warden along with the other two cooks. Not a single one of the workers spoke.

Mr. Warden tightened his grip on the tortured page. "I won't tolerate this. There will be more security by the end of the week, I assure you." He crumpled the paper until it disappeared inside his fist. He strode back into the office and slammed the door behind him.

Katya was too shocked to know what she thought beyond an automatic fear for her own safety. Workers throughout the carnival buzzed with assumptions and judgments. She heard every sentiment from a worried "Who would do that?" to a hard-edged, mumbling "It's about time."

Heinz muttered to himself, "Does he think it's somebody who works at the carnival?"

Katya glanced at the food stall again. If someone were planning to murder Mr. Warden, she didn't like Magdalene working twenty feet from his office.

Heinz's thick elbow nudged her arm, firm but not impatient. "We're finished here. Go see if anybody else needs help."

Katya walked away, rebuffing his order and heading straight for the food stall, making sure the door to the office remained closed. She did not usually worry about Mr. Warden's reaction when she disregarded Heinz's directions, but under the circumstances, she felt she should. It was not every day Mr. Warden lost his head in front of his employees. Katya needed to reassure herself about Magdalene's safety if not find a good answer to Heinz's query before concern ate a hole through her stomach.

The cooks had returned to work, cleaning counters and smuggling unsold food into sacks to carry home. Magdalene worked her way closer to Katya, scrubbing the surfaces around her with a darkened rag.

Katya leaned toward the high counter, running any possible suspects through her head. "You don't think it's the carriage driver, do you?"

Magdalene kept her voice even lower than Katya's. "It doesn't matter. Whoever it is, they're only angry at Mr. Warden."

Katya's eyes widened in disbelief. "It doesn't matter? After multiple threats? We're alone with the driver every night. If he's that angry, we'll be lucky if the police find us in one piece in the morning."

Irina, her dull eyes anchored deep in her pudgy red face, threw Katya a disapproving scowl. She turned her broad back to the young women to scrub blackened bits from the bottom of an iron skillet.

Katya let out a puff of agitation at Irina's dismissal. "Every paper would report it," she insisted to Magdalene. "That's not how I wanted to get in the paper. I haven't gotten in for getting married yet."

The third cook, an Englishman with a dark, tidy moustache, shoved a cast iron pot into Magdalene's hands. She wiped it down while she answered Katya with distracted assurance. "I don't think it's the driver."

Katya pictured several other workers she didn't know very well. "One of the ticket sellers, maybe. Or the woman who cleans the water closets. We have to ride with her, too."

The Englishman leaned toward Katya. "We don't need your help here. Take your gossip somewhere else."

Katya looked up at him. "You're not worried about the threats?"

The man ducked down to store the clean pots in the cabinets. "Why should I? We've all wanted to take a swing at Mr. Warden on one day or another. I'm sure they'll go straight for him."

Irina peered at Katya, her voice slow and hinting. Her accent was thicker than Katya's with hard vowels and complex, shifting consonants. "Why don't you offer your help to Mr. Warden? You've gotten closer to him than any of us have from what I've heard."

Katya filled her chest with indignant air. She set her hands on her hips, searching every piece of her mind for the best retort she could think of. Only the sharpest and cleverest would do.

Before she could find it, Magdalene waved her away. "Wait for me at the front. I'll only be a few minutes."

Katya sulked at the pompous glint in Irina's eyes and stalked off toward the front of the carnival. She was willing to bet an entire week's salary Irina had never had anything brash or romantic happen in her whole life. If she was not jealous, she should have been.

Walking alone, Katya felt the toll of the chaos and cacophony of the night creep over her. She dotted old sweat off her forehead with the wrist of her glove. The soles of her feet throbbed from strolling the grounds for hours with little time to rest.

Katya passed the Beast, the towering roller coaster at the carnival's center, its metal and wooden frame eerily silent and still. The stage for the band in front of it lay empty, all of the music stands folded under their chairs and the instruments gone home with their musicians. Katya knew every inch of the property and at least one thing about everyone who worked there. She stopped at the corner of the stage, playing Mr. Warden's outburst over in her head. She glanced behind her, where the three cooks rushed to organize their space and Mr. Warden's office stood behind them, tantalizing her. Katya respected Magdalene's request, but there was only one person who could ease her apprehension. She would hurry back in time to meet the carriage. Katya retraced her steps with determined strides, keeping her eyes on the small dark building to avoid Irina's disapproval as she whizzed past the food stall.

Behind the wooden plaque labeled OFFICE, the door remained closed. Katya held her ear against it, her hat shifting to the other side of her head. She grabbed hold of the brim to keep it on. Two muffled voices entered her ear, Mr. Warden and the man glued to his side, Mr. Lieber, head of security. They sounded intense but reasonable. Katya pulled her ear back, straightened her hat, and opened the door.

The first room held two sofas, both of them empty. The two men lurked in the back room through the open door. Mr. Lieber stood on the left, his almost-white blond hair parted on the right and his blue eyes suspicious. Mr. Warden leaned into view from the right where he sat at his desk. Their conversation stopped the moment Katya opened the door.

Mr. Warden eased into a smile, the same twist of his features that made people love and hate him. "It's not a good time to ask for a raise, Katya," he teased.

"I didn't come about that." Katya closed the door. "I was concerned for you when I heard you'd been threatened."

Mr. Warden made a cavalier gesture with no hint of his prior irritation. "It's nothing. We're forming a plan to make sure it doesn't amount to anything."

"But there has been more than one threat?" Katya passed through the first room to linger in the doorway. She focused purposefully on Mr. Warden. She barely knew Mr. Lieber, but his very presence could unnerve her into shivers. Although both men wore expensive, well-fitting suits, the absence of steampunk additions made Katya all the more aware of the gears and clock hand-shaped buttons on her own costume. She handled the guests, and they did not.

Mr. Warden nodded to the nearly full wastepaper basket beside his desk. "Number three."

"Do you have any idea who might be writing them?"

"No."

"Some of us are worried it might be someone close to us, someone who could do us all harm." Katya ignored the impulse to look for Mr. Lieber's response. She could imagine him sneering in approval of the workers meeting bad ends.

Mr. Warden gave no reaction except to warm his voice. "I'm sure you're quite safe. We'll have new security soon."

"Do you think that will be enough?"

"Why not? How is anyone going to kill me if he can't get to me?"

An uncomfortable reflex curved Katya's lips. "Why would somebody want to kill you?"

"I don't know."

Mr. Lieber took a step toward them, his boots thundering on the wooden floor. "Miss Romanova, we have other matters to discuss."

Katya nodded, wanting to talk to Mr. Warden further but feeling Mr. Lieber's brush-off as surely as if he had escorted her out. "I'm sure you do. I'm sorry."

Mr. Warden considered her, his expression hanging between humor and condescension. "If anyone tries to kill you, let me know right away, won't you?"

Katya flashed a forced grin. "Of course." If the joke was meant to relax her, she did not find it very reassuring.

Katya turned and let herself out. She had not learned as much as she wanted to, but she did feel slightly comforted. Mr. Warden would not take any chances with the carnival. He would protect his interests – professional and economical. That meant the staff's safety, too.

Katya rounded the food stall. It sat silent and empty now. Magdalene and the other cooks walked up ahead of her, approaching the ticket booth at the front of the grounds. Katya hung back, keeping her distance until the mustachioed Englishman parted from the women to make his way home on the public, horse-drawn streetcar. Katya resented having to ride with Irina in the private carriage. Mr. Warden spared its expense because the sides of it advertised the carnival to all who saw it. It only served the four women employed there, driven by a man who rarely spoke. Katya did not really believe he hid the kind of anger that led to murder, but he certainly possessed the opportunity since he had so little work to do. He waited in the front of the carriage outside the gate, and Katya climbed up into it after the others. The charwoman already sat inside, her gloved hands folded over her lap. She spoke even less than the driver.

Katya settled in next to her across from Magdalene. Out the window beside her stood the carnival's impressive iron gates and its plethora of signs advertising its wonders. To one side hung the original signboard naming it *William H. Warden's Astonishing Public Carnival, Open to All*. Beneath it hung the newer, slightly larger sign proclaiming, *Come See The Famous & Amazing Steampunk Carnival You've Read About!*

The carriage heaved forward. Katya addressed Magdalene although she knew the others were listening. "I talked to Mr. Warden. He says there's no immediate danger."

Magdalene brushed her fair, curled bangs back from her forehead. "Do you believe him?"

"Of course. He might've told me more if Mr. Lieber weren't there."

"He intends to keep us safe?"

Irina looked over from the view out the window. A streetlight beam radiated off the cogs and metal parts sewn to her hat. "We're a barricade, my dear. We're part of the security he's talking about. If somebody carries a gun through the gate, he'll pass all of us before he gets to Mr. Warden. Or *she*. There are plenty of women who'd like to see him dead, I'm sure."

Katya said nothing. She resolved to wait until Irina and the charwoman had been dropped off at their houses to continue her conversation with Magdalene. When they finally left the two young women alone two stops later, Katya gave a heavy sigh in the dim light of the carriage. "How does everyone know what happened between me and Mr. Warden?"

Magdalene slipped off her red silk gloves, engine gauges embroidered on the backs in pure white thread. "Did you really think he wouldn't tell anyone? Or that nobody would guess? He created a job for you, Kat. He doesn't do favors for anybody else."

Katya thought back to the brief entanglement that had created so many rumors and cynical outbursts. "I needed the work, and I'd rather work for the carnival than anywhere else. It was easy for you. He needed a cook, and you're a cook. If getting close to Mr. Warden got me a job, so be it. It's not like I let him under my corset, just over it." Katya laughed at her boldness. "He let me name my own salary after that."

Magdalene paused, her eyes falling on the dusty floorboards. "Maybe Irina's right. Anyone could be writing those letters."

"Mr. Warden won't let anything happen to the carnival. He can't afford to let word of the threats get out. If the papers knew he was being threatened, there'd be a stockholders' meeting tomorrow. Half of them would want to pull out."

"And Mr. Warden would sweet-talk them back in again. He always gets his way."

"He won't if he's dead. What would happen to the carnival? Who would run it? Mr. Lieber?" Katya imagined reporting to Mr. Lieber, the stern German seated in Mr. Warden's office chair. She shuddered. "I won't work for him. I'd rather sell cookbooks under the guise of charity and keep the money for myself."

"We can't worry about that. He'll get his new security, and maybe there won't be any more threats."

"Maybe." Katya doubted it, but she hoped it was possible.

Chapter Three

Katya spread a thin layer of butter over the broken halves of her roll. As usual, she sat at the head of the large table despite being the newest arrival to the boarding house. The owner, the white-headed Mrs. Weeks, sat at the far end, paying as much attention to the evening newspaper as she did her supper. Her daughter Mary sat beside her, the frizzy curls of her hair drooping from the heat of helping her mother in the kitchen. Lizzie blathered on across from her about a play she had seen recently at the theater. Magdalene, trapped between Lizzie and Katya, munched quietly on sausages and a casserole of baked tomatoes. Katya waited impatiently for Lizzie to stop recounting every person she recognized in the theater crowd, setting her knife down with a sharp *clink* against the edge of her plate.

The metallic clang only seemed to refocus Lizzie's busy mouth. She let her fork dangle from her hand, loosely pointed at Katya. "We finished your embroidery at the shop today. I was supposed to tell you to drop by and pick it up."

The thought of an extra jacket to wear at the carnival preoccupied Katya for a moment. She liked the deep, rich blue of her regular jacket, where Lizzie and her employer had embroidered a large pale-blue and tan compass. She couldn't wait to see the new jacket, a shiny baby-blue satin, embroidered across the back with a design of gears one of the carnival mechanics had drawn up for her. Thoughts of the carnival dragged Katya back to the question she wanted to ask. "Have you heard any recent gossip about Mr. Warden?"

Lizzie raised her eyebrows. "No. Should I?"

"I just wondered if he had done anything particularly rakish lately."

Mrs. Weeks laid her copy of the *News* on the table. "Is he rakish, Katya?"

"Only when it pleases him."

Magdalene spoke up with a more direct answer. "Not everybody likes Mr. Warden as much as others."

Lizzie tittered. "I'm surprised Katya doesn't like him more. He's exactly what we're looking for. He's rich, not too old, and he could charm the bustle off anybody, even Mrs. Weeks."

Katya took a delicate bite of her roll even though she was starving. "Mrs. Weeks wouldn't be interested in a man like that."

Lizzie looked Katya over and clucked her tongue. "He spurned you, didn't he?"

Katya hunched behind her roll. "Wouldn't you like to know?"

Mrs. Weeks lifted the *News* and turned the page. "Another article on Frances Cleveland. You know, of all the first ladies I've seen in my lifetime, she's the youngest and the loveliest. I'm so glad President Cleveland's moved on after all that scandal about the woman in Buffalo."

"What scandal?" Lizzie asked, perking up.

"Don't look at me to repeat it. It happened before your time, and they dug it up during the election." Mrs. Weeks composed herself and tapped her newspaper. "Here's an ad for another one of those cure-alls. Coughs, consumption, headaches, nausea."

Mary stretched her neck up and peeked over the top of the paper.

Mrs. Weeks bent the page down so Mary could see it. "I swear by Ayer's, but I don't know about this one. How can it cure an ache up in your head and take out the swelling way down in your feet? What do you think, Mary? Is it worth a try?"

Mary spoke up in her smooth, gentle voice. "I don't know. It could work."

Lizzie jumped into the conversation. "How much is it?"

Mrs. Weeks consulted the paper. "A dollar twenty-five. You can get Ayer's for a dollar a bottle."

Lizzie threw a grin down the table at Katya. "I bet Mr. Warden could sell anything at any price."

Katya finished her roll and wiped her fingertips on her napkin. "Have you ever met Mr. Warden?"

"No." Lizzie leaned forward, her eyes eager at the thought.

Katya doubted Mr. Warden would give Lizzie the time of day. Despite his faults, he was a dapper gentleman, and Lizzie stayed as common as they came. Katya did not consider Lizzie fit to stand in the same room as Mr. Warden, and she expected he would quickly surmise the same. "Ride out to the carnival, and I'll introduce you."

Lizzie's eyebrows scrunched up, and her shoulders sank forward. "To the carnival? It's so loud there and hot. I much prefer the theater."

"The theater's just as hot, and there's no breeze."

"You don't have to do any walking at the theater."

"Don't expect to meet Mr. Warden, then. He spends all his nights at the carnival."

Lizzie narrowed smoldering eyes at Katya.

Katya finished her dinner and patted her napkin to her lips. She left it on the table as she stood up. "If you'll excuse me, I have to change for work."

"In case your clothes weren't gaudy enough," Lizzie muttered.

Katya slipped her hands down the slim curves of her corseted waist. She liked her clothes bold and bright, and she did not care what Lizzie thought of a single piece of her wardrobe. "Coming, Mags?"

Magdalene took the last bite of her sausage. "Yes, in a minute."

Lizzie straightened her back and squared her shoulders, balancing on the front edge of her chair to see Katya over Magdalene's head. "As if you didn't take longer to get ready than anybody else in the house."

Katya smirked. "As if Mr. Warden didn't want me looking my best."

"You're bluffing. Everybody knows he wants everything about the carnival to be perfect. There's nothing special about you."

Katya folded her hands on top of her chair back. "No? All the guests will see me at one time or another, probably more than once. Mr. Warden stands to gain from having a beautiful, well-dressed woman at the center of everything. Otherwise, I wouldn't be paying you for such detailed embroidery."

Lizzie laid her napkin on the table. The haughtiness drained from her rounded features. "I don't know how you got your job, and I don't care. Get your clothes altered somewhere else if you like. But don't act like I'm nothing because I don't work at the carnival. If it weren't for the seamstresses, the builders, the sign makers, and even the farmers, you and Mr. Warden would have no carnival to speak of."

Katya bent towards Lizzie over the back of her chair. "If it weren't for Mr. Warden's brilliant ideas, none of that business would've happened."

Katya strolled out of the dining room into the long hall running through the middle of the house. She climbed the back stairs and let herself into her room, the second door on the left. Her carnival outfit stretched across the bed, the royal-blue jacket with bronze buttons shaped like gears, a black and white striped dress, and her cream-colored gloves embroidered with a compass on the back of each wrist.

Katya picked up the hat she had selected for the evening. It was completely covered in black velvet, the brim turned up at the sides and in the back. A bronze buckle adorned the band, and green ostrich feathers fanned out liberally over the crown. She set it on her head, arranging the tilt of it in the mirror. She did not care what Lizzie said. Katya was the most extravagant attraction at the carnival, and she aimed to remain that way.

A few light knocks on the door preceded Magdalene easing it open. She stepped into the room and closed the door behind her.

"If Lizzie doesn't know anything about Mr. Warden's death threats, nobody outside the carnival does."

"That's good for him and good for business, but it doesn't help us escape any danger."

"You said you believed him that we were safe."

Katya selected a black-beaded hat pin from the white porcelain holder on top of her dresser and speared it carefully through her hat. "I believe he'll do what he can, but anyone angry enough to send three letters might be willing to take out anyone who gets in their way."

"Don't you think the letters might be empty threats?"

"I haven't had time to think about that. I've been too busy worrying we'll be murdered while we work."

"You don't think the added security will be enough?"

"I'm not sure." Katya turned to look at Magdalene. Magdalene's white and red striped day dress was cut more conservatively than Katya's mint and hunter-green one. Not even the crimson dresses Magdalene wore at the carnival came close to matching the fine details of Katya's costumes. She wondered what Magdalene did with all the money she saved.

Magdalene glanced at Katya's elaborate clothes laid out between them. "I'll get dressed, and we can meet the carriage."

"I wish I had my own carriage. Then we wouldn't have to ride with Irina."

Magdalene tilted her head to one side. "You should be kind to her. She's lost three children."

"I save my kindness for Mrs. Weeks. She lost her husband."

"You don't think Irina suffers?"

Katya tested the placement of her hat pin, and the arrangement barely swayed. "I'm sure she does, but Mrs. Weeks is kinder to me on her worst days than Irina has ever been to anybody."

Magdalene reached for the door handle.

Katya put her hand out to keep her from leaving. "What does she say about me when I'm not there?"

Magdalene clasped her hands in front of her lap. After a pause, she admitted, "She thinks you're privileged."

Katya's mouth dropped open at such a judgmental word. "Privileged?"

"Yes. Spoiled by people like Mr. Warden."

Katya closed her mouth. She could not argue with that. "I buy my privilege with charm. Irina should try it. The results would be much better than what she gets with that sour face."

Magdalene popped the door open. "I won't mention it."

Chapter Four

Lizzie was right about one thing. The carnival made the loudest noises Katya had ever heard.

Outside the gates, the muffled buzz combined the excited chatter of children, the murmuring of adults, and the clacking horses' hooves pulling carriages. Inside, past the ticket booth, two game stalls welcomed patrons with the crashes of baseballs knocking into bottles and the stall runners calling to anyone within their sight. Energetic shouts rang out from the spinning Kaleidoscope on one side while the oohs and ahhs from the rising Tower on the opposite side fell away even at a near distance.

Almost at the center of the carnival, the twenty-eight-piece band played compositions written specifically for it, most of which surged with the same grace and flair as Chambers' *Trombone Section* or Sousa's *Gladiator March*. Competing for the pounding eardrums of patrons and employees stood the Beast, the grandest coaster, an iron monstrosity at the hub of the racket. The loudest shrieks issued from its cars as they climbed to the highest peak and raced through the hollows, curves, and dips back to their starting place. Two smaller coasters contributed surprised to fearful screaming from either side, mixing with calls and applause from the judging of contests held in front of the eastern L-shaped coaster known simply as the El.

In the rear of the carnival, besides the roar of the Beast, the air was surprisingly calm. The third and final game stall rested in the great shadow behind it. The two food stalls flanked the impressive Warden wheel, giving a wide berth to the carnival's most popular attraction. In one of twenty compartments, couples and children could sit and turn higher along the path of the wheel to look out over the southern neighborhoods of the city. The ride would only stop to let new passengers on or old passengers off, returning its riders safely to the ground in a usually awed hush. Except for Mr. Warden's recent door-slamming, the two buildings hidden away behind the food stalls were the quietest, his office and the maintenance men's storage building. Katya kept her distance from the water closets as much as possible, determined not to make herself an expert in their sounds as well. The imposing coaster behind them, the Cannon, served wonders to mask the sound and the smell.

Katya felt at ease striding the grounds, greeting patrons and offering her help. She looked smart in her new pale-blue jacket, and she smiled even wider whenever she caught children pointing excitedly at the painstakingly detailed embroidery. She escorted a family with six children to the western food stall for popcorn, licorice, and root beer. Before Katya could think about crossing the back of the grounds to visit Magdalene, a young couple stopped her to ask about the height of the sky-scraping Tower.

As instructed by Mr. Warden, Katya walked while she talked. "The Tower itself stands sixty feet, but the cars only rise to fifty."

The young man spoke up for his wide-eyed companion. "Is it safe?"

"Perfectly. We've had no injuries since the opening of the carnival, unless you count stomach aches from the eating contests."

"You host contests for eating?"

"Oh, yes. At least once a week. Have you stopped by the side stage? There's pie judging tonight. You should try a piece. It's always the tastiest in the city."

"We might do that."

"Try whatever you like. There's plenty of time left in the evening."

Katya stopped, and the couple looked up, having been led unknowingly to the waiting line for the Tower.

"Enjoy your stay," Katya said and left them to decide if they wanted to ascend it or not.

Katya barely reached the nearest game stall when she saw a woman in faded green step past the ticket booth. She did not know her, but she knew she had seen her several times before. Many guests came to the carnival again and again over the course of its open season, but none of them frowned as much as this woman. In a sea of giggles and shining eyes, this woman was never happier than solemn. Katya kept her distance but trailed along behind her, anonymous in the ever-shifting crowd.

The woman was not in the trimmest shape despite her slender shoulders. Her mossy-green jacket hung bulkily on her frame, loose where it should hug tightly. More than anything else, her hat betrayed her poor economic station or at least her modest choice in fashion. Her bonnet slumped low against her head, its long ribbons tied beneath her chin. Her hair shone black in the light of the gas lamps distributed across the grounds. Aside from her frown, what intrigued Katya were her feet, moving quickly and much more surely than the leisurely pace of all the other patrons. Katya tailed her past the thundering Beast and watched her drift away from the crowd. The woman glanced around nervously before slipping away behind the food stall toward Mr. Warden's office.

Her curiosity fully piqued, Katya swept toward the food stall, eager to tell Magdalene what she had seen. A tugging on her skirt brought her attention to a short, sweet-faced boy in search of his mother. Katya took him by one small, dirty hand and led him through the crowd from one attraction to another until they found his parents. She dotted beads of sweat off her forehead with the finger of her glove, inspecting the palms to find the boy had left a smudge of dirt across the right one. Mrs. Weeks could wash it out for her.

New customers floated through the gates, pointing at Katya, then at the Tower, then to the games and the band playing behind them. Katya beamed, still in love with the thrill of the carnival, knowing she could never be happy to be a patron. She had to work there, in the bustling center of the modern world.

A couple passed by several yards away, the woman piercing Katya from the corners of her eyes. Katya's mouth dropped open as she recognized Lizzie smirking with self-congratulations. Lizzie tightened her elbow's crook around the arm of a doctor Katya had ridden in the park with one afternoon some months before. Katya hardly cared if she lost him to Lizzie, but she gawked at Lizzie's audacity to flaunt it in front of her.

Katya wove through the crowd, headed straight to the food stall where Magdalene would probably be too busy to talk. Sure enough, Magdalene was working with both hands at all times. She took money from patrons, counted out pieces of hard candy from a bowl on the counter, and passed fried dough desserts wrapped in paper from Irina to reaching hands of all sizes.

Katya stepped up to the side counter, standing apart from the line of customers. Magdalene did not slow her pace, pouring a small glass of lemonade and handing it down to a little girl. She glanced at Katya, and that was all Katya needed to know Magdalene was listening. "It's a fine night Lizzie picked to come to the carnival."

Magdalene gave no answer. She took a dollar from the girl's father and passed him back a few quarters in change.

Katya continued. "She's got Dr. Kirby on her arm."

"I thought he was *your* Dr. Kirby." Magdalene raised her eyebrows at the next customer in line.

"He was. He's hers now."

The young man ordered potato chips for himself and peanut brittle for the lady beside him.

Katya spoke up again. "Not that I mind. His mustache is always crooked. You'd think a doctor could afford a better razor and mirror."

Magdalene cracked a smile. She wrapped a piece of peanut brittle in thin paper and handed it to the young woman.

Katya wiped at the dirt smeared across the palm of her glove. "It's been so busy, I haven't been able to ask you about something. There's a woman who comes here – she's here tonight – poking around Mr. Warden's office. Have you noticed her?"

Magdalene took a paper cone full of fried, salted potato chips from the Englishman and passed it to the young man. "What does she look like?"

"Black hair. Not very tall. Awful, sad-looking bonnet. She's too pretty for it and far too young."

Magdalene paused. If she was thinking any condemning thoughts about Mr. Warden, she held them in. "Yes, I've seen her."

"Do you think something's going on? Do you think she might have something to do with the letters he got?"

"Do you mean, has she been writing them?"

"Not necessarily. He could have a situation like Lizzie and I do, where he's seeing two different women close together. Or perhaps she has a suitor who's jealous of him."

Magdalene picked through the change in her palm, restarting her murmured count. "Any of it's possible. We won't be able to figure it out in the course of two nights."

Irina turned to give Magdalene another swirled circle of fried dough. She narrowed her eyes at Katya as a warning.

Katya leaned toward Magdalene and tipped her hat at Irina. "Mr. Warden should use her as head of security."

"Be kind," Magdalene persuaded, dipping her hand into the bowl of candy.

Katya walked away, pulled back into the nightly grind of greeting guests and guiding them all over the grounds. She thought very little of Lizzie and Dr. Kirby, filling her mind with story after story about Mr. Warden and the mysterious woman in green.

Chapter Five

Railroads entered the city from almost every side, welcoming those who could afford to travel as businessmen and tourists. Katya did not normally mind this. She was not born there and had traveled by train to get there herself. She understood the draw of the city and the carnival. She appreciated what the local and traveling carriage trade did for the success of both.

Only when an exceptionally long-winded guest bent her ear did Katya find herself regretting the city's easy access. The woman prattled on for such an inescapable length of time, Katya completely lost track of it. The large woman was stuffed into a golden outfit that made her complexion fall sallow and sickly by comparison. The height of her hat threatened to rival that of the Tower, and although Katya was pleased with herself for getting away with some light rouge across her cheeks, this woman had applied hers with too heavy a hand.

Every time Katya attempted to slink away or open her mouth to interrupt, the woman met the subtle movements with a new or repeated point. "It's been three years since the world's fair in New Orleans," the woman drawled offhandedly. "If New Orleans can have one, so can Chicago. It'd be nice to see something so extensive and universal without traveling."

Katya parted her lips to agree with her.

The woman settled her shoulders. "It's nothing against New Orleans, of course. It's just that Chicago could use the positive publicity."

A short, lanky boy zipped past Katya, making her skirt rustle against the petticoat beneath it. She stared after him, taken aback by his rush during the standstill of her own evening. He clutched a stuffed bear under his arm, its black eyes staring back at Katya with the round hopelessness of the recently kidnapped.

It was one of the toy prizes from the rear game stall, and the man who ran it was close on the boy's scuffed heels.

"Excuse me," Katya muttered to the woman. She left the patron discoursing to herself to follow the game runner and the boy.

The man snatched the boy by the sleeve of his brown jacket. The boy spun and soon got over the surge of courage or mischief that had made him run off with the animal. He stared at the game runner, jerking his arm away from the hand that held his sleeve in place. His short shouts rose on the way to hysterical screaming.

"I'm not going to hurt you," the game runner insisted, his thick Irish voice gentle despite the effort of running after the boy.

The boy was still panicking, tugging his arm repeatedly. "Let go of me."

The game runner let go immediately, and the boy remained in front of him, hugging the stuffed bear. "Do you really need that bear?" the man asked.

"Yes. You can't prove I took it. I won it fair and square."

"I'm sure you did." The game runner looked over his shoulder toward the game stall and Mr. Warden's office beyond it, both of them blocked from view by the Beast's vast inner workings. "If I let you keep it, will you promise not to take – I mean, win – anything else?"

The boy's head bobbed up and down.

"I want an honest promise now, not a lie. Shake my hand like a man." The game runner held out his hand, and the boy gripped his fingers loosely with his own. "That's an oath, then. Can you find your parents by yourself?"

The boy nodded and sped away on his scrawny legs.

Katya blew out a breath. The game runner had been more than generous with the boy, probably risking his job if Mr. Warden found out about the lifted merchandise, and the boy raced off without so much as a thank you.

Katya retraced her steps. The woman from Chicago had wandered off into the crowd. The game runner passed Katya as he returned to his game stall. He apologized briefly to his waiting customers and encouraged the next one in line to take a turn.

A member of Mr. Warden's additional security caught Katya's eye, moving slowly through the crowd. Dressed in a plain, loose suit, the patrons would never know he worked for the carnival rather than attending as a guest. Katya strolled past him, only partially aware that she was looking for the woman in ill-fitting green, half expecting her to emerge from Mr. Warden's office at any moment.

A woman's scream both interrupted Katya's thoughts and merged with them. She darted toward the sound, wondering if it was one of Mr. Warden's proposed mistresses or if fresh death threats were making their way around the carnival. A woman wailed outside the eastern food stall, pointing a bare finger into one of the trash bins positioned around the roofed, open structure.

"My ring," she cried, looking to the others around her. Her eyebrows tented imploringly. "Please. My ring is in there."

Katya laid a light hand on the woman's shoulder. "Did you drop it?"

"I only took my gloves off for a minute, and it slid right off. It's down in there somewhere. It couldn't have fallen far. I don't know how to get it out."

Katya peered into the giant drum. Nothing sparkled up at her. The top of the collected garbage was littered with sheets of paper soaked translucent with cooking oil. Discarded potato chips, unfinished bites of fried dough, and roasted peanuts nestled in among the pages.

The woman wept into her loose gloves until the man beside her, his own ring glinting in the lamplight, handed her a handkerchief.

Katya took a deep breath and pulled off her gloves. "I'll find it for you. Hold on." She passed her gloves to the anxiously watching husband and unbuttoned her jacket. He accepted that, too. Katya rolled her sleeves up and cringed as her bare fingers reached the top layer of trash. She watched her smooth, luminous skin disappear into the refuse, once-desired food items cast aside to turn slimy and lukewarm. Katya dug further, her face twisting at the dozen different sensations that brushed against her from slick oil to rough salt. She tried to erase her disgust for the on-looking couple, knowing full well she would sift through the whole barrel if she had lost a wedding ring.

Katya leaned farther over the rim. The longer she took, the more determination furrowed her face. She would find that ring, and she hoped Irina was watching. How many privileged, lazy busybodies dug through the garbage of countless strangers? Her fingers brushed the sides of the drum and reached deeper. The edge of a paper wrapper scratched at her elbow. Katya stretched her other arm another inch. The tip of her index finger circled a shape it had not found before. She clenched all of her fingers, carefully lifting them up through the garbage to the top.

The woman sniffled, brightening a strained smile as she hung in the balance between drying up and crying new, happy tears. Her husband patted her back.

Katya sighed with relief to see the ring shining amidst the sopping papers. She dropped everything but the ring and brushed as much oil off as she could with slippery fingers. "I'm so sorry. There you are. You should be more careful around the rubbish bins."

The woman accepted the ring with glimmering and gracious eyes. "I will. Thank you so much. I'm sorry for all the trouble I caused you."

Katya looked over her greasy arms. "I'll clean up all right. I might attract a few stray cats before I do."

"Thank you again." The woman slid the ring on and wiggled her finger to test the fit. Despite the shiny trail it left along her finger, she put her gloves on over it. "Can't be too careful now."

Her husband raised his eyebrows at Katya, holding up her jacket and gloves. Katya gestured to the food stall. "Would you mind leaving them at the stall for me? I'll pick them up when I'm clean."

The grateful couple drifted away, and Katya returned her attention to her hands. She cringed in disbelief, trying to shake off some of the clinging residue. On top of the pile, in the packed garbage Katya had dredged up from the deep, rested a stained, cloth-covered notebook. Katya glanced around, but everyone near the food stall was focused on its numerous treats. They were either speaking with Magdalene or reading the priced menu supported above her. Katya took a soiled finger and flipped the notebook open to a random page. She could hardly believe what she saw, not just a drawing of the Warden wheel, but a technical one. Numbers marked the penciled lines, and other figures had been added in black ink. Katya closed the notebook and carried it with her, being careful to hold it close without brushing it against her dress.

Katya picked her way across the grounds, excusing herself as she hurried around slow-moving patrons. A door to one of the water closets swung open. A young lady stepped out, and Katya quickly claimed it behind her. She latched the door and turned to the white porcelain pedestal sink. A small pump hung above it on the wall, and a bar of soap sat waiting in its tray beside it. Katya ignored them both and spread the notebook open across the front edge of the sink. She turned page after page, her dark eyes scanning the detailed drawings, moving swiftly through the excess of information. She had never seen anything like it. She flipped back to the first page, but no one had written a name or a date there.

"It must be Mr. Warden's," Katya murmured. She unrolled a long stream of toilet paper and wrapped it carefully around the notebook. Katya set the mummified blueprints on the toilet seat and began pumping water over her greasy hands. She rubbed her forearms with soap until the oil loosened and left her skin moist but clean. She looked the notebook over while she dried herself, wondering where she could hide it until she could show it to Magdalene. She thought of trying to hide it behind the toilet where none of the patrons would want to touch it, but she did not want to risk the charwoman throwing it out.

Katya stuffed the notebook under her arm and let herself out of the water closet. With her usual air of professionalism, she nodded politely to the patrons as she passed them, crossing the back of the grounds to the food stall. She walked around to the rear of it, where the Englishman was popping corn in an iron skillet of shining oil.

"Did a man give you my things?" she asked.

The Englishman nodded.

"Can you pass them to me, please?"

The Englishman ducked down briefly and extended Katya's belongings over the counter.

Katya offered her thanks and turned away from him, knowing he was already focused on the popping corn instead of her. She unfolded her jacket and tucked the notebook into the shoulder of one sleeve, pressing it in snugly. She folded her jacket up and raised it to the Englishman. "I've changed my mind. It's such a warm night, and it reeks like garbage. I'm sorry for the inconvenience."

The Englishman lifted the jacket from Katya's hand and set it out of sight. His haggard features betrayed the slightest furrow of annoyance. Katya fitted her gloves on and followed the side of the stall toward the endless sea of patrons. She glanced up in time to see Irina shaking her head at her. Katya gave her the cold shoulder and wove herself into the crowd.

Chapter Six

Unlike the night Mr. Warden flared his temper, Katya followed Magdalene's renewed suggestion to wait for her at the front gate. She held her jacket in front of her as she walked, the notebook still disguised inside its sleeve. She wished the others would hurry up. The carriage would not leave without Irina and the charwoman. Irina would not leave the food stall until every pot and inch of counter had been scrubbed to the highest standard. Katya looked over her shoulder as she passed the Beast. The three cooks remained busy inside the stall, not one of them having stepped a foot outside.

Katya heard a familiar voice up ahead that slowed her pace almost to a stop. She pulled her mind away from the notebook, trying to pick out the words in Mr. Lieber's terse expulsions. She did not know more than five words in German, but she understood his tone perfectly.

The carriage waited just past the gates, almost centered between them. The driver sat stiffly in his seat, his eyes pained in a blank expression. The whip hung limply in his hands. Mr. Lieber stepped into Katya's view from where the ticket booth had obscured him. She only saw his face for a flash, but his neck strained with taut muscles.

Mr. Lieber continued his tirade in English. "I've seen you look at her. Do you think she even sees you? The driver of a women's carriage?"

The driver interrupted politely. His English accent was one Katya rarely heard, the vowels loose and slurred between softened consonants. "Mr. Lieber—"

The German raised his hand in a swift jerk. "Mr. Davies, I don't think I need to argue that I have the more commanding stature. Women's eyes are drawn more to me than they are to you."

"I haven't been–"

Mr. Lieber reached up and wrestled the whip from the driver's hands. He swept it up above his shoulder, holding it high. "Are you calling me a liar?"

The driver grimaced and raised his arm in self-defense. "No."

Katya stopped walking, her stomach tightening in a sickening knot. She lingered twenty feet from the ticket booth, hoping that if Mr. Lieber turned, it would partially hide her from him.

Mr. Lieber shrieked at the driver. "Have I not caught you looking at her?"

"Maybe," Mr. Davies agreed. "She is a human being. My eyes might have fallen on her without knowing it."

Mr. Lieber screamed at him. "I should think you would know. Do you pay no attention to the things you see? Are you saying she's unworthy of being looked at on purpose?"

"No, sir."

"Do you see me now?"

The driver nodded, his voice fumbling. "Yes, Mr. Lieber."

"Do you see this whip in my hand?"

"Yes."

Mr. Lieber strode away, disappearing behind the ticket booth and soon retracing his steps. He raised the whip higher, the tips of its falls dangling against his back. "Do you see me whipping your horse?" Mr. Lieber cracked the whip down hard in front of him.

Katya jumped aside so the ticket booth obscured Mr. Lieber's actions. She shuddered uncontrollably, hunched over the jacket in her hands.

The driver interjected again, desperate and forceful. "Mr. Lieber–"

"Mr. Davies, do you or do you not see me whipping your horse?"

The whip slashed the air and cracked when it landed. The horse whinnied, and Katya covered her mouth to keep from crying out.

"I see you," the driver hissed.

"Are you sure?"

"Yes, I'm sure."

Mr. Lieber cracked the whip twice more.

The driver leapt down from his seat. Katya hid herself completely behind the ticket booth. She could barely hear anything aside from the whip slicing the muggy summer air and the horse reacting in protest. Half a minute pounded past before the whip fell silent. Four boots stomped and dragged in the dirt.

"Give me the whip," Mr. Davies demanded.

Something or someone slammed into the side of the carriage.

Mr. Lieber's voice picked up again. "Pay more attention to what you're looking at, or I'll whip your eyes out of your head."

A pair of boots landed nearer to the ticket booth.

The driver called a little louder. "I should've known getting me fired was an empty threat. That wouldn't be good enough for you."

Mr. Lieber's voice sounded closer to Katya. "Pray it is, Mr. Davies. Pray it is."

Katya heard Mr. Lieber walking toward her. She tried to catch her breath, knowing he would be rough with her if he thought she was listening. If he found the notebook, clearly Mr. Warden's property and not hers, very little might keep Mr. Lieber from whipping her, too. Katya stepped out from behind the ticket booth in a smooth motion as if she had been walking the entire time. She tried to lighten the fear tensing her face. She flicked her eyes to Mr. Lieber's, but he was not looking at her. His arm slammed into her shoulder as he passed her, knocking her a few steps to the right. She stumbled forward, determined not to stop and glare at him.

The driver climbed back into his seat, resting the whip across his knees. He rubbed his head through his curly hair.

Katya did not know what to say to him. She opened the carriage door and boosted herself inside. She sat down on the far side of the bench, feeling through the fabric of her jacket in the dim light. Her fingers followed the squared contours of the notebook, still hidden and still safe.

In a matter of minutes, Magdalene and Irina climbed into the carriage with the charwoman not far behind them. Katya forced a smile at Magdalene, content for once to listen to the silence or chatter of the others, whichever they chose. The Englishman and a few other men – game runners, mechanics, and ride operators – made their way toward the gates as well, but the carriage rolled away before they reached them.

Only Magdalene and Irina talked, carrying on a conversation that moved so slowly, Katya might have preferred the monotonous turning of the wheels beneath them.

"He uses too much oil," Irina insisted.

Magdalene shrugged. "It doesn't matter. Unless Mr. Warden has a problem with it, I'm not going to argue with him about it."

Irina leaned toward her. "Oil costs money. When does Mr. Warden ever not care about money? A little oil here, a little oil there. That doesn't matter. But when it's night after night, we're pouring money out into the grass. What if it's too much money? It could be my job."

Magdalene shook her head. "It would be his job, not yours."

"Not with Mr. Warden in charge. Have you ever seen me take money from the customers instead of sweating over the stove?"

"No."

"And you won't. He hides me. He would have me organizing the tools and spare parts in the maintenance building if he could. The lamplight is for pretty faces only."

Katya barely registered that Irina's remark might have been aimed at her. She could feel the flat cover of the notebook pressing against her thigh as her arm rested on top of her jacket.

Irina continued, her words dropping with resignation. "I would be the first to go."

Magdalene shifted on the edge of the bench, her skirt and the bustle beneath it taking up the rest of the seat behind her. "I'm sure with your skills, you could find another job."

Irina cocked a thick eyebrow. "And be asked about the carnival for the rest of my life? I don't think there *is* a life after the carnival, not that many would know. I think it haunts you. It's too big to slink away."

Katya pictured the drawings and plans of it riding in her lap. She wondered how long it had taken Mr. Warden to think of it and sketch all those schematics. It had obviously taken great effort, more effort than most people would pour into their dreams, which only brought her back to her most nagging question. How did the notebook end up in the trash?

Magdalene and Irina's interminable conversation did not end until the carriage stopped in front of Irina's house. Katya glanced out the window at the narrow building with cursory interest.

Irina reached over and patted Magdalene's hand as she stood up. "You're much too kind. I'll see you tomorrow."

Irina let herself down from the carriage and started up the sidewalk to the porch. The carriage lurched forward. The charwoman across from Katya let her eyes drift closed.

Magdalene spoke up gently. "I never get over how quiet it is in the city after the chaos of the carnival."

Katya nodded absently.

"For every engine and instrument and child that screams all night, twice that moves off the street by the time we get out. There's not even a dog barking."

Katya rode on, deciding she definitely preferred silence to unimportant words.

The carriage braked, and Magdalene reached across the middle of the carriage to tap the charwoman's knee. Her eyes flew open, and she offered a sleepy hum of gratitude as she ambled out of the carriage.

As soon as the carriage jolted into motion, Katya leaned her head close to Magdalene's, unable to keep herself from grabbing Magdalene's hand. In a low voice, she confessed, "I have something extremely important to show you when we get home."

Magdalene looked at her with curious eyes, her head dropping to one side.

"It's about Mr. Warden."

Magdalene's expression sobered with concern. "Are you all right?"

"Yes, but what I show you must be our secret."

"Of course."

Chapter Seven

The carriage slowed to rest in front of the grey-sided boarding house. A wooden sign out front spelled the name in easy-to-read letters: *The Weekly Boarder,* followed underneath by the scrolling words *Mrs. Ophelia Weeks, Proprietor.* Magdalene opened the carriage door, and Katya followed her out.

For the first time, Katya felt aware of the driver sitting behind the horse. He was not a nameless fellow worker but someone who had braved Mr. Lieber's wrath. She paused while Magdalene walked ahead to the porch. The driver did not look down at her, his eyes lost in thought against the horse's back.

"Thank you, Mr. Davies," Katya said. "Have a good day." She went up the sidewalk without waiting for a reply. When she reached the porch, she glanced back, and Mr. Davies raised his hand to her in a subtle wave.

Magdalene unlocked the front door, and Katya trailed her into the hall. She started up the front circular staircase while Magdalene bolted the door. Katya opened her room and left the door ajar for Magdalene. Magdalene joined her, closing the door quietly, and Katya turned to face her. She tossed her gloves and jacket onto the bed, holding up the paper-wrapped notebook.

Katya explained in a hush. "I found this in the garbage." She unwrapped the greasy toilet paper, too preoccupied with the notebook to take the oil-soaked strand to the trash. She let it fall to the rug.

Magdalene kept her distance. "What is it? Did you look inside?"

"The first chance I got. Do you know what this is?"

Magdalene shook her head. "What's the big secret? Did you find someone's diary?"

"Better." Katya opened the notebook so Magdalene could see it. "It's Mr. Warden's notes on how to build the carnival rides."

Magdalene pulled off her white gloves and tossed them on the bed next to Katya's. She took the notebook gingerly in her hands. "Why would he throw this away?"

"I don't know."

Magdalene turned the pages slowly. Her cornflower-blue eyes scanned each drawing fully. "It's not just the rides, Katya. There are pages on how to lay them out across the grounds."

Katya stepped around to Magdalene's side, and they stood staring at the notebook together in the middle of the room.

Magdalene turned back a page and pointed to the bottom. "This one puts the food in front behind the ticket booth as one long stall." She showed Katya the next page. "This one has two smaller food stalls but still in the front of the carnival."

"Why would he throw this away?"

"Are you sure it's Mr. Warden's?"

"Whose else could it be? There's no information in the front. I checked."

Magdalene perused the first few pages of the notebook. "It's just pictures of engines and how they work."

Katya remembered her trembling fear while Mr. Lieber argued with Mr. Davies and beat the carriage horse. "You understand why we have to keep this a secret, don't you? Mr. Warden obviously wanted to hide this. He never thought anyone would find it. It was halfway down the trash bin, the one closest to his office."

"It smells like it, too." Magdalene extended the notebook a few inches away but continued to flip through it.

"Why would he want to destroy this?"

"I don't know. Do you think it has something to do with the death threats?"

Katya tried to connect the two but could not. "Everybody knows Mr. Warden built the carnival. Destroying his notebook isn't going to erase everybody's memory."

"Maybe he wrote something else in here, something personal." Magdalene turned the pages more quickly. "It's just one drawing after another, isn't it?"

Katya watched the schematics flip by, plans for the Tower and other attractions she did not recognize. A few of them were crossed out with a simple ink line. "If it weren't for the circumstances, I'd love owning this book."

"What circumstances?"

Katya grimaced at the thought of Mr. Lieber's whip cracks. "I'm afraid to have it. I like Mr. Warden, but I don't trust him. If he really were trying to destroy this and finds out we have it – *I* have it – I could be in big trouble."

Magdalene turned past pages of several different plans for the Warden wheel. "Maybe Mr. Lieber threw it away."

"He wouldn't do it unless Mr. Warden told him to."

"Unless they're not as close as everyone thinks."

Katya walked to the dresser and unpinned her hat in front of the mirror. "If that's the case, we don't know anything for sure."

"Are you still trying to solve the death threat mystery?"

Katya dropped the hat pin into its holder and laid her hat on the dresser. She turned to Magdalene, a new realization chilling her blood. "Mr. Warden hired the new security to keep us safe."

"Yes."

"No. I think Irina was right. The security is to keep Mr. Warden safe. Everything is to keep him safe. I passed one of the new guards tonight within fifty feet of the woman who screamed when her wedding ring fell in the trash. I was the only one who responded. I never saw security again. If the security is there for everyone, wouldn't one of them come forward to help a screaming woman?"

Magdalene reached the last page of the notebook and folded it closed. Despite its exhilarating content, she set her mouth in a frown. "I'd hope so."

"Did you find anything personal in there?"

"No. Most of it's filled with plans. The last third or so is blank."

Katya took the notebook from Magdalene. "Where can we possibly hide this that not even Mary or Mrs. Weeks will find it? You know how thoroughly they clean."

Magdalene glanced around the room. "You could wrap it in fresh paper and hide it in your underwear drawer."

"And have all my corsets smelling like old peanuts and stale popcorn? No, thank you."

"Do you have a better idea?"

Katya's eyes searched every drawer and corner of the room. "I could put it under the dresser."

"It's too high. They'll clean there."

"I could keep it in the sleeve of a jacket I leave hanging in the armoire."

"Then all of your clothes will smell."

Katya opened the top drawer where she kept her corsets, an array of blue, purple, and silver silks adorned with lace. "I could keep the notebook here and move my corsets to other drawers."

"Now you're thinking."

"We don't have anything to wrap it in."

Magdalene took a moment to think. "Mrs. Weeks puts her old newspapers in the garbage before she goes to bed. Today's issue should be pretty clean."

Katya passed the notebook to Magdalene. "Do you think she'll miss it?"

"Grab the middle pages. She'll never notice."

Katya sat down on the bed and loosened the lacings on her boots. She pulled them off and set them on the rug. "Which garbage are they in?"

"The kitchen. She cleans it up before she finishes reading the news."

Katya searched Magdalene in wonder. "How do you know all this?"

"I've lived here much longer than I've worked these crazy carnival hours. I used to see her do it every night. If there was a paper in the house, this is what she'd do with it."

Katya grabbed a book of matches from the dresser. She struck one and lit a small glass lamp from the dresser. "Wait for me. I'll be right back."

Katya slipped out of the room and took all the care she needed to close the door with only the slightest bump. She hurried to the front staircase where she could disturb only one person, the gently snoring Mrs. Weeks. The other front room belonged to the awake and elsewhere Magdalene. Katya descended the stairs almost silently, not stopping when she reached the first floor. She continued into the basement, the air noticeably cooler against her skin. She turned and entered the first room on the right, a spacious kitchen stocked with everything Mrs. Weeks needed to cook for her boarders. The fireplace sat cold and dark.

Katya had not visited the kitchen for anything but her afternoon hair curling for months. She was grateful the lidded trash bin was easy to see, tucked under the edge of the large prep table. She slid it out and set the cover on the table. Like Magdalene predicted, Mrs. Weeks' newspaper sat neatly folded on top of the fragrant garbage. For the second time that night, Katya reached into the trash and lifted out something valuable.

The headline shouted, *Bell's Latest Experiment Another Failure*. In smaller letters beneath it, bolded words elaborated, *Alexander Graham Bell insists he will perfect the machine that could replace the telegraph, but a decade of failures leaves many skeptical.*

A pang of homesickness struck Katya for New York and the family she had left behind. She remembered her parents talking about Alexander Bell when she was a girl and how close he thought he came to passing the human voice through telegraph wires. Even though a widely publicized accident with battery acid scarred his hands almost beyond use, his assistant Thomas Watson stood by him through every experiment while their benefactors came and went. Katya wished more than ever someone would invent something better than the telegraph. Letters and telegrams took too long for her youthful impatience, and she would have welcomed the chance to hear her mother's voice from so far away.

Katya pulled the middle sheets of the newspaper out and left the outer pages in the garbage. She eased the lid onto the bin and crept back to the stairs. She climbed them, careful to keep the newspaper away from the flame in the lamp. With a little maneuvering, Katya freed a few fingers from the newspaper and opened the door to her room.

Magdalene sat in the corner chair, staring intently at the drawings in the notebook.

Katya closed the door. "You wrap it, and I'll make room."

Katya passed the newspaper to Magdalene and crossed the room to the dresser. She set the glass lamp aside and rearranged the contents of her drawers, listening to the crisp crinkling of the newspaper behind her.

Magdalene carried over the tightly wrapped notebook and set it in the empty drawer. "It's such a shame. It should be on display somewhere, not hidden in here."

Katya blew out the light in the lamp and returned it to its place on the dresser. "I know, but it's too dangerous for that now."

"Maybe Mr. Warden is dangerous, which means the carnival will be dangerous as long as he owns it."

Katya pushed the drawer closed, shutting the package out of sight. "Mr. Warden can't be all bad, or he wouldn't need Mr. Lieber to do things for him."

"That's who you're really afraid of, isn't it? Mr. Lieber?"

Katya nodded stiffly.

"Have you told Mr. Warden he frightens you?"

"No. There's no point."

"I thought maybe he would listen to you. None of the women are comfortable around Mr. Lieber."

"There are only four of us. He wouldn't fire Mr. Lieber if I took all my clothes off and danced around his office. The two are inseparable. It's hard to talk to Mr. Warden without Mr. Lieber there."

"But you were alone with Mr. Warden when he..." Magdalene chose her words discreetly. "...gave you your job?"

"Yes." Katya appreciated Mr. Lieber's absence on that cool afternoon. She remembered introducing herself to Mr. Warden, noticing how handsome his definite features made him. She could not have guessed they would share a tight embrace in the back room of his office. He proved more than pleasing to look at, employing strong, supple fingers. His mouth explored hers expertly. The pressure of Mr. Warden's hands against her corset and her breasts beneath it raised goose bumps on her skin just to think about it. And she had thought about it countless times since then. With a breath, Katya returned her focus to Magdalene and Mr. Warden's less-appealing qualities. "It may have gotten me a job, but it taught us from the start what kind of man Mr. Warden is."

"And you're sure he's not as bad as Mr. Lieber?"

"Quite sure."

"What do we do with the notebook now?"

Katya lowered her eyes to the unassuming surface of the closed dresser drawer. "We wait and see if anyone mentions it. We wait and hope we're not the next to get death threats."

Chapter Eight

The youngest employees at the carnival were boys, the same ages as some of the carnival's biggest fans, between eight and fourteen. Like the inconspicuous security, few guests noticed them in their dark attire, but Katya watched them at work. They stayed mindful of the crowd as they wound their way through it, carrying buckets of water from the pumps in the rear of the carnival to whichever ride needed them the most. They rarely spilled a drop, developing their arms, shoulders, and chests to three times the size of their peers. Katya did not trouble herself with all the politics she saw complicating the front pages of Mrs. Weeks' newspapers, but she found herself supporting talk of more laws against child labor. Mr. Warden defended his hiring practices by saying these boys' families needed the additional income and he hoped their nights at the carnival would build the foundation for a dependable work ethic. Laboring at the carnival kept them out of the factories and off of the farms. From what Katya had heard around the dinner table, she was more inclined to agree with Mrs. Weeks. Mr. Warden and other business owners like him were cutting costs by hiring children. They saved money on women's wages, too, which made Katya duck her head with guilt at her higher salary. It was common knowledge that carnival employees made more than the average worker, but it did little to make Katya feel better.

A pair of boys waddled toward the Kaleidoscope at the front of the carnival, low-hanging buckets weighing down each arm. They set the buckets on the ground beside the ride's operator, waiting for him to open the hatch to the boiler tank, as Katya had heard it called. Next to the boys, the ride operators' costumes seemed all the paler and brighter. Mr. Warden meant the boys to blend in and all but disappear in the night. The ride operators and game runners dressed to be seen, their well-tailored jackets and pants embroidered with curling steam ripples or gleaming golden gears. Seamstresses had fastened many of their jackets with clasps and hooks rather than buttons. Their top hats, like several of Katya's, sported metal buckles on the bands.

After a few hours near the front of the carnival helping various guests, Katya wandered toward the rear. Another pair of boys carried buckets toward the engine tucked neatly beneath the Beast. Without warning, they scampered away, ditching the buckets, which landed hard in the grass. An explosion thundered out of the engine. Katya's arms flew up to shield her, but nothing touched her. Little debris decorated the air and the ground, mostly small metal scraps and bolts. Katya wrapped her arms around herself to try to stop her body from shaking.

Now the security appeared, revealing themselves in their plain clothes by approaching the Beast while the patrons shrank back. Katya lingered where she was, a safe distance from the coaster's west side. She had a perfect view of the band stage where two security men briskly motioned the musicians to safety. For the first night since the carnival opened, the marches stopped, leaving the air bombarded only by voices and grinding machinery. The giant Beast rumbled to silence as the moving cars slid down the track and turned into the resting station behind the vacated stage. One of the operators helped the patrons out of the cars, reassuring them that they were completely safe.

Katya knew the real drama unfolded behind the coaster where the workers accessed the engine. She crept past the Beast, numerous patrons pausing to watch the activity before moving on to working attractions. Mr. Warden strode from his office toward the Beast faster than Katya had ever seen him move. Mr. Lieber kept in step beside him with a plainly dressed security man on his other side.

"What happened?" Mr. Warden bellowed at the ride operator studying the engine hatch.

"I don't know. It just blew."

Mr. Warden shoved the man out of the way. "What do you mean you don't know? Do you know how much money this makes in a night? It's second only to the wheel. Where's maintenance? They'd better be on their way."

"Security went for them."

Mr. Warden turned toward the maintenance office, meeting Katya's gaze in the process. He returned her watchful stare for several seconds before shifting to greet the maintenance man hurrying toward him.

"Can you fix it?" Mr. Warden barked before maintenance had even reached the engine.

"Let me have a look, sir." The maintenance man stepped past Mr. Warden, lowering his tool box to the ground. He examined the engine parts with thickly gloved fingers and heavy-lidded eyes. His drab, dark brown clothes turned him into part of the machine, he stood so close to it. "Here's the problem, Mr. Warden. This valve right here leading up from the boiler."

Katya stretched her neck for a better view but could not see past the posts to what the man was indicating. She relaxed a little at the hope the incident was over.

"Can you fix it?" Mr. Warden repeated.

After half a minute, the man answered, "No. I'm not sure I can. I could look at what tools I have."

"Tools!" Mr. Warden exploded. He adjusted his jacket and lowered his voice. "I expect this machine up and running by the time we open tomorrow, or you are never stepping foot on these grounds again. Do you understand me?"

"Yes, sir. I'll just get more tools."

"Get your tools," Mr. Warden growled amidst the sounds of the running coasters.

The man slunk away toward the maintenance building. Mr. Warden led Mr. Lieber and the plain security back to his office. Katya couldn't see where the ride operator had gone, likely around the front of the coaster to help the other man appease the disappointed crowd.

Katya almost walked away, the spectacle of danger and argument completed. An unexpected figure passed beneath the giant coaster to the broken engine, rekindling Katya's interest. The bearded game runner spent more than a minute there, his cream-colored suit with pale blue embroidered smoke wafting over it standing out against the dark metal and wood. He returned to his stall by the time maintenance returned holding a few extra wrenches in his hands. Katya strolled on, continuing her rounds. As she passed the Beast's engine, she heard the last words she expected from the maintenance man.

"It's fixed."

Katya stopped and stared at him.

The man glanced around, as confused as she was but much more enthusiastic. He toggled a few levers and swiped his finger over a hole where a bolt might have been.

"It's been fixed?" Katya called to him.

The man nodded and tested the sturdiness of a vertical pipe. "The valve's working. I'll have the rest of it fortified by tomorrow."

Katya doubled her pace, avoiding eye contact with the game runner as she passed his stall. He explained the rules to his customers as if he had never left the booth, as if he understood nothing more complicated than its game. She swept straight across to the food stall and the opening at its back. She grabbed Magdalene's arm, making the light change jump in her hand.

Magdalene barely held her composure. "What are you doing?" she asked.

"We have to talk." Katya pulled on her arm.

"We're very busy." Magdalene managed to pass the change to the first person in line.

Katya forced a wide smile for the customers. "We'll be right back."

Katya dragged Magdalene out of the stall. Irina cussed loudly under her breath in Russian, but Katya moved on, steering Magdalene past the harmonica-playing contest on the side stage to the vibrating end of the El. Its cars whizzed down the track above them, curving back the same direction they'd come from.

"You're going to get us fired," Magdalene insisted.

Katya stuck her head close to Magdalene's. "The game runner just fixed the Beast."

"What?"

"The Beast. Steam pressure broke a valve or something. Maintenance wasn't sure he could fix it. He was gone for one minute, and I swear, the game runner fixed it before he got back."

"Who are we talking about?"

Katya hesitated. "I don't know his name. He's the one everyone calls the Mick."

"I don't know his name, either," Magdalene admitted regretfully.

"I thought you knew everybody."

"Not him. Nobody knows him."

Katya pulled back a few inches to look Magdalene in the eye. "Everybody knows one thing: he's a game runner. That's all. How can he fix the Beast when maintenance can't?"

"Maybe he had access to the notebook you found. He could've stolen it from Mr. Warden and thrown it out when he was done."

"Everybody's a crook around here." Katya folded her arms and recalled the only clear memory she had of the game runner, watching him chase down the bear-stealing boy. He seemed too gentle and conscientious to steal Mr. Warden's private papers and leave them in a garbage bin. "What do you think he could've gained by learning about the rides? Do you think he'd rather work with them than the games?"

"I don't know. Mr. Warden seems more the type to take what he wants."

"He hasn't taken me," Katya grumbled.

Magdalene grabbed hold of Katya's arm, shocking her with the firm, sudden grasp. "Who would know these machines better than anybody?"

Katya searched her face, too dumbfounded to pull away. "Mr. Warden."

"Not a name. Who?"

"The person who invented the carnival."

"What if that person wasn't Mr. Warden?"

Katya pointed halfway across the carnival to the game stall. "You think that haggard man who spends his nights talking people into spending their hard-earned money to try to win stuffed toys and trinkets invented this carnival?"

Magdalene raised a hand in defeat. "Then you tell me how he knew what to do."

Katya remained silent, trying to find another explanation.

"I think he started the notebook, and it ended up in Mr. Warden's hands one way or another. Mr. Warden built the carnival, knowing it wasn't his. It explains why there are two kinds of marks in that book. The original pencil, and Mr. Warden's fountain pen."

"Why would the game runner come here?"

"How could he stay away? If he imagined all this, of course he'd be here. He might've sent those death threats to Mr. Warden."

Katya shook her head. "I don't know, Mags. He seems so nice."

"Even the nicest of men would be driven mad by something like this. If he created all this, he's a genius, and he deserves the fortune Mr. Warden's been amassing from it."

"Maybe he gave the notebook to Mr. Warden. Maybe he's a silent partner."

"Silence and the Steampunk Carnival don't go together, Kat. If he were a partner to Mr. Warden, somebody would know about it. He'd be doing what Mr. Lieber's doing, wearing a nice suit and sitting around the office while the rest of us work for our money."

Katya could not argue with Magdalene anymore. Her head spun from the suggestion that the biggest scandal at the carnival was its very existence.

Magdalene took Katya's hand between hers. "Do you agree we should talk to him about the notebook?"

Katya stared at her, petrified. "Mr. Warden?"

"No, the game runner."

"Do you really think he'd talk to us?"

"Let me do the talking. I'll figure out exactly what to say."

Chapter Nine

Katya escorted the last of the patrons past the ticket booth and waved to them as they meandered through the gates. The plainly dressed security had already disappeared from the grounds. Katya busied herself until Magdalene finished cleaning up the food stall. She rounded the entire carnival, offering her services to every employee she saw except the bearded game runner. Katya ended up in the other food stall, scrubbing browned and blackened sausage bits from the bottom of a cast iron skillet. She kept an eye on the game runner while he closed up his stall, arranging the toys and souvenirs so they sat straight and welcoming on the shelves.

The game runner exited his stall, pausing to look over his work. Katya's panicked heart shook her ribs with its pounding. If he left the carnival, she and Magdalene would have to wait even longer to talk to him. She wiped the skillet dry and set it on the counter. She hurried out of the stall and approached the game runner before he could disappear.

"Excuse me," she said breathlessly.

The game runner tipped his hat, lowering his eyes with self-consciousness. "What can I do for you, Miss Romanova?"

Katya started. "How do you know my name?"

"Everyone knows who you are, miss."

By the game runner's tone, Katya assumed he meant this as a casual compliment more than a jab at her reputation. "I'm afraid I don't know yours."

The game runner offered a small, wry smile. "You don't need to."

Katya gestured to the game stall. "I was wondering if you wouldn't mind showing me the way the game works. Do you have time?"

"Of course." The game runner walked over to the stall. He did not sound as accommodating as he was trying to be, but Katya could not let it bother her.

Katya glanced at the far food stall. Magdalene was still there beside Irina and the Englishman.

The game runner lifted several glass bottles from underneath the counter and arranged them on the table below the prize shelves. "You're sure you haven't played this before?"

"Never."

The game runner held out several painted wooden rings. "It's simple. You stand behind that counter there and try to toss the rings so they land around the tops of the bottles."

Katya leaned toward him. "No, how does it really work? I know the games are rigged. I'm just not sure how."

The game runner pursed his lips ruefully and lifted three more wooden rings from underneath the counter. "Some of the rings are a little smaller." He held the second set out near the ones in Katya's hand. She might not have noticed the difference if she did not see them side by side. "These are sized to barely fit over the mouths of the bottles. Even a direct hit would be hard to catch around them."

The game runner ducked down and rose with a third set of rings. "The ones I gave you are the normal ones. These are sized a little bigger so it's easier for certain people to win a prize."

"What sorts of people?"

"I can't give them to children very often. If they all start winning prizes, people will get suspicious. Mr. Warden's very strict about that."

The rule seemed to pain him to say it, but Katya could not tell if it was the name or the restriction that stuck in his throat.

The game runner flipped the rings over in his hands. "I usually give them to a parent or sometimes the man in a young couple so he can win a prize for his lady."

"That's very kind of you."

The game runner shrugged. "More suggestions from Mr. Warden."

Katya studied the game runner. She had never stood this close to him before or paid him this much attention. He was younger than his beard and the unruly hair escaping his hat made him look from a distance. Katya realized she had mistaken him for five or ten years older. Whether he was younger or older than Mr. Warden, she could not guess.

"Do you want to play?" he asked.

Katya nodded. The game runner stepped aside, and Katya bought Magdalene's plan a few more minutes. She edged up as close to the counter as she could.

The game runner smirked good-naturedly. "I can't let you lean over the counter."

Katya inched back. "What's the point in rules if the whole game is rigged?" She tossed the rings one at a time, each ring bouncing off the bottles before she tried the next one with no success. "I'm a horrible aim, aren't I?"

"Try these." The game runner offered her the larger set of rings.

"Do these really work?" Katya made sure she was not bowing over the counter and tossed the first ring. It danced around one of the bottles' lips before diving to the side. Katya whooped with delight and steadied herself before she tried again. The ring landed around one of the bottles on the right. "It only took me five tries."

"Some people never get it."

Katya handed the final ring to the game runner. "How do you keep all the rings straight?"

"It takes a practiced eye for slight variations in diameter." The game runner collected the rings from the ground, the table, and the bottle's neck. He put them away under the counter. "There are several sets down here. Sometimes a customer asks for another set if he thinks the ones he has are rigged. I have to give him another identical set, or he'll know they are." The game runner stored the bottles away.

"You haven't worked here the whole time the carnival's been open, have you?" Katya asked, trying to remember.

"No, miss. It was open a few months before I came here."

"Do you know what happened to the man you replaced?"

The game runner adjusted the fit of his hat. "I don't know exactly. I offered to work dirt cheap because I needed the job, and within a few days, there was this opening for me."

Katya stopped herself from asking more questions. She sighed gratefully as Magdalene breezed up to her side.

"Good evening, Miss Harvey," the game runner greeted her.

"Good evening." Magdalene brushed sweaty curls back from her forehead. "How are you?"

"I'm fine, miss. And you?"

"Fine, thank you. I'm glad you're still here. We wanted to talk to you."

The game runner raised his eyebrows, but he did not look completely surprised. "Oh? What about?"

"We found something we think might belong to you. We found a notebook full of plans for the carnival."

The game runner's mouth dropped open, his composed facade breaking quickly. He wiped his sleeve at his forehead. "You found the journal."

"So it's yours?"

The game runner motioned with his hand for her to keep her voice down. "We can't talk about this here. Would you be willing to meet with me?"

Magdalene nodded.

"Do you know the church St. John the Evangelist? They've been leaving their doors open to the homeless at night. We can talk in there."

"Yes. Mr. Davies will take us."

"Thank you." In a desperate whisper, the game runner added, "You don't have it with you, do you?"

"No, I'm sorry. We've kept it hidden. It's safe with us."

"It's better that way, at least for now." The game runner stepped out of his stall. "I'll take the streetcar. I'll be there as soon as I can."

"We'll wait for you."

Katya and Magdalene walked away. When they passed the Beast and saw the carnival carriage waiting for them outside the gates, they moved a little faster. Magdalene sidled up alongside Mr. Davies and gestured for him to lean down to her. Katya climbed up into the carriage with Irina and the charwoman. Irina looked her over sharply, and Katya pretended not to mind.

Mr. Davies uttered a quiet, "Yes, miss," and Magdalene claimed the empty seat next to Katya.

Mr. Davies drove them into town, straight up Madison Avenue toward the city's circular heart. Katya tapped her foot impatiently to the striking of the horse's hooves. Mr. Davies stopped to let Irina and the charwoman off at their homes in the western neighborhoods before changing his route and turning east down Washington Street. The carriage turned again when it reached Circle Park and slowed to resting outside the twin towers flanking the gothic facade of St. John's Church.

Katya and Magdalene descended to the sidewalk.

Mr. Davies slid to the near end of his seat. "Are you sure you want to be here at this time of the morning?"

Magdalene considered the church, her expression pensive. Katya could see the concern in her eyes. "We're waiting for someone. We won't be alone very long."

"You're meeting a man, Miss Harvey?"

"Not for the reason you think. Do you think I would?"

Mr. Davies' bunched shoulders relaxed. "No. Please be careful, ladies."

"We will," they chimed in together.

Reluctantly, Mr. Davies returned to the center of his seat and flipped the horse's reins. He rode away down Tennessee Street.

Katya listened to the retreating carriage and night sounds of animals prowling the maze of nearby allies. "Do you think we're safe?"

"We have no choice." Magdalene studied the church's architecture, a large round window high in the center above an impressive, peaked doorway. "I'm sure we're fine. Just be quiet until the game runner gets here."

Katya nodded. "I wish I wasn't dressed so well."

"You could take your jacket off."

"Not at this hour."

Magdalene walked up to the church and reached for the door handle. Katya stayed close behind her, and they slipped into the front hall. Except for occasional rustling in the next room, the church sat still and silent. Katya and Magdalene crept forward toward the sanctuary, the largest room Katya had ever seen. Even in the dim light of a few lamps, she could see the ceiling arching up two or three stories to curve over their heads. At least two dozen rows of pews stretched out in front of them before the dais. The rustling continued from some of the pews as people shifted positions, their heads, elbows, and feet occasionally knocking against the wood.

Magdalene ushered Katya into the first pew on the right, and they sat huddled, looking around the room. Katya did not know how many homeless had crawled into the church pews for a secure place to rest. She hoped the game runner knew what he was doing meeting them there. Their voices could carry anywhere in the cavernous room, waking the sleeping and feeding them the unfortunate business of the country's most interesting attraction.

Chapter Ten

Katya remembered Mrs. Weeks following the newspapers closely for months while the inventor Thomas Edison struggled with his experiments on electricity and light. Katya had paid the most attention to the articles that mentioned how his work, if successful, could be applied for purposes of entertainment. Unlike Mr. Warden's carnival, the visionaries speculated, rides and coasters could be run on electricity rather than steam. Instead of so many gas lamps creating heat and fire hazards, light bulbs would more efficiently illuminate the night. Some said the bulbs would stand on posts as the gas flames did already, and others ruminated the bulbs could be hung in strands strung over the grounds. Light bulbs could brighten the top of the Tower, the spokes of the Warden wheel, and the tracks of all three coasters.

At the time, seated comfortably in the Weekly Boarder's dining room, and even now, occupying the solid wooden pew waiting to find out if the carnival could indeed be referred to as Mr. Warden's, Katya denied the idea that the carnival could be improved through such an innovation. Whoever had created it put the best technology of the times to new uses, and Katya respected that. The withering heat of the gas lamps, exploding valves, and chugging machines were small prices to pay to work there or enjoy it as a patron. Katya had fallen in love with the carnival's grandeur the first time she saw it advertised on a poster: *Management seeks qualified workers for all positions!* She had lost her breath when she saw it in person and entered its hallowed grounds. It still struck her with its ingenuity and gleaming presence every night she worked there. Electricity could no more improve it than a phonograph could replace the musicians in the band.

Katya glanced toward the door, but no one had moved much in the time she and Magdalene had been waiting. The more she thought about the carnival, the more she wanted to know the truth. Was it Mr. Warden's success, or did it belong to this man whose name no one knew?

The front door of the church creaked open. Katya exhaled with relief and patted Magdalene's hand.

The game runner stole into the room, and Magdalene waved to catch his attention. He sat down beside her in the pew, lowering his hat to rest on his thighs. Katya leaned forward to see him past Magdalene.

"What's your name, sir?" Magdalene whispered.

"Brady Kelly."

Katya spoke up with insistence. "How come you'll tell her and not me?"

Brady's apologetic eyes flicked to Katya's face. "It's nothing against you, Miss Romanova. I didn't want to speak my name at the carnival. Mr. Warden knows that name, or at least he should. He stole that notebook from me. I've spent three years trying to get it back."

"You invented the carnival?"

"Yes."

Magdalene picked up the conversation again. "That's what we don't understand, Mr. Kelly. How did Mr. Warden use your ideas to do what he did?"

Katya interrupted. "More importantly, how did you ever think of the carnival? What inspired you to draw such fabulous things?"

Magdalene glanced at Katya, not so much condemning as wondering how creative brilliance rivaled the underhanded nature of Mr. Warden's accomplishments for what they needed to discuss.

Brady moved his hat to the empty space beside him, his fingers clutching the brim. "I'm not sure I can answer all your questions, ladies, but I'll try." He fiddled with his hat, rotating it one way and then the other. "I had a family once, in Illinois. My wife, Sarah, cleaned houses so we could afford our own to raise our little boy, Nathaniel. They made me so happy, I would've lived with them anywhere. I was already working with engines and machinery, fixing and designing them. I thought, what would be more perfect than a place for families to go where they could enjoy themselves and see something they couldn't see anywhere else?"

Brady pulled his hat into his lap, his fingertips tapping a jittery dance against the band. "Nathaniel caught diphtheria when he was three. I'd already started the journal – my notebook, as you call it. I had some basic ideas of how to connect the steam engines to the gears that would make the rides move. He died never seeing more than that, just my drawings." Brady tore at his hat brim, pulling it and folding it. "Have you ever listened to someone dying from diphtheria?"

Katya and Magdalene shook their heads.

"He couldn't breathe. He coughed and coughed, but he couldn't breathe. He could barely swallow, his throat hurt so bad. Sarah sat with him as long as she could. She wiped the drool from his lips and the blood from his nose. He shook from the chills but burned with fever. We buried him." Brady nodded slowly, his eyes unfocused as he remembered it. "They shouldn't build coffins so small, but there are a lot of them, aren't there?"

Katya nodded. One of her sisters had not lived past her first few weeks.

"My wife," Brady continued, "Sarah. She caught consumption the year after. I gave up my job to care for her, but nothing helped. We sold the house, and she passed much the way Nathaniel did, coughing and fighting for breath. She sweated all night, no matter how much I fanned her. When she died, I took whatever jobs I could, and I threw myself into that journal. I dreamed of a place where families – anybody – could go and enjoy themselves and be together."

Katya interjected gently. "Did you know how you were going to build it?"

"No. I got lost in those drawings. I didn't know if it would ever really happen. Then the notebook disappeared, and I had no idea what to do." Brady raised his hand, resting it over his face for a moment.

Magdalene's voice fell soothing and quiet. "Did you know William Warden?"

Brady composed himself with several blinks. "Loosely. He stayed at the same boarding house for a while. We worked together at a factory. He was a friend of the foreman, so he didn't spend very long fixing machines before he was simply supervising the rest of us. He didn't really have the technical knowledge needed for the job, but he could discipline."

"Did you tell anyone what you were working on?"

"No. I always figured Warden was a petty thief. He must've stolen bigger, more expensive things than my journal, although the journal did pay off."

"Do you have any idea how he turned your journal into the Steampunk Carnival?"

"Not exactly. He's a smooth talker, Warden. People like him. People who don't know much about him, that is. It's easy to picture him in a boardroom of some city skyscraper with a cigar between his teeth, selling my inventions to a group of builders and investors."

Katya recalled multiple headlines and articles about the carnival. She could not resist sharing its colorful history with Brady. "It wasn't called the Steampunk Carnival in the beginning. People weren't sure what to think of it when the workers were building it. I think they were excited, but they were also quick to condemn it. The night we opened, reporters from the *News* and the *Journal* and the *Mirror* were all there taking photographs and interviewing people. Everything was so disorganized, only the children seemed to enjoy themselves. The newspapers called us the steam-run carnival for punks, writing us off, thinking we wouldn't last long." Katya felt proud to reveal the change in public opinion. "The carnival caught on like wildfire, and there wasn't enough room in the papers to keep calling us that, so they shortened it. Mr. Warden liked the phrase so much and so many people repeated it, he had it printed on that sign put up outside the gates even bigger than the original name."

Magdalene adjusted her position on the edge of the hard bench. Her next question came almost inaudibly. "Mr. Kelly, did you send those death threats to Mr. Warden?"

Brady lowered his gaze. "Yes. I got the job at the carnival to see it for myself and be a part of what I dreamed about for so long. It's not exactly what I had in mind, but it's close. I wasn't sure what to do then." Brady's eyes widened as he focused on Magdalene's face. "I'd never kill Warden. I only meant to scare him."

"You might have scared him into throwing out the journal. He might've been trying to get rid of the evidence against him."

Katya leaned closer to Magdalene and Brady. "Why doesn't Mr. Warden recognize you?"

Brady sighed a dry, short sound. "My appearance isn't what it used to be. I used to keep my hair trimmed, my beard trimmed. It's amazing what losing your family and everything that means something to you will do to you. He's never recognized me by voice or any other way. I never gave him my real name when I approached him about the job."

"And that was good enough for Mr. Warden?" Magdalene guessed, her sad tone revealing her lack of surprise.

Brady shrugged. "He didn't want to know the workers he managed before. This is the way I wanted it, Miss Harvey. I kept to myself as much as possible. I didn't start calling myself the Mick to gain friends. Everybody has kept their distance except the two of you."

"I saw you with the boy," Katya admitted. "The one who stole a stuffed bear from your game stall. You were so pleasant to him. Even if you did threaten Mr. Warden, I didn't think you'd hurt us."

The trio fell silent. The homeless lay still in their pews, either straining to listen or dead asleep.

Magdalene's voice cut into the silence. "What are we going to do now?"

Brady shook his head. "I don't know. I've thought of every possible plan."

Katya broached the crux of the problem. "We can't even go to the police. They'd never believe us. Mr. Warden has too much influence over every corner of the city."

"I know. If I accused him of anything, they'd pin the death threats on me, and I'd never see the light of day again except on a chain gang."

Magdalene peeled her gloves off and laid them in her lap. "We have the journal as proof. There's enough of your handwriting in it that experts would be able to link it to you. Mr. Warden obviously hasn't looked at it in a long time, or he might have recognized your handwriting in the letters."

"It's not enough," Brady insisted. "Unless I get a public confession out of Warden, the police will never believe me. People have to see him for what he is, a cheat who got lucky off other people's work."

"Is that what you want us to strive for, Mr. Kelly?" Magdalene asked.

Brady rubbed a smudge on his hat brim with his thumb. "I don't want to drag you ladies into it. Lieber's as dangerous as they come, and Warden would do anything to hold onto the carnival."

Katya revolted against the idea of leaving Brady to take care of things himself. She struggled to keep her voice low. "We've worked at the carnival longer than you have. We've been in the city longer. We know everybody better. I might not have much pull with Mr. Warden, but I do have some. Where do you think you'd get by yourself? It's too important to tell us to go on our way. It's all we're going to be thinking about anyway."

Brady hesitated, pressing his thin lips together.

"Mr. Kelly," Katya tried again. "Let us help you. Please. The carnival means everything to me. It's the only job I ever wanted, the only place I've ever loved with every bit of my soul. You designed it that way. If the carnival is a lie, how can I feel good about helping the patrons spend their money when it all goes into Mr. Warden's pockets?"

Brady nodded reluctantly, his grey eyes preoccupied and darkly shaded. "All right. You can help me. We just need to figure out what to do." He ran his fingers through his thick, unkempt hair.

Magdalene rested her hand on his arm. "We'll think of something, Mr. Kelly. I don't think we should threaten Mr. Warden anymore. Any additional security might make it harder for us to take action."

"I won't do anything unless we decide on it."

Magdalene stood up. "It's been a long night. We should all get some sleep."

Katya and Brady rose to their feet.

Brady met their eyes intensely. "I appreciate this. I do. I never thought I'd see that journal again. I wasn't sure how I was going to expose Warden's fraud."

"We'll find out what we can about Mr. Warden's schedule. We'll let you know what we discover."

"But we have to be careful."

"We will. It'll be easy for Katya to stop by your stall long enough to ask you to meet with us."

"Should we have a code phrase?"

Magdalene nodded. She thought for a moment.

Katya remembered what Mr. Warden had said about the great wheel. "'The wheel is very popular tonight.' It's true every night, but the patrons won't know that."

"I look forward to hearing that phrase," Brady said.

Brady turned and led the two women out of the sanctuary. They crossed the front hall, and Brady eased one of the double doors open into the slow summer wind.

"Can you get home all right?" he asked.

Magdalene looked up the street for the streetcar. Horses' hooves struck the road several blocks away. "We'll be fine. How are you getting home, Mr. Kelly?"

"I'll walk this way and see if I can't find another horsecar." Brady set his hat on his head, adjusting it briefly. "Thank you again, ladies. Good day."

"Good day, Mr. Kelly," Katya and Magdalene replied.

Brady walked away down Tennessee Street, and the two women started in the opposite direction. They soon spotted the horse-drawn streetcar and waved for it to stop.

Magdalene loosened the drawstring of her purse. "How much from here to Plum Street? It's just over the river."

The driver tipped his hat, revealing neatly combed grey hair. "You ladies work for the carnival, don't you?" He beamed. "I'll let you ride for free. I can take you straight there. There's nobody else at this hour."

"Thank you so much."

Katya wasted no time in climbing up the step behind the driver at the front of the streetcar. She sat down in the second seat, leaving room for Magdalene to sink down beside her.

The streetcar turned to the right, taking the angled Kentucky Avenue away from the five-point intersection toward the river. Katya craned her neck and caught a glimpse of Brady walking alone through the hazy gas lamplight before the buildings at the next corner blocked her view.

Chapter Eleven

Katya double-checked her appearance in the oval mirror above the water closet sink. She made sure the perfect number of dark curls showed over her forehead beneath the brim of her hat. She had worn her largest hat tonight, angled heavily to one side. It was covered in royal-blue silk with thick, fluffy ostrich feathers cascading from the band. Lizzie's employer had altered it for her, gluing charms and discarded watchmaker's gears amidst the feathers.

Katya smoothed the front of her cobalt-blue jacket and the skirt of her silver gown. She needed to look her best, and she finally satisfied herself she could look no better. She let herself out of the water closet, almost bumping into the charwoman carrying a bucket of murky water. Katya jumped back to avoid soiling her clothes. The charwoman ducked back as well, sloshing water out over her shoes.

"I'm sorry," Katya said quickly. She meant it, and she was doubly sorry she did not sound sincere.

The charwoman bobbed her head, her eyes scanning the ground as she strode past Katya.

Katya pushed on through the edge of the crowd to the nearest food stall. She stood at the side counter, apart from the customers, trying to get one of the cooks' attention. "Excuse me."

The cooks continued working, frying and plating and doing it again.

"Excuse me, I need a snack for Mr. Warden. He's waiting for it."

Without looking up from plopping a long sausage on a thin bun, the nearest cook blurted, "What does he want?"

"Anything. He's just hungry. He wants it fast."

The cook passed the prepared plate to the worker at the counter for the customer line. He set down a fresh white plate, dropped a bun on it, and used his pair of tongs to center a sausage across it. He squirted a steady, practiced stream of mustard down one side and handed it to Katya.

"Thank you." Katya hurried away with it, swinging out around the line of ravenous customers. She carefully avoided meeting Brady's eyes as she passed his game counter. She steered clear of Magdalene working the front of the other food stall, simply noting the modest red hat and jacket brightening the corner of her vision.

Katya stepped into the shadows leading up to Mr. Warden's office. She pulled a small, folded slip of paper from the left shoulder of her dress and hid it under the plate. She did not listen at the door this time, well prepared for Mr. Lieber's presence. Katya knocked a few times before she opened the door, finding the two men in the same places she usually did. Mr. Lieber glared from his standing position on the left side of the back office, and Mr. Warden leaned over from his desk chair on the right to see through the doorway. Whatever they had been discussing, it had left a thoughtful frown on his lips.

"I brought you a snack," Katya greeted him, passing through the front room. "I thought you might be hungry."

Mr. Warden waved his hand flippantly. "I don't want anything."

Mr. Lieber snatched the plate from Katya's hand before she could pull it away. She barely managed to hide the slip of paper in her gloved fingers as she closed them.

Katya turned her back to Mr. Lieber. On the desk in front of Mr. Warden, a thick ledger lay open, column after column filled in with numbers by the ink pen discarded nearby. She rested her loose fist on the desk. "You're not working too hard, are you?"

Mr. Warden leaned his head back to look up into Katya's face. His dark eyes shone with adoration and mischief. "I don't pay myself to do nothing."

"How do you keep it all straight?" Keeping the note tucked against her palm, Katya traced her finger down the far left column of abbreviations.

Mr. Warden's demeanor tightened into worry again. "Why don't you leave that up to me?"

"All right."

Katya could hear Mr. Lieber behind her, slurping at the juicy sausage and muffling bun. She pressed the note into Mr. Warden's hand and tilted her head to whisper closer to his ear. "Keep this between us."

Mr. Warden nodded subtly.

Katya stepped away to leave the room.

Mr. Lieber's hard voice stopped her cold. "Miss Romanova."

Katya forced herself to meet Mr. Lieber's gaze over her shoulder.

Mr. Lieber sucked sausage grease off his thumb. "Tell those good-for-nothing cooks to buy some real German mustard next time. I'm sick of this *scheisse*."

Katya nodded although she had no intentions of helping him and let herself out of the building.

Within an hour, Katya felt Mr. Warden's fingers take hold of her elbow. She stood in the opposite corner of the grounds from his office, having reassured several ladies that the Kaleidoscope did not rotate quickly enough to render them ill. Mr. Warden had been bare-headed before, but he had put on his top hat to come find her, a clean, gleaming black. He guided Katya away from the crowd, further into the corner by the fence. Behind her, the Cannon roared as its cars raced and turned along the sloping, jet-black track. Katya watched the Kaleidoscope gyrate behind Mr. Warden, set on a raised platform so people could see it more easily. Eight color-tinted booths spun on a round disc which turned at a slightly slower pace. Excited shouts rang out from the passengers at irregular intervals, expressing everything from uncertainty to exhilaration.

"You wanted to see me?" Mr. Warden asked, his expression solemn and distant.

"Yes."

"Are you still worried about the death threats? I told you you shouldn't be. I hired more security, and I haven't gotten any more letters."

"That's good." Katya tried to think of the best way to change the subject toward what she needed to know. She kept her voice light and casual. "I was there when the Beast broke down, but I never heard anything about it getting fixed. How am I supposed to keep the guests informed if I don't know what's going on?"

"It was only down for one night. It's running now. What else do you need to know?"

"Maintenance said he didn't know how to fix it."

Mr. Warden cracked his mask and chuckled warmly. "You have to know all the gossip, don't you?" His eyes wandered her costume before meeting her gaze with a twinkle. "I'll indulge you, Miss Romanova. Yes, that fool. He was a whiz when we had problems with the Tower last year, but he hadn't a clue when it came to the Beast. He was a terrible liar. I knew he didn't fix it."

"Do you know who did?"

"No, and I don't care. One of the other maintenance workers was covering for him, I suppose."

"With how important the Beast is, someone could've lost their job over a mistake like that."

"Someone did. That idiot won't be coming around here anymore. I've hired his replacement already."

"Are you sure you're not overworking yourself? Seeing to the coasters, firing a man, interviewing new staff. You're at the carnival every night."

Mr. Warden pursed his lips, urging her on.

"You must have meetings to attend," Katya guessed.

"Once or twice a week."

"Do you ever have time for fun?"

Mr. Warden broke into a grin, more humored than he was annoyed. "Surely I must have as many dates and suitors as you do."

Katya grimaced. She could picture Lizzie smirking at her, ecstatic on Dr. Kirby's arm. Katya kept the subject about Mr. Warden and herself. "No one can possibly have more dates than the genius behind the Steampunk Carnival."

Mr. Warden brushed a soft leather glove along Katya's jaw. "You underestimate the effect you have on men."

"Do I?"

Mr. Warden moved closer. "You're as beautiful as ever." He ducked his head and kissed her.

His lips felt inviting and deliberate. Katya returned Mr. Warden's affection without thinking, her chest swelling with a dizzying breath. She lost herself in the confidence of his sturdy arms and the smooth blend of his cologne. Mr. Warden pulled away, and Katya remembered what kind of a man he was. She held onto Brady's words. Mr. Warden was a petty thief who had stumbled across the discovery of a lifetime and nothing more.

Mr. Warden's hand lingered on Katya's arm. "Are you still worried about me?"

Katya gathered her thoughts. "A little. I worry about your health. There are so many diseases going around. I'd hate for you to catch one in your exhausted state."

"I'm not exhausted. Far from it. You're the one walking all over the grounds every night in those boots. I'd hate for you to injure one of those delicate ankles."

Katya blushed at the thought of her boss becoming acquainted with the slenderness of her ankles. "I'll be careful."

"I know you will." Mr. Warden set his gloved hand under Katya's chin. "You'll let me know if you see or hear anything you think I should know about, won't you?"

"Of course."

"If there's one thing I won't tolerate, it's a dishonest employee. Let me know if you need to speak to me alone again."

"I will."

Mr. Warden tapped his finger against Katya's chin and walked away. Katya lingered in the corner between the fence, the rattling Cannon, and the churning Kaleidoscope. She considered it an apt place to be, trapped with no easy way out, her heart shaking and her thoughts swirling in circles.

Chapter Twelve

Katya folded the last music stand closed and tucked it under its paired folding chair. The band had moseyed off twenty minutes before. Katya did not mind being assigned such basic tasks at the end of the night. She liked to prove she earned her salary. Katya could pour herself into her work, not just with words and gestures, but with muscles and sweat. She only wished Irina or any of the others could see her. They would still call her lazy, but at least she would have solid evidence to the contrary.

A single sheet of music rustled across the stage. The wind sailed it along the wooden boards and off into the grass. Katya chased after it, pinning it under the narrow toe of her boot. She crouched down to pick it up, two men's hard voices diverting her attention. Mr. Lieber and Mr. Davies strode towards her. Katya assumed they were headed for the front gates and backed up to let them pass far by her.

Mr. Lieber spat on in German.

Mr. Davies clenched his jaw so tightly, Katya was surprised he could speak when he interrupted. "As much as I don't want to talk to you in any language, would you mind joining me in English so we can finish this conversation?"

Mr. Lieber obliged him without a pause. "You have a job to do, Mr. Davies. Don't go looking for ways to expand it. Just do what you were hired to do."

"When Mr. Warden created the carnival, they called it entrepreneurial spirit. When I make a suggestion that could expand the business and create additional opportunities for all of us, it's put down as overstepping my boundaries."

"Nobody asked you to think for the carnival."

Mr. Davies looked past Mr. Lieber at Katya. He tipped his hat briefly and softened his voice. "Do you really need to escort me to the exit? Don't you have something better to do?"

"As head of security, it's my duty."

"It'd be your pleasure to escort me out for the last time."

"Perhaps one day, Mr. Davies."

The two men strode on in silence, a heavier ignoring of words than Katya had felt in a long time. She retreated to the band stage and secured the piece of sheet music under one of the heavy metal stands. She sat down in the chair above it, content to wait for Magdalene here rather than hear any more of Mr. Lieber and Mr. Davies' argument.

Katya could not see or hear the two men from where she sat. The front two game stalls and the ticket booth blocked her view of them. Katya untucked the sheet music from its impromptu paperweight and studied it. She wondered how the musicians knew what to do, what to make of all the black shapes skittering over the thin, horizontal lines running the length of the page.

Heavy, purposeful boot steps pounded the dirt. Even though Katya knew it would be Mr. Lieber, she could not resist looking up. When he noticed her, he stalked towards her and loomed at the edge of the stage.

"What are you paid for, Miss Romanova?" Mr. Lieber demanded.

Katya lowered the sheet of music to her lap to keep her nerves from shaking it for Mr. Lieber to see. "You know what my job is, Mr. Lieber. I take care of the guests. I do what nobody else has time for."

"Is that how you sold yourself to Mr. Warden? You're a clever one, aren't you?"

Katya maintained her composure, breathing steadily and keeping her spine straight with help from her corset. "It's the truth. Who else greets the guests? Who else helps them? I'm the only one who doesn't have something to sell them."

"And therefore, Miss Romanova, you're no use to the carnival."

Knowing Mr. Davies probably remained within earshot in case she got into trouble, Katya pressed her point. "How are the guests going to spend money at the Warden wheel if they can't get to it?" Katya almost choked on calling it Mr. Warden's wheel when Brady had designed it.

Mr. Lieber leaned toward her, his eyes level with hers. "How could they miss it? It's a hundred feet tall."

"Actually, it's eight stories..." Katya let her knowledge drift away as it only served to narrow Mr. Lieber's pale eyes at her. "I know they can see it from a distance, Mr. Lieber, but I assure you. Once inside the carnival, new guests have no idea where it is. They get disoriented by the band and the games and the coasters. I'm of more use here than anybody knows."

"You're fortunate the carnival earns as well as it does. Your salary disappears in all those facts and figures intriguing you so much. If patronage dropped, you'd be the first to go."

Katya recalled Irina saying Mr. Warden would fire her, the disgruntled cook, first in the case of a money crisis. Mr. Warden might be willing to shell out dollars for beautiful faces, but Mr. Lieber focused simply on the worth of one's labor. "I could learn to do something else," Katya insisted.

Mr. Lieber curved his lips in a malicious smirk. "You cling to the carnival. Or do you cling to Mr. Warden like the other girls?"

Katya's eyebrows scrunched down over her penetrating eyes. "I do not."

"Do you think he considers you special because he gave you this job?"

Katya snapped at him. "Do you think you're special because you're head of security? It must be hard to oversee the carnival from the back room of Mr. Warden's office."

Mr. Lieber reeled his hand back at shoulder height. Katya flinched, her whole body tightening against the back of the chair. Mr. Lieber held it there, reconsidering. "You want to talk about usefulness? If you want to make yourself useful, Miss Romanova, squeeze a few brats from between those legs and give the factories some fresh workers before the law tells a man whom he can and cannot hire."

Shock kept Katya from speaking. She watched Mr. Lieber march away and disappear behind the mammoth Beast. She did not know Mr. Lieber well enough to guess if he would repeat his arguments to Mr. Warden or not. Katya imagined Mr. Lieber standing silently in Mr. Warden's office, brooding and smiling to himself about his verbal conquests. He would nod when Mr. Warden addressed him and accept all of Mr. Warden's decisions. In his heart and mind, Mr. Lieber would be in his own world, one which he dominated unequivocally.

The wind tore the loose page from Katya's hands. It flipped and circled on the breeze, landing in the grass far beyond her reach. Katya let it go. One of the band members would miss it the next night, but that was not Katya's responsibility. She wondered if any of the carnival's employees valued her presence besides Magdalene and Mr. Warden. Even his appreciation was suspect in the light of Mr. Lieber's tirade.

Katya stood up and crossed the grass between the two game stalls to the front of the carnival. By the relief in the voices approaching from the rear of the grounds, Magdalene, Irina, and the Englishman had finished cleaning their food stall. Katya reached the gates and Mr. Davies waiting in the high seat behind the carriage horse. She nodded congenially to Mr. Davies, who tipped his hat solemnly in return. She climbed up into the back to sit down and wait for the others in peace.

Chapter Thirteen

Katya made a point to stay as far from Mr. Warden's office as possible. She wanted to guide each patron to his or her destination, but coming too close to Mr. Lieber set her nerves on edge. Several times, she chose to keep her distance, gesturing the guest the rest of the way to a food stall or the Warden wheel. They did not seem to mind or notice her lapse in quality of service, but Katya did. She was disgusted with herself and furious at Mr. Lieber for being so harsh with her. Instead of strolling the grounds and greeting guests with a natural effervescence, she sulked her way through the crowd, waiting for the patrons to approach her with their needs. If a guest looked lost or overwhelmed, she left them alone to figure it out or ask someone else.

Katya strode past the bandstand, trying to put extra space between herself and the rear of the carnival, when she spotted a lazy figure propped up against one of the narrow lampposts. She blew out an irritated breath at the ignorance. The most she could make out from the back was the rectangular figure of a man – although slightly short – and certainly a carnival employee. His top hat sported a flashing silver buckle on the back of the black band, and his dark brown suit fit him neatly with rounded seams following his shoulders.

Katya sped toward him on anger-fueled limbs. She started spewing at him even before she saw his face. "You should know better than to lean against the lampposts." Katya folded her arms and stopped in front of him. He was much younger than she anticipated, close to her own age or a few years older. With the flame of the lamppost backlighting his hat, she could not make out the color of his eyes or hair. Even with a smudge of dirt or oil on the left side of his forehead, his clean, smooth features gave him a level of attractiveness Katya chose to ignore.

The man cracked an off-guard smile. "What?"

"Don't lean against the lampposts. It's a public health concern. There's gas filling the pipe. Any day now, there's going to be a law against it." Katya waved him away from the post. "I'm not kidding."

"I'm sorry. It seemed sturdy enough to me." Now that he spoke in longer sentences, Katya could hear the Irish brogue in his voice, the round O's and sharp E's muffled by a gentler influence. He peeled his back off the iron lamppost. "I didn't know."

Katya let some of her annoyance ebb so she would not embarrass herself. "It's all right. Just don't do it again."

"I don't think we've met. My name's Maddox O'Sullivan."

"Katya Romanova."

"Oh," he said, his voice rising in pleasant surprise. "You're Katya Romanova."

Katya eased back a step, further rattled by the lyrical sound of her name in his accent. "Why? What have you heard about me?"

Maddox shrugged. "Nothing, just your name."

He sounded sincere, but Katya took another step back. "It was nice to meet you, Mr. O'Sullivan."

"Do you have to run off? We barely got acquainted."

"I have a job to do, Mr. O'Sullivan, and so do you."

"What is your job here, Miss Romanova?"

Katya bristled at having to explain herself again, her argument with Mr. Lieber ringing bitterly in her ears. "I help the guests find everything they need." She turned away.

Maddox continued the conversation anyway. "I joined the maintenance crew just this week."

Katya swallowed her exasperation and faced him once more. "Mr. Warden told me he'd hired new maintenance. I can tell by your suit what you do."

"You must know everything about the carnival."

Katya could not give a glib answer to that. "I know the workers. I know the rides. I know the guests."

"You've worked here a long time."

"Since the beginning."

"Do you like it?"

"I'd rather be here than anywhere else."

Maddox stepped forward to close the gap Katya's footfalls had created. "Would you like to go for a walk with me sometime?"

Awkwardness tightened Katya's chest, and she searched for the most polite rejection. "I apologize, Mr. O'Sullivan, but I shouldn't." She glanced around them at the carnival guests, some watching the games being played fifty feet away and others watching the band perform yet another rousing march. "I should get back to the guests."

"They look like they're doing fine without you, not that they don't need you."

"I appreciate the offer, but I really don't think it would be in our best interests to see each other socially."

"Aren't you friends with someone who works here?"

Katya looked Maddox over, worried he had heard more than he was letting on. "Yes."

"Thick as thieves, they told me."

"That's different. We're friends."

"Maybe, but what happens if you have a falling out? It'd be the same situation, making it uncomfortable for you to work here."

Katya felt forced to be more direct. "I apologize, Mr. O'Sullivan, but I'd be wasting your time. You're not the kind of man I'm looking for."

Maddox raised his eyebrows. "So you've got him picked out, do you? What kind of man is it?"

Katya straightened the hem of her jacket to fit it more squarely across her shoulders. "Let's not fool ourselves. The best way for a woman to get by is to attach herself to a man who's established and well off."

"I suppose so." Maddox licked his lips. "Do you ever think about having fun instead of money?"

"The pursuit of money is fun except when they won't part with it."

Maddox laughed deep in his chest, honest and entertained. "I mean real fun. You know, like the carnival's fun for all these people."

"I don't have time for that kind of fun. I'm glad for you if you do."

"Is there anything fun to do in the city? I haven't been in town long. I've been out east the last couple of years."

Katya's heart leapt to think of the east, of the big house in New York where her family stayed. She redirected the pictures in her mind to the city she had moved to. "There's the English Opera House in the center of town. They put on good productions there. You can hear music any time you like. If you're tired of marches, there're orchestras playing Wagner and Handel. There's almost more music in the city than anything else. There are parks to explore. You could join a sports club if you like, but I don't know much about them."

"I'm surprised. You know so much about everything else."

Katya decided to stick with the truth. "I haven't had any dates there, so I'm not as familiar."

Maddox's eyes sparkled with mischief. "Suppose I want to ask a girl out. How will I know where to take her unless you show me all the best places?"

"I'm not naive. I know what you're trying to do. My advice is to find a woman who isn't me and ask her to the carnival. There's not a better place in the whole country. If she isn't mad for you after one night here, she isn't worth your time. Have a good evening, Mr. O'Sullivan."

Katya turned and strolled away before Maddox could reel her back into the conversation. She heard his parting remark called to her over her shoulder.

"Have a good night, Miss Romanova."

Katya gave no sign she had heard him. She walked on until she reached the crowd gathered around the eastern side stage, dozens of people engrossed in watching six men gorge themselves in a pickle-eating contest. Katya immersed herself in the dense crowd, smiling brightly at those around her and asking if they needed assistance. They shook their heads and turned back to the gradually slowing action. Katya remained there for some time, until the man in charge, dressed in a sharp black suit, presented a winner's ribbon to the contestant who was barely more than translucent skin wrapped around thin bones. A spokesman for the canning company stepped forward to elaborate on the exquisite taste and crunch of the product. Certain that Maddox had either stayed near the lamppost or moseyed to the back of the carnival where the maintenance building was, Katya went on her way, trying to avoid either location.

Chapter Fourteen

Katya sat on the front edge of the hard wooden pew in the back of St. John's Church. She tried not to yawn, hiding each involuntary stretch of her jaws behind her yellow satin glove. Next to her, the early hour did not seem to affect Magdalene as strongly. She smelled like popcorn and frying potatoes but sat as patiently as if she had just woken up from a pleasant sleep.

Brady slipped into the sanctuary and lowered his hat from his head. He sank into the pew on the other side of Magdalene. He looked tired and old, new creases forming worried ravines across his forehead. "I was glad to hear the wheel was popular tonight, Miss Romanova. What have you learned?"

Katya dropped her hand from her face, where she had stifled another yawn. "Not as much as I hoped. Mr. Warden spends all his nights at the carnival. He has a few meetings a week, but I don't know where. He goes on dates during the day, but I don't know whom he's seeing or where."

Magdalene turned to Katya. "Do you think we could ask at the Opera House if Mr. Warden has been there? Maybe we could find a pattern. If we say we're looking for him, I'm sure they'd be happy to help."

Brady answered before Katya could decide either way. "He could change those plans too easily. We need to know exactly where Warden's going to be. If we can learn his schedule and anticipate his movements, we'll be able to find the best place to expose him."

"It's not over yet," Katya insisted. "Mr. Warden was tight lipped when I talked to him, but he said I can talk to him anytime. Alone, without Mr. Lieber, if I want."

Magdalene spoke up. "The death threats have them both on edge. We don't want to come across as suspicious by probing for information."

"You could ask Mr. Warden," Katya suggested. "Everybody trusts you. They all seem to think I'm after Mr. Warden's money." Katya stopped before she shared too much about her personal life in front of Brady. "He'd talk to you, Mags. If you wait a week or two, Mr. Warden might give you the information we're looking for."

Brady interjected, rubbing his palms against each other. "Could we set him up? Could we get him an interview or have him make a speech at some event?"

"I don't know," Magdalene breathed.

Katya rested her hand on Magdalene's arm with a new thought. "Do you know who Mr. Warden's seeing now?"

"No."

"I haven't seen the woman in green for a while. I haven't seen any women near his office in weeks."

Brady broke in with another question. "Do you think any of Warden's girlfriends would betray him by talking to you?"

"They might." Katya considered her own complex relationship with her boss. "Mr. Warden never keeps anyone near him whom he can't use for something. If they're aware of that or we point it out to them, they might open up and tell us something."

"There are too many *if's*." Brady ducked his face and laid his hands over it. The pads of his fingertips smoothed his forehead, and his thumbs slid across the planes of his closed eyelids.

Magdalene spoke up, soft and soothing. "No man is impenetrable, not even Mr. Warden. He has his weaknesses. We just need to make them work for us."

Katya forced her mouth closed against an impending yawn that slurred her opening words. "That's not good enough. Mr. Warden's being too cautious, even with me. We have to try what we know will work. Mags, you have to try. If I keep bothering him, he'll know we're up to something, and we'll never learn anything."

A few pews away, a swish of fabric against hard wood preceded a few hollow knocks as one of the invisible homeless rolled over.

Katya lowered her voice. "No one would suspect you."

Magdalene whispered back. "What do you want me to do?"

"Talk to Mr. Warden in front of Mr. Lieber. If you try to get him alone, he might think you're up to one of my tricks."

"I think you should keep trying. If he's willing to see you again, he's willing to talk."

Or do more than talk, Katya thought, but she kept that concern to herself.

"I have no reason to talk to Mr. Warden," Magdalene added.

"Of course you do. When I ran into Mr. Lieber, he wanted the cooks to buy German mustard instead of what you're using. It'd be easy to appease him and buy a few minutes learning Mr. Warden's schedule."

"You don't think it's going to be suspicious if I try to spin a conversation out of German mustard?"

Brady leaned past Magdalene to see Katya better. "I have to agree with Miss Harvey. If Warden's come to expect you, Miss Romanova, you stand the best chance of slipping past his defenses."

Katya wanted to keep arguing to the contrary, but there seemed to be no point. "What do you expect me to talk about?"

Magdalene laid her hand on Katya's, her eyes wide with eagerness to convince her. "Anything. Tell him one of the reporters wants to interview him, and you want to arrange a time. Tell him one of the patrons wants a date with him, and he should meet with her downtown."

"At the Opera House?" Katya grumbled, her voice dragging.

"Yes, that's good. A mystery date at the Opera House."

Brady reached out and took Katya's free hand between his own. "Miss Romanova, I'd appreciate it greatly. Please try one more time. If Warden won't talk to you, we'll find another way."

Faced with Brady's hopeful, weary eyes, Katya conceded.
"I'll try."

"Thank you."

They all rose at once, Katya slipping her hands free of her
friends' outreaches. They moved to the door of the sanctuary
and filed out of the church onto the sidewalk.

Brady's Irish accent reminded Katya of Maddox, and she
wondered if she should ask him if he knew anything about the
young maintenance man. She decided he probably would not.
Even though she was coming to know Brady's past and current
situation, no one else at the carnival knew the first thing about
him. He kept to himself, and that included staying away from
those who gossiped and those who were gossiped about.

"Be careful, ladies," Brady said, breaking away from them to
walk south on Tennessee Street.

"Good night," Katya and Magdalene chimed in.

The two women turned north, looking and listening for the
streetcar they expected at any moment.

"Do you think he knows?" Katya whispered without
forethought.

"Knows what?" Magdalene stretched her neck in search of
the carriage.

"About me and Mr. Warden."

"I don't think so."

"I don't want Mr. Kelly to think I don't want to help him."

"He's not going to think that." Horses' hooves struck the
road higher up the street, and Magdalene relaxed her angled
pose.

"Don't you think it's strange to be stuck between your boss
and someone you barely know?" Katya asked.

Magdalene adjusted her rosy gloves at the ends of her
crimson sleeves. "I would've found it stranger if the carnival had
nothing uncommon about it. It was never designed to be normal.
It's too ambitious to be average in any way."

The pair of horses pulled the streetcar toward the corner. Katya hoped the driver had not yet ridden into earshot.

"Yes," Katya agreed under her breath. "For a place that has everything, that's exactly what we stand to lose."

Chapter Fifteen

Katya rehearsed the story over and over in her head as she crossed the grounds. A woman had approached her near the front gates, a radiant young woman, not unlike herself. Katya knew this was the only way Mr. Warden would keep listening. This young woman, who did not supply her name, desperately wanted to meet Mr. Warden, not in a quiet back office at the carnival but out on the town for a date. Pressing her for more, Katya learned the young woman was smitten with the theater, and Katya would proceed to talk Mr. Warden into a romantic rendezvous at the English Opera House. She could suggest a dinner at Bates House, too, a one-block walk from the theater and a mere two blocks from the church where the plan had been hatched. Katya appreciated the irony of it, especially since Mr. Warden might not be able to appear in public again for some time if the trap succeeded.

Katya imagined Brady revealing his true identity in front of the Opera House, removing his hat to make sure the lamp lights caught his face. Mr. Warden would freeze immediately, knowing his lies had been exposed. The crowd would form a circle around the two men, chattering and whispering. Mr. Warden's reputation would be ruined, and once the police arrived, all his freedoms would be cut off. There would be no rendezvous with a beautiful woman, and Mr. Warden would drop his sullen gaze as the truth of the ruse dawned on him. The police would secure his wrists in handcuffs and lead the silent, disgraced carnival owner to their wagon.

Katya slipped past the food stall where Magdalene's red gloves were busy reaching out in front of her for money and then to the side for food. Katya brushed a few curls back from her neck and opened the door to Mr. Warden's outer office. She was completely unprepared to find the small building packed with chaos, several policemen active inside.

Through the open doorway to Mr. Warden's office, Katya spied Mr. Lieber lying motionless on the carpet. She stared at the blood. It seemed to cover everything, adding a bright red to his throat, jaw, and shirt while it darkened the carpet around him. Katya took another step, mesmerized by the horror of it. She could not tell where the blood was seeping from.

A policeman caught Katya by the elbow. "You shouldn't be in here, miss. We need to collect evidence and move this man's body."

"Mr. Warden," Katya heard herself call in a detached, yearning voice.

Mr. Warden poked his head into the doorway, not seated in his chair but standing. One bare hand rested on the back of his neck. Concern pulled Mr. Warden's features into a deep, thoughtful frown. Katya could still envision Mr. Lieber standing on the left, peeking through at her with disapproval. In his place, another policeman occupied the office with Mr. Warden, a pencil and notebook in his hands.

"You shouldn't be here," Mr. Warden said, so agitated he sounded disappointed to see Katya.

"Please tell me what happened." Katya struggled to make sense of it. She worried if they forced her to leave with only those raw, grisly images filling her mind, she would break down in tears.

Mr. Warden stepped past Mr. Lieber's body, prone with his head almost in the doorway. His face was thankfully turned away toward the corner he had often brooded in. His pale blond hair rested much the way it always had, straight and precisely parted. Only a few short locks curled out of place toward the carpet.

Mr. Warden reached Katya and held onto her arms. "Are you all right? You look frightfully pale."

"Mr. Lieber's dead," Katya said, as if saying it meant believing it.

"Yes," Mr. Warden answered wryly.

"How?"

Mr. Warden hesitated, glancing around him at the policemen. There were three of them crammed into the waiting area. The fourth remained behind Mr. Warden in the office. "Someone took a letter opener I had lying on my desk and gouged a hole in the side of Mr. Lieber's neck with it."

Katya pictured the scene better than she anticipated, and her knees wobbled, threatening to buckle. She locked them in place, holding onto Mr. Warden's arms as he held hers. "But he can't be dead. I just saw him."

One of the policemen stepped closer and raised his bushy black eyebrows. "When did you see him, miss?"

"A few nights ago."

"Where?" The policeman turned a page in his notebook.

"Near the front of the carnival. At the band stage." Katya's memory obliged her, pulling her away from the bloody image of the lifeless Mr. Lieber. She saw him stalking towards her while she sat at the corner of the stage.

"What was he doing?"

No, further back, Katya's mind directed her. Mr. Lieber had come towards her from the other direction with Mr. Davies arguing at his side.

Mr. Davies. Katya felt weaker. She could hear their words tearing at each other. Katya had once suggested Mr. Davies was responsible for the death threats against Mr. Warden. Now he might have had good reason to take down Mr. Lieber.

"Miss?" the policeman prompted.

"Where were you, Mr. Warden?" Katya asked. "When this happened?"

Mr. Warden's shadowed eyes swam, preoccupied. "I was out. I was speaking with customers."

The policeman edged closer. "Miss, I need a statement, please. And your name."

"Katya Romanova. I spoke briefly to Mr. Lieber. I didn't know him well, and we had no reason to talk. It was the end of the night, and we were both worn out."

"Do you remember anything he might've said to you?"

The exact words eluded her, but Katya felt the echo of her ensuing anger. *She should pump out brats to work in factories.* If Mr. Warden had not been standing in front of her, blocking her view of Mr. Lieber, Katya might have spat at his soulless corpse. She shook her head in answer to the policeman. "No. It was nothing unusual."

"You work here at the carnival?"

"Yes, sir."

"Do you know of anyone who would've wanted to harm Mr. Lieber?"

Katya held Mr. Warden's gaze. She could not tell what he was thinking, if he wanted her to keep quiet or if he would agree that most everyone wanted to hurt the abrasive head of security. "I can't think of anyone."

The policeman in the inner room stepped through the doorway. "Mr. Warden, you mentioned receiving death threats."

Mr. Warden barely turned towards him, his arms still interlocked with Katya's. "Yes."

"One theory, obviously, would be that someone came in here looking to attack you."

"Yes."

"I don't think that's the case. Why would a murderer come unprepared? And the damage to the deceased." The policeman tipped his hat to Katya. "My apologies for being blunt, miss. This was a crime of passion aimed directly at Mr. Lieber. I don't believe he was killed by someone trying to carry out those threats."

Mr. Warden nodded.

"I still need to get a complete statement from you, Mr. Warden."

"Yes, I'm coming." Mr. Warden squeezed Katya's arms. "Will you be all right, Miss Romanova? Do you need an escort somewhere?"

Katya shook her head. "No, I'm fine."

The nearest policeman finished making notes in his book. "Miss Romanova, we're requesting that you keep quiet about what you've seen here. Mr. Warden has made it clear that the details of the murder are to be kept out of the papers."

"Yes, I'll be quiet."

Mr. Warden patted Katya's arm as he pulled his hands away. "Good girl."

Katya stepped back toward the door to the outside, the portal to fresh and innocent air. "Do you need anything else from me?"

"No. Thank you."

Katya could guess Mr. Warden's next move, but she did not feel as reassured about it as she had been before. "You'll hire more security, won't you?" Katya hoped he could not hear the anxiety belying her flat tone.

"Of course. I can't have someone running amok at the carnival, taking out my best workers." Mr. Warden regarded Katya with personable, protective eyes. "I only hire the best, and I consider you all most worthy of personal safety. We need our patronage to stay where it is and not fall flat on its face."

"Thank you, Mr. Warden. Thank you, officers." Katya let herself out the door, never more relieved to close a door than she was to shut herself out of the same room as Mr. Lieber's dead body.

For a moment, Katya hung close to the office, simply breathing the summer air and letting the noises of the carnival inundate her ears. She breathed in the careful spicing of sausages and the cinnamon-sugar powder sprinkled over the fried dough desserts.

Katya sped off at a run, turning sharply at the rear of the nearest food stall and arriving at Magdalene's side. Katya grabbed at her friend's wrist clumsily.

"Hey," Magdalene blurted out. Her wide, alarmed eyes searched Katya's face. "Are you all right?"

"I have to talk to you." Katya's words jumbled together. "I saw..."

"I can't talk now." Magdalene took a plate of dessert from Irina's large, square hand and gave it to the first customer in line.

"It's incredibly important." Katya cut herself off before she could cry. Mr. Davies had been so angry. He would be too smart to kill Mr. Lieber with his whip. The letter opener would have presented itself as the perfect, most convenient choice of weapon. "Please. Just one minute."

Irina answered for Magdalene, her voice exploding in Katya's ear. "We don't have a minute to spare."

Magdalene glanced over her shoulder at Katya. "Can't it wait? Please?"

Katya nodded, not knowing what else to do. She wandered out of the food stall, wondering how she was going to work the rest of the night with Mr. Lieber's flushed white face waiting behind her eyelids every time she blinked.

Katya wound her way into the crowd, slowly returning to her duties of greeting and guiding. The man who had said her job was unneeded lay dead. She was not surprised she did not feel sorry for Mr. Lieber. She did not miss him, but she noted his passing left a strange, vacant hole. She did not imagine that another three or four or five security men were going to be more trouble than a single Ernst Lieber.

But Katya still worried. What kind of man could take down Mr. Lieber with a simple, just-found letter opener? And would it be the same man waiting to drive them home in just a few hours?

Chapter Sixteen

An hour before the carnival closed, Mr. Warden's plain-clothes security spread out over the grounds. They visited every worker, delivering the message that Mr. Warden would share an announcement after the guests emptied out.

Katya led the last patrons past the ticket booth, noting the security stationed on both sides of the gate. The band members sat silently in their seats, instruments resting beside them or in their laps. The rides came to their final stops for the day, turning no more revolutions and sending no more cars along their tracks.

Mr. Warden waved all of the employees toward him as he strolled past the Beast and the bandstand. Katya lingered on her side of the anxious crowd of workers, spotting Magdalene in red on the other side, standing with the impatiently frowning Irina. The rest of the fifty or so employees filled in the loose and jagged circle forming around their boss.

Mr. Warden offered no poetic versions of the truth. "Ernst Lieber is dead."

Katya did not catch Mr. Davies' face when Mr. Warden issued the news. The thought of looking at him, a possible murderer, spooked her into a shudder. As it was, Katya saw the open mouths and dumbfounded stares of the others as they gasped and swore under their breaths.

"There'll be an investigation into his murder," Mr. Warden continued, having regained his businesslike certainty since the last time Katya saw him.

The employees' confusion graduated to shrieks and urgent questions.

Mr. Warden patted his hand against the air to quiet them. "The details don't need to be known. I'll be hiring new security in the next few days."

The fear and speculation continued to buzz, and Mr. Warden waited until it fell away. Katya glanced aside, finding a glimpse of Maddox off to her left. He fixed his eyes on Mr. Warden and did not seem to notice her.

"Police are confident," Mr. Warden added, "this was a crime carried out specifically against Mr. Lieber. None of us should be in danger. It's my biggest concern that the carnival remain a happy, contented place for those who work here and those who visit."

Irina folded her bulky arms, and Katya found humor in knowing what Irina must be thinking. *When was the carnival ever a happy place for its employees?*

"You can close up and go home," Mr. Warden concluded. He sounded tired, having used all his energy to keep his crew from committing landlocked mutiny.

Mr. Warden slipped away through a gap in the circle. The employees slunk back to their duties, and Katya thought only of how soon she could tell Magdalene about her terror of Mr. Davies. She busied her hands helping the band fold up their music stands, trying to decipher if she could feel Mr. Davies' eyes on her back or not.

This time, Katya waited until Magdalene and Irina reached the band stage to approach the front gates. The Englishman parted ways with the three women, and they climbed up into the carriage. The charwoman already sat drooped in the back corner, her dreary eyes gazing out the window into the black night. Katya settled into the seat across from her with Magdalene at her side.

The carriage jerked into motion, and Katya bit her lip. She longed with every muscle in her body to turn to Magdalene, press her face as close to her friend's ear as she could get, and whisper, "I think Mr. Davies did it."

The carriage ride lasted twice as long as usual, or at least, Katya imagined it did. No one spoke. Irina caught the hem of her dress in the bottom corner of the door as she climbed down to the sidewalk and spent several unending minutes working it free. The charwoman nodded off by the time Mr. Davies stopped the carriage in front of her house. Magdalene needed a minute or two to shake the woman awake. She drowsily collected herself and ambled out of the carriage.

Finally alone, Katya snatched Magdalene's wrist. The carriage picked up its pace for the final leg of the journey.

Magdalene eyed Katya with tilted eyebrows. "What's wrong? Is that what you're so upset about? Someone murdered Mr. Lieber?"

Katya explained herself with breathless adrenaline. "He was. I saw him. I went into Mr. Warden's office to talk to him, and Mr. Lieber was lying on the floor." Katya's hand flew over her mouth. "I'm not supposed to talk about it."

"I won't repeat anything you say to me. Was Mr. Warden telling the truth? Somebody planned to attack Mr. Lieber?"

"I don't think it was planned. They used a letter opener that Mr. Warden had out on his desk." Blood rose in Katya's vision, and she swallowed hard to wash it away.

"You don't think it was Mr. Kelly, do you?" Magdalene asked. "He wouldn't have acted so irrationally."

"No. I didn't think of Mr. Kelly." A whole list of suspects ran through Katya's head. Maddox O'Sullivan. The charwoman. Mr. Warden. He had said he was out of the office meeting with customers, but whom? He had never done that before.

The carriage rocked to a stop in front of the Weekly Boarder.

Katya reset her grip on Magdalene's wrist. "No, I think it might be–"

The carriage door flew open, and Mr. Davies stood on the other side of Magdalene below them on the sidewalk. He showed his teeth in a genteel, easy smile. "Ladies, if you wouldn't mind, I'd like a few private words with Miss Romanova."

Magdalene turned to Katya, her eyebrows rising in interest and suggestion. Katya hoped she did not think Mr. Davies wanted a romantic conversation, as that was surely the last thing lurking in his mind.

Katya's eyes bulged at the thought of being alone with him until she feared they would drop out of her head. "No, I'm sorry, Mr. Davies. I'm exhausted. So much has happened tonight."

Magdalene patted Katya's hands as she scooted along the bench toward the open door. "Now, Kat, it'll only take a minute. Won't it, Mr. Davies?"

Magdalene swept down past Mr. Davies. His dark blue eyes sparkled in the dim lamppost light. "It shouldn't take very long at all."

Mr. Davies swung the door shut, and Magdalene waved to Katya from the sidewalk. Katya inched toward the door, but the carriage started up much sooner than she anticipated. The horses pulled it swiftly through the neighborhood, past houses Mrs. Weeks could recite the extended histories of. Katya had declined sipping tea with several neighborhood ladies, and she wished more than anything she was safe in any of their houses now.

The carriage's sharp right turn lurched Katya to one side. By the time she propped herself up, a skidding left turn swayed her body the other way. The carriage bolted down Washington Street while her heart pounded out of rhythm. Katya stared out the window at the road, watching the hard granite blocks speed past. She thought about jumping out, but she would ruin her dress at the very least if she was lucky not to break her neck.

The carriage sped over the river bridge, plummeting Katya's stomach into her belly. Mr. Davies would not need a letter opener if they stayed near the water. Arms strong enough to subdue Mr. Lieber could easily hold her under its surface. The carriage turned again, slowing a few blocks later at the military park.

The park featured mostly open ground, laid out with narrow paths in the same design as the city streets around it. Four paths converged from the four corners into a circular drive in the center. Mr. Davies followed the nearest path, stopping the carriage in the middle of the lane where a scattering of trees blocked Katya's view of the surrounding streets.

Despite the hammering in her ears, Katya tried to hope for the best. Maybe Mr. Davies had not stabbed Mr. Lieber in the neck with a borrowed letter opener. Maybe all of Katya's terror and dread stemmed from a simple misunderstanding. Then Katya realized something else. Not only had she seen Mr. Davies arguing with Mr. Lieber, Mr. Davies had likely heard her exchange with Mr. Lieber. He might have his suspicions about her. Maybe that explained this nightmarish ride.

The carriage door gaped open, and Mr. Davies stepped up to sit next to Katya. She shrank away from him, grasping for the handle on the door to her right.

Mr. Davies' sleeve brushed hers, he sat so close to her. "You think I killed Mr. Lieber."

Katya had not expected the solemn, almost apologetic tone in Mr. Davies' voice.

"I didn't kill him, Miss Romanova," he insisted.

Katya hung back in the corner. "I didn't, either."

"I know."

Katya relaxed in the dim light, wishing she was home in her safe room in her soft bed, but glad her heart was slowing to its normal pace. "Then why did you bring me here?"

Mr. Davies shook his head. "I'm sorry if I misjudged you. I don't know you very well. I only know what they say about you."

Katya averted her eyes. "What did you hear?"

"That you have a close connection with Mr. Warden. I thought if he were angry about Mr. Lieber being killed, he might press you for information. You might've told him or the police that you saw me arguing with him. Not just the other day, but before."

"I was afraid you might've killed him," Katya admitted.

"It wasn't me. I'm sorry if I scared you, but I had to talk to you before you had a chance to think otherwise."

"I didn't tell Mr. Warden or the police anything. I didn't even mention that you were there that last night I saw Mr. Lieber. You won't tell Mr. Warden I had words with Mr. Lieber, will you?"

"No, and I don't imagine it would matter if I did. Nobody liked Mr. Lieber."

"Mr. Warden did. I don't want to give him any reason to think I might've killed him." Katya took a handkerchief out of her bag and dotted it across the top of her forehead under the brim of her hat. "Next time, Mr. Davies, please tell me what you want to speak to me about. I thought you were going to kill me. I've had enough excitement for one day."

"I apologize again."

Katya tried to make out Mr. Davies' features in the shadowed carriage. For all of her recent thoughts and suspicions about him, she knew very little about him. "What were you arguing with Mr. Lieber about? What idea did you have for expanding the carnival?"

Mr. Davies shrugged. "Maybe it was too far from the theme of steam and gears. I wanted a job I could do at the carnival during the evening without having to make my money all over town. I suggested to Mr. Warden that we expand the carnival to include a small corral where children and perhaps adults could ride horses. Not everyone has been on a horse."

"I haven't," Katya ventured. "I think it sounds like a good idea."

"Mr. Warden didn't like it, but he was more polite about it than Mr. Lieber was."

Katya held her tongue to keep from saying what she was thinking: *Mr. Warden might not be making those decisions much longer.* "Do you have children, Mr. Davies?"

"No. I've never been married. I see the children around the carnival sometimes, and I thought they might want something else to do here."

Katya thought of Brady's original vision for the carnival, one for families and wonder. "I'm sure you're right. How do you know so much about horses?"

"I used to work with them over in Cornwall. It's a part of England, surrounded on three sides by water."

"And now you live here," Katya teased him. She had heard of the Great Lakes north of the state, but she had seen mostly mere ponds since leaving New York.

"It took some getting used to," Mr. Davies obliged her. "I drove carts for the tin mines there. I got to know my horses very well. It's why I took this job for the carnival."

"Maybe someday you could work with more horses at the carnival."

"I like your optimism, but I won't hold my breath for it." Mr. Davies reached for the door handle beside him. "That's all I wanted to say. I should see you home."

Because Katya knew Magdalene would find some way to feel sorry for Mr. Lieber, she voiced one last question. "Mr. Davies, are you sorry Mr. Lieber's dead? Because I'm not, and I'm not ashamed of it."

Mr. Davies' eyes flicked around the dark carriage. He met Katya's gaze before he answered. "No, Miss Romanova, I'm not."

Mr. Davies slipped out of the carriage and returned to his high seat. The carriage bounced forward and carried Katya to the park's center circle before making its way down the next path to Market Street.

Katya closed her eyes, trying to recover as much as possible during the ride home. She usually had enough energy for anything, but her harrowing ride had spent all her reserves, leaving her limp, supported mostly by the dependable sturdiness of her bustle and corset.

When the carriage stopped, Katya looked out the window at the Weekly Boarder. She dragged herself out of the carriage, pausing only to wish Mr. Davies a good night. Katya climbed the three stairs to the porch and let herself into the front hall. As quietly as she could, Katya ascended the front staircase, gliding her hand up the curving railing to steady herself. She reached her room and unlocked that door as well. She had barely hobbled inside when Magdalene crept up behind her.

"What did he say?" Magdalene whispered.

Katya faced her with eyelids drooping for need of sleep. "He's not the killer, and neither am I. Good night, Mags. I'll tell you the rest when I get up."

Chapter Seventeen

The changes at the carnival did not present themselves as obviously as Katya expected. She scrapped the plan to lure Mr. Warden into a mysterious date downtown, and pending a better idea, she avoided his office as much as possible. She felt freer knowing she no longer needed to worry about Mr. Lieber's imposing presence, but she also felt hemmed in. Katya could not tell which men roaming the carnival night after night were paying guests and which were Mr. Warden's newly hired security.

Katya stopped mentioning the carnival around the boarding house. The only person there who wanted to talk about it with her was Lizzie, who smirked slyly every time they occupied the same room. Katya would ask for a platter or a pitcher to be passed to her at the table, and Lizzie would hand it to Magdalene between them with a sidelong glance at Katya. Katya always imagined Lizzie thinking pointedly, *You can have this, Katya, but the doctor and his rich friends from the east side of town are all mine.*

The rooms and halls at the boarding house grew quieter by the night. Lizzie disappeared on dates for and after dinner a few times a week. Mrs. Weeks buried her white head in the newspaper every afternoon, offering more and more snippets of news about President Cleveland's upcoming goodwill tour across the country. "It'll be five thousand miles," Mrs. Weeks announced with punctuated syllables. "His private train will take him as far west as Omaha, Nebraska, and as far south as Montgomery, Alabama. He's taking his wife, of course, and about half a dozen other people."

Mary shared a small portion of her mother's enthusiasm, reserved but pleasant. "That'll be nice."

Mrs. Weeks gasped loudly, clutching the locket over her chest. The rest of the ladies swung their heads to look at her. Mrs. Weeks raised her eyes with a proud, beaming smile. "President Cleveland is including us on his goodwill tour."

"How exciting," Lizzie murmured, sipping her tea.

Mrs. Weeks read some more and squealed with delight. "They're going to be meeting and greeting people down at the statehouse."

"You should go, Mother," Mary encouraged.

"I think I will. I should try, at least. You know, Mrs. Cleveland has refused to say what she'll be wearing on the trip. I'd love to see her and report to everyone I know how fashionable she is. My friends talk about her all the time. They'd simply die to know that I met her."

Katya and Magdalene listened with interest, but they had little choice about where they would be when the president arrived in the city. They climbed into bed early that morning, several hours before his arrival, and slept right through the president's visit.

Mrs. Weeks sat aglow at the lunch table, regretful to say the *Presidential Special* had already whisked the presidential party off to its next stop in Terre Haute.

"You should've seen Mrs. Cleveland," Mrs. Weeks reminisced, her blue-grey eyes floating toward the ceiling. "She looked radiant. Her dress was green silk, and her bonnet was stunning. The carriage drew up to the statehouse pulled by eight grey horses."

Lizzie glanced up from buttering her roll. "You're so formal, Mrs. Weeks. Everybody else calls her Frankie."

"I know, but I think she deserves all the respect in the world. She's better educated than the president, you know."

Mrs. Weeks' demure conversations at the Boarder soothed Katya's mind after her nights at the carnival. In the early morning, she left the grinding of machinery, her ears pounding with it, and woke up hours later to the pleasant, innocuous trickle of afternoon discussion. When weeping and screaming woke her from a sound dream two days after the president's departure, Katya took a few moments to realize she lay in her own bed. The tidy room stood organized around her, bombarded by the vibrating slam of the front door downstairs. Katya leapt out of bed and tore her dressing gown out of the armoire. One hand fumbled to tie it around her waist as she opened the bedroom door.

Mrs. Weeks clambered up the front stairs with Mary and Lizzie behind her. She waved a copy of the evening paper. "President Cleveland is dead!"

Magdalene's door popped open next to Katya's.

Mrs. Weeks stopped in the middle of the hallway with the four young women pressed in around her. "The president was assassinated in St. Louis."

Magdalene flattened her hand over the heart of her blue-flowered dressing gown. "What happened?"

Mrs. Weeks lifted the newspaper closer to her face. "President Cleveland arrived in St. Louis yesterday. A chorus of twenty-four thousand children welcomed him in song. Afterward, five of the children presented Mrs. Cleveland with a floral shield, which she received with hugs and kisses. What a remarkable woman she is, always so graceful, so gracious."

Mrs. Weeks untucked a handkerchief from the end of her sleeve and wiped tears from her cheeks. She lifted the paper once more. "The president was well received at the Merchants Exchange, where the applause was so great, he often had to pause his speech. It was during one of these moments that an unknown gunman took aim and shot the president through the head."

Magdalene stumbled closer to Katya and latched onto her arm for support. "That's terrible. Poor Frankie."

Mrs. Weeks nodded. "Mrs. Cleveland was at a luncheon. She wasn't there when it happened. He was dead when she reached him. The article says they were only married for thirteen months. They didn't even have a chance to have children."

Mary dotted her handkerchief to her face. "Who's going to be president now?"

Mrs. Weeks consulted the paper. "Following President Garfield's assassination six years ago, President Cleveland had the foresight to review the Succession Act when his vice president, Thomas A. Hendricks, passed away from ill health in 1885. The act was officially changed last year, now leaving Secretary of State, Thomas Bayard, to accept the presidency. He's to be sworn in as soon as possible.

"You know," Mrs. Weeks added, sniffling, "Thomas Hendricks' widow just helped welcome the Clevelands to our city. If Mr. Hendricks hadn't died, our former governor would've been president. How proud we would've been."

Katya leaned against Magdalene. Her heart ached for Frankie. She barely recognized Thomas Hendricks' name from the papers, but she admired Mrs. Weeks' devotion to her home city.

Magdalene hung onto Katya's sleeve. "It wouldn't erase what Frankie's going through."

"No, it wouldn't," Mrs. Weeks admitted.

Slowly, Mrs. Weeks turned to the spiral staircase and followed it down. Mary trailed after her, blowing her nose quietly.

Lizzie lingered in the hall, her usually sharp gaze blurred by the solemn news. "Is the carnival going to close tonight?"

Katya steeled herself against Lizzie's superior expression. "I doubt it."

Lizzie raised her shoulder indifferently, her eyelids fluttering. "It seems to me your carnival won't be needed tonight. Nobody wants to ride a roller coaster after finding out their president's been shot."

"I think you're wrong. I think attendance will be higher than ever."

When attendance proved roughly the same, Katya refused to let it bother her as she walked the grounds that night. The carnival opening its gates for those who wanted to forget their sorrows seemed victory enough. The band played the stately, rousing *Hail, Columbia* and *The Star-Spangled Banner* every hour. The side stage, where Lizzie's employer judged an embroidery contest, stopped its activity for a few minutes of silence between each round.

The unusual repetition grated on Katya's nerves and challenged the strength of her patriotic spirit. She was almost glad when the carnival closed in the morning. She strolled past Brady's game stall on her way to check for lingering visitors in the water closets when she noticed him waving her over. Katya made sure no one watched her before she stepped up to the end of the counter. "Do you need some help closing up?" she asked.

"Yes. I need you to rearrange the boxes and things on the shelves there." Brady gestured to the two long shelves under the counter.

Katya sank down on her haunches as best she could. She heard the strong but delicate clinking of the glass bottles as Brady collected them from the platform behind her. He dropped several into the grass between them. He crouched down, taking his time to pick them up as he spoke in a low voice.

"I wanted to talk to you, Miss Romanova," he said. "Miss Harvey, too. I hope you'll pass along what I tell you."

Katya nodded. Her gloved hands moved the boxes of painted wooden rings around on the shelves, not accomplishing a thing.

Brady spoke up evenly. "I didn't harm Mr. Lieber."

He sounded so genuine, Katya felt guilty for including him on her list of suspects, even temporarily. "I know."

"I didn't want you to be afraid of me."

"We're not."

Brady pulled a larger box off the bottom shelf and stood the bottles up in it side by side. "The security's tighter than ever."

"How can you tell?"

"You can always tell who they are. Look at their eyes. They're too watchful to be guests. They're too serious to feel amusement in their lives." Brady stood up and collected the last few bottles from the platform. He crouched down again to set them in the box. "Have you noticed them?"

"No, but I've tried to seek them out."

"Warden picked them well. They all look like ruffians, even the ones who shave on occasion."

"Do you know anything about them? Names or what they might've done before?"

"No."

"Do you think it's too dangerous for us to keep meeting?"

"Not at the church." Brady lifted the box of bottles onto the bottom shelf. "I think we're safe there."

Katya turned frightened eyes on Brady. "What about the carnival? Do you think we're safe here?"

Brady took a moment to answer, which froze Katya solid despite his reassurance. "We're safe for now."

Chapter Eighteen

Within a week of President Cleveland's assassination, the carnival returned to its normal routine. The band restored its passionate, upbeat repertoire. The side stage hosted uninterrupted contests and demonstrations. Katya noticed the same woman arriving almost every night, although a far cry from the woman in poorly fitting green she had seen weeks before. This woman strutted with confident purpose, her golden head held high. Katya wondered if she was also coming to visit Mr. Warden, and a brisk walk across the opposite side of the carnival from her confirmed Katya's suspicions. The woman stepped gracefully past the food stall, her deep purple jacket melting into the shadows as she let herself into Mr. Warden's office.

Katya waited near Heinz operating the Warden wheel until the woman reappeared. Katya tugged on his sleeve and tilted her head at the woman. "There. The woman coming out of the office. Who is she? Do you know her?"

Heinz squinted at the woman and cocked an eyebrow. "Know her? That's Isolde Neumann. No man in the county isn't in love with her or her money."

"Why? Who is she?"

"Her father brought his ornament-making business here from Germany years ago. They're very popular around Christmastime."

Isolde strutted through the crowd, passing the food stall and heading for the front of the carnival.

Heinz looked Katya over, one eyebrow askance. "She gives you a run for your money, doesn't she?"

Katya could not deny Isolde dazzled, even at a distance. The lamplight flickered off her smooth, even skin, illuminating the strong line of her jaw. Her hair gave off every shade between honey and lemon chiffon. She eased out of sight behind the Beast's supporting beams.

Katya kept her irritation at Heinz to herself and crossed the grass to the food stall. Magdalene stood at the counter, handing small paper bags rattling with hard candy to the waiting customers. Katya stood off to the side where Magdalene could still hear her. "Did you see Mr. Warden's latest girlfriend? She just walked past."

"What makes you think she's his girlfriend?" Magdalene scooped more hard candy into a pair of white paper bags. "He can't be dating every woman who passes within fifty feet of him."

"This woman's gorgeous. Rich, too." Katya leaned her shoulder against the counter. She could not ignore a small twinge of jealousy. "She let herself right into his office the way the other woman used to."

"You haven't seen her around anymore?" Magdalene handed out the newly filled bags of candy.

"No. It appears he's traded up."

"Did you get her name?"

"Yes, Heinz gave it to me."

"Well, hold onto it in case we need it. She might need to meet him downtown for something very soon."

Katya wrinkled her nose. "I'm glad we changed plans. We don't need to make any more trouble for this woman. She's already dealing with Mr. Warden."

"That's more trouble than anybody deserves." Magdalene glanced at Katya. The humor blanched from her voice. "I need to talk to you."

"Can you get away?"

"I don't think so."

Irina shuffled in front of Katya in the booth, looking for something among the pots and jars on the shelf. "What are you two whispering about now?"

Magdalene turned away from the line of customers toward Katya and Irina. "I feel like I'm being watched."

"We're all being watched," Irina assured her, her deep voice gruff with resentment.

Magdalene pressed on. "I feel like every time I look up, someone's staring at me. They don't want candy or sausages. I don't know what they want. They never get in line."

"Maybe you should try offering them something." Irina picked up a long-handled iron dipper, the wide, flat ladle poked through with holes. She moved back to the other side of the stall to retrieve frying dough from the pan.

Magdalene leaned closer to Katya. "I'm serious, Kat. It scares me." Her arm shook where it propped her up against the counter.

Katya tried to sound reassuring. "It might be nothing. Mr. Kelly told me Mr. Warden's new security looked a little rough. But you have to remember they're not after us. We didn't have anything to do with Mr. Lieber's death."

"But they'll be looking for who did." Magdalene straightened up and began scooping candy into another set of bags. "They'll be looking for whoever sent Mr. Warden those threatening letters. I'm sure he hasn't forgotten those."

"We're innocent. He has to know that."

"I hope so." Magdalene turned to the waiting customers. "I'm sorry about your wait. Please have some candy on the carnival."

Katya ambled away from the food stall. She half expected one of Mr. Warden's mysterious goons to stand staring at her, barely visible through the shifting crowd. Just as Katya would be able to memorize his face, he would certainly disappear behind a large figure in a top hat and never show up again.

No such security appeared. The only faces surrounding Katya were fascinated, awestruck, and eager for more. The men tipped their hats to the ladies around them, and the children munched happily on salted popcorn. Katya waited for one of

Mr. Warden's observant, stone-faced lackeys to break the sea of contented people, but they were all that she could see. She passed the enormous roar of the Beast. A few couples danced and applauded in front of the bandstand. The musicians seemed to respond by playing louder and with even more gusto, lending a triumphant tone to the swirling march.

Katya did not doubt Magdalene was being watched. She felt convinced she was being studied as well, along with most if not all of the carnival staff. She felt it in her long, delicate bones, although for the moment, she did not feel their eyes weighing on her. It was only a matter of time until she saw them, perhaps partially concealed at the edge of a shadow, possibly much bolder. Katya spent the rest of the night looking for Mr. Warden's hardened security, helping the patrons as much as she was paid to. As sharply as she looked for them, not a single one caught her attention.

Chapter Nineteen

Isolde continued to visit the carnival, every outfit more elaborate than the last. Katya watched her from safe distances, Isolde's rounded curves and neatly cinched waist draped in fine silks of bold purple, ivory, and gold. Katya began designing new costumes for herself in her head, embroidered silk jackets imported from Asia and fitted with metal clasps down the front. She envisioned a sky-blue jacket displaying a working clock face on the back, the thin metal gears turning for the guests' delight. New gloves could hold small, functioning compasses on the back of each wrist. Lizzie's employer could cover new dresses in even more complex and colorful embroidery. Katya imagined patterns of gauges and clouds mixing with sheet music and hard candy.

Every time the gilded Isolde strolled past with smugness lighting her bright blue eyes, Katya quenched her jealousy with a new design. Sometimes Katya followed her to the back of the carnival, and sometimes Katya beat her there by crossing the other side of the grounds. Isolde never visited the world's greatest attraction without visiting Mr. Warden's office, and Katya never stuck around to see how long Isolde stayed inside. Katya took her sulking to another area, letting the happiness of the other guests boost her spirits.

Katya did not expect to see a woman other than Isolde at the office one night when she glanced at its door. Isolde had not arrived yet if she was going to. This woman did not enter as if she were expected. Her shoulders drooped lower than Isolde's confident lines, and her blonde hair was faded within a few shades of translucent. She huddled close to the door, knocking in a few brief wraps. The door remained closed, and the woman knocked again in a desperate fury. Katya moved closer to the Warden wheel but not so close that Heinz would shoo her away.

The office door opened, Mr. Warden standing backlit in the doorway, his hand resting on the handle. He did not look surprised to see her but greeted her with a formal tip of his hat and a familiar recognition in his eyes.

The woman erupted in emotion, her mouth moving in quick bursts of speech. Katya could not hear her words for the chug and grind of the wheel looming over her. The woman wiped a handkerchief swiftly under her sagging eyes.

Mr. Warden regained his calm, speaking in slower, calculated motions.

The woman took a step back and swung forward. Clutching her handkerchief in her hand, she pounded her fists on Mr. Warden's chest, the material flapping and waving with every movement.

Now Mr. Warden changed his response to her. Creases around his eyes gave him a pained expression, but his smooth mouth denoted nothing but patience. When the woman collapsed against him, her mouth gaped open in weeping, Mr. Warden stretched his arms around her. He said something, and she nodded. He led her slowly and carefully inside as one might guide someone sick or injured.

Katya barely noticed the man on her right until he spoke. "That's Agna Lieber."

Katya jumped, her heart striking the inner curve of her ribs. She stared at the man next to her, brown eyes sharp above a trimmed beard. He dressed in a simple suit as well made as any carnival goer wore, but as Brady had said, his gaze regarded Katya much too seriously to be there for fun. Katya could not place his accent, something muddled, like a softened German. Katya could only repeat what the man told her, as perplexed as he had been sure of himself. "Agna Lieber?"

"Yes."

"Is she related to Ernst Lieber?"

The security man took his time to answer. "She's his widow."

"I didn't know he was married." Katya tried to imagine Mr. Lieber perhaps five years younger, nervous and sweating as he asked Agna to marry him. She tried to picture Mr. Lieber at home, eating dinner with his wife in front of a steady fire. She would pass him a dish of sausages served with sauerkraut, followed by a cup of authentic German mustard. Katya could not dream of him saying thank you or doing much more than slathering the sausages in the yellow sauce and stuffing them into his mouth.

"He had a little girl," security added.

"A little girl?" Katya knew she must sound stupid, but she could not fathom Ernst Lieber having a family. Not just any family, but a wife upset enough over his passing that she would accost the great William Warden on his own turf. "How old is she?"

"Seven, maybe less."

"I've never seen Mrs. Lieber here before."

"She had no reason to come before."

"Did you know she was coming?" Katya watched the door to Mr. Warden's office, wondering how long it would stay closed this time. The security guard gave no answer, and Katya glanced over. He no longer stood beside her or anywhere else she looked.

"So I was right," Katya murmured to herself under the great Warden wheel. "They do move and disappear through the crowd like ghosts."

Katya decided not to wait for the reemergence of Agna Lieber. She drifted back to the patrons and their numerous questions and problems. The sneaking suspicion tickled her brain that she should have known Agna existed, and by the end of the night, Katya remembered where she had first caught wind of a woman in Mr. Lieber's life.

The original argument Katya heard between Mr. Davies and Mr. Lieber had been about a woman. Katya had assumed she was a girlfriend or hopeful acquaintance of Mr. Lieber's, but now she realized Mr. Lieber had raged on behalf of Agna. She wondered if Mr. Davies had actually been interested in her or if Mr. Lieber had taken a simple glance as the only trigger he needed to rip Mr. Davies in two.

Katya did not think it mattered. Mr. Lieber was dead and buried. She did not expect to see Agna again, and she did not mention Agna's visit to Mr. Davies when she left the carnival for the night.

Three days later, Katya passed Agna in the crowd and almost did not recognize the widowed Mrs. Lieber. Katya stopped in her tracks and studied the woman. Agna's hunched figure continued toward the water closets, clad in the pale, muddy colors the charwoman always wore. Against the wood and metal backdrop of the carnival, Agna labored nearly invisibly. She carried a bucket in each hand, one arm straining longer than the other. She set them down outside one of the water closets and eased the door open before she carried the buckets inside.

That night in the carriage, the charwoman's silence seemed more purposeful than usual. She pursed her lips as she stared out the window, her eyes focused on something Katya could never see.

In the morning, Mr. Davies made his usual stop after picking up Katya and Magdalene from the Weekly Boarder. Irina's form shifted the weight of the carriage as she stepped inside. She settled in across from Katya in her dark brown jacket and lighter brown dress. The carriage did not stop for the charwoman.

"Is she sick?" Magdalene asked.

Katya felt a pit deepen in her stomach. "I think she's been replaced," she said.

Irina looked up from brushing at the fabric of her skirt. "Because of the security? Did they find something out?"

Katya thought back to the scene Agna had played out with Mr. Warden. "It's because Mr. Lieber was murdered. I think she's been replaced by Mrs. Lieber."

Irina's dark eyebrows shot up under her parted bangs. "There's a *Mrs.* Lieber?"

"Yes. She paid a visit to Mr. Warden the other night. I saw her again last night. She was cleaning out the water closets."

Irina nodded slowly, her eyelids heavy for thinking. "Any one of us could be next."

"No, I think she just needs a way to support herself. She has a little girl to look after."

Irina's eyes widened again. "Mr. Lieber had a little *girl*?"

"I was as surprised as you are. It's hard to imagine him being a father, isn't it?"

"It's hard to imagine a monster like him at all."

Magdalene spoke up. "He must've had a softer side we never saw."

Irina guffawed with gusto and raised her hand to cover her mouth. "Excuse me, dear, but there was nothing soft about Ernst Lieber. I'm sure his widow was well acquainted with the back of his hand."

Katya wondered if Mr. Davies could hear them from his high seat behind her. She hoped, if he did care anything for Agna Lieber, that the wind was drowning in his ears.

"I feel sorry for the woman," Irina admitted. "Marriage to Ernst Lieber couldn't have been kind to her. She must've felt freer than a jay bird when he went to meet his maker."

"I'm not sure," Katya said. "She seemed pretty upset."

"Well..." Irina trailed off. "Sometimes the more they bruise, the more used to it they become."

Mr. Davies stopped the carriage at the carnival gates. It pained Katya to see Mr. Warden's name in huge letters near the opening. Mr. Kelly's name deserved to be there, not someone who used the carnival to lure every eligible woman to him within fifty miles.

"I wonder if Mrs. Lieber will be riding with us," Katya said as she stepped down from the carriage.

The next morning, only Katya, Magdalene, and Irina were dropped off.

That evening, Mr. Davies made a new third stop, and Mrs. Agna Lieber climbed into the carriage.

Chapter Twenty

Agna settled into the back corner of the carriage, keeping her head down and her mouth shut. Katya felt too uncomfortable at her unexpected appearance to greet her.

Magdalene attempted a polite "Good evening," but Agna gave only the slightest nod in return.

Irina, like Katya, sat without speaking.

Maybe because Katya felt so aware of Agna's presence, she saw Agna much more during her nights at the carnival than she had ever noticed the previous charwoman. The usual woman had proven no slacker. Katya knew from glimpses of her bare hands that the woman's palms and fingers were worn into rough, peeling patches of what could loosely be called skin.

Agna worked every bit as hard if not harder. Katya observed her time and time again carrying buckets weighing her hands down to her knees. Agna did not just clean and tidy the water closets, making sure they smelled fresh and kept a full supply of toilet paper. She ducked in and out of Mr. Warden's office quite often with a bucket of cleaning supplies. Katya learned from listening in on the maintenance men that Agna had even organized their storage room for them without being asked.

If Katya had heard about Mrs. Lieber before meeting her in such a peculiar way, she would have prepared herself to dislike her. But as the nights wore on, Katya realized that Agna never enjoyed herself. The charwoman she replaced had not been a bundle of mirth, but Agna's frown sank deeper. Her movements were not simply purposeful and efficient. They were labored, desperate to please, and hurried to complete each task.

Agna's misery tore Katya's heart to pieces until she could not stand to ignore the woman anymore. Katya approached her in front of the maintenance office behind the western food stall.

Agna let her buckets down with a controlled drop, one full of dirty water and the other brimming with supplies.

"Mrs. Lieber?" Katya said, her voice lilting. "We haven't met formally. I'm Katya Romanova. I help direct the guests here."

Agna squinted at Katya with a guarded expression that could have hidden anything from suspicion to physical exhaustion.

"I'm sorry about your husband," Katya added. She did not clarify that she was only sorry that Agna had lost her husband and not that Ernst Lieber no longer walked among the living.

Agna opened the door to the maintenance office and hoisted the bucket of supplies inside. Katya followed her. She had not ventured into the small building since she toured the carnival before its opening. Like Mr. Warden's office, a wall and door split it into two rooms. The front room surrounded Katya with shelves and bins of tools and spare parts. A work bench stretched across the right-hand wall. Through the open doorway to the inner room, Katya could see a few chairs around a table where maintenance could sit and relax. Finding no men in the building, Katya closed the door.

"What do you want?" Agna asked in a hoarse voice, her back to Katya. She lowered the bucket of supplies on the workbench.

"I thought you might want a friend at the carnival."

Agna chuckled ruefully by the time Katya finished her sentence. "I don't need a friend."

"What do you need?"

Agna faced Katya, her dim blue eyes dissecting her. "I don't know you."

"I saw you talking to Mr. Warden. You have a daughter to take care of, don't you? You need this job."

"Yes, and he gave it to me. What do you want from me?"

"I think you deserve better. That's all." Suddenly doubting her ability to reach Agna, Katya fumbled for the door handle.

"Wait." Agna stood as proud as anyone in her position could. Her head was pulled back, even her shoulders lifted, but her face stretched taut with anguish. "I have one question. Nobody can tell me where my husband died. Do you know where he was when it happened?"

As every heartbeat pounded in Katya's ears, she remembered promising Mr. Warden she would keep the information to herself. Faced with Agna's grief, she heard her lips break that promise. "He died in Mr. Warden's office, in the back room."

Agna's fingers grasped at her throat. "I was in that room."

"I'm sorry."

Katya opened the door and let herself out. Twenty feet away, Isolde Neumann strolled past the corner of the near food stall. She tilted her head back, taking in the sights rising into the sky around her. Katya imagined she had just come from Mr. Warden's office and was finally convinced to spend some time getting to know the rest of the carnival.

Katya stayed by the maintenance door to give Isolde time to move farther away. Katya did not take more than a few steps to her left when Maddox approached her from the opposite direction.

Maddox beamed in recognition and tipped his hat. "Miss Romanova. I never thought I'd see you over here by the maintenance storage. Don't tell me one of the customers wanted to borrow a hammer?"

Katya tried to sweep past Maddox. "No, Mr. O'Sullivan, they did not."

Maddox turned to follow her with his gaze. "Have you been reading the papers? The police arrested the man who shot President Cleveland. He'll be going to trial soon."

"Yes, I heard."

"The maintenance men are putting bets on whether or not he'll be hanged. I think he will be. The man who shot President Garfield was."

Katya nodded and tried to slip away.

"I barely remember that," Maddox rambled on. "I was only fourteen when they hanged him. It was exciting, though."

Katya huffed. "Mr. O'Sullivan, I have work to do, and I'm sure you do, too."

Maddox angled his hat back a little, his good mood only brightening. "I heard you're not above shirking your work every now and again."

Katya lowered her chin. "You've started hearing bad things about me."

"Nothing that bad, Miss Romanova. I'm sure you'll hear some interesting things about me."

"I don't talk to maintenance very often."

"Let me fill you in, then. I've been roaming half the country most of my life. Never been here before. I just spent over two years on the east coast, like I said."

Katya sighed and put off her thoughts of running away from him. "Did you like it there?"

"It was all right. There's excitement to be had everywhere. You don't have to go west for it."

"The West is supposed to be one of the most exciting parts of the country."

Maddox shrugged. "I like it here. They don't have machines like this out west."

"No, they don't."

Another maintenance man draped in a suit of drab colors called for Maddox, and with his attention diverted, Katya stole away into the crowd. She passed the water closets and the Cannon firing its cars onto the sloping tracks behind them. She did not know how to react to Maddox's presence at the carnival. Katya felt more like herself when the patrons began asking for help: Which flavor of hard candy tasted the best? Was the Warden wheel safe for rambunctious little boys? Katya was not used to avoiding such a pervasive, moving target. Not even Mr. Warden pursued her that incessantly.

Chapter Twenty-One

Every time Katya saw Agna Lieber – riding in the carriage or working at the carnival – she remembered Mr. Lieber's violent argument with Mr. Davies.

Mr. Davies never spoke to Agna in any special way. He greeted her stiffly, as if he, along with everyone else, knew Agna primarily by the way she had come to work at the carnival. She was a struggling widow first and a fellow worker second. Katya listened closely to Mr. Davies' scant words, trying to discern the least amount of secret desire or hidden feeling. She could never find any, but she knew it could be due to a certain cleverness or great respect for Agna's mourning on Mr. Davies' part.

Katya could picture the scenario either way. Perhaps Mr. Davies' eyes had only fallen on Agna a single time, and Mr. Lieber had taken his protectiveness to the extreme. Katya liked the other path better, a story she wove to be larger than life. Poor Mr. Davies, unmarried and childless, pined for Agna from the driver's seat of his carriage. He rarely dared to sneak glances at her, much less speak to her, and the only time he let his eyes linger too long, Mr. Lieber's jealous temper wrung him out for it. Poor Mr. Davies, with his lonely job of driving four women who shared the good fortune of having each other's company for support and conversation. He had only the horse to mutter to in the sparsely populated hours of the early morning.

Katya spun wild tales as she rode in the carriage or waited for carnival patrons to approach with a need. Mr. Davies would break from his normally mundane routine and reassuring manners. He would drive off with Agna into the night instead of escorting her home. The horse's sprinting speed would frighten her, but Mr. Davies' presence would comfort her. At last the carriage would stop, and Mr. Davies would fling himself down from the driver's chair. Agna would climb down to meet him, only farmers' fields surrounding them now. Her eyes would water with a rise of affection she had barely acknowledged when her husband lived. She would throw her arms around Mr. Davies, and he would kiss her with unrivaled passion. He would press her back against the side of the carriage, reaching for the buttons on the front of her jacket...

"Do you know what contest is being held tomorrow?"

A man's harsh German accent splintered Katya's fantasy. It could hardly be mistaken for Mr. Davies' lyrical, rustic English speech.

Katya blinked at a young blond couple watching her expectantly. Two small, pale-haired boys stood at their sides. Katya tried to remember what Mr. Warden had told her. "I believe it's a dancing contest. It starts over every hour. The best couple in each group wins a five-dollar certificate to Montani and Company grocers."

The young woman turned to her husband, her eyebrows raised as she nodded at him. The young man tipped his hat to Katya.

"You're welcome," Katya gushed. "Enjoy the carnival. Make sure you get some snacks for the children."

The family walked away, and Katya returned to her tales of Agna and Mr. Davies. She passed the rest of the night uneventfully, and once she had helped the two men in the ticket booth chase down loose tickets blowing away across the grass, Katya set her sights squarely on Mr. Davies. She left the band to fold up their own music stands and strolled over to the gate as soon as the carriage pulled up.

Mr. Davies tipped his hat as Katya approached him. "Good morning, Miss Romanova. Are you early, or am I late?"

"I'm early, Mr. Davies. I wanted to ask you something, but I'll warn you. I'm sure it's none of my business."

Mr. Davies tilted his head, waiting.

"Do you mind if I climb up and talk to you?"

"Not at all."

Katya stepped up into the driver's seat and settled in next to Mr. Davies. He set his horse whip aside.

Katya cringed to see the tool up close. "I'm sure you remember the night Mr. Lieber used your whip against the horse."

Mr. Davies' back stiffened. "You saw that. Yes, I remember."

"I heard you arguing about a woman." Katya paused to see if Mr. Davies caught on to what she was saying. "Now that I know Mr. Lieber was married, I wondered if you weren't arguing about Agna."

"In a way," Mr. Davies replied. "No argument with Mr. Lieber was ever about anything but power and his need to control everything."

"He accused you of being interested in his wife."

"I remember."

Katya paused again, on the verge of truth after so many of her own detailed versions of it. "I wanted to ask you if you were. Are you interested in Agna?"

Mr. Davies chuckled. "I wouldn't have imagined you for a busybody, Miss Romanova."

"I try not to be. I only wondered because you and Mr. Lieber were having such a terrific argument. I wondered if there was any shred of truth to what he said. And I also wanted to ask because she works here now. You see her twice a day. I thought if you did like her, it might be torture for you."

"No, I was never interested in Mrs. Lieber. She deserved better, but everyone knows that. I believe I ran into them a few times around the city. At a restaurant or a park. I might have looked at her in passing before I realized whom she was with. I was always keen to avoid Mr. Lieber, as I'm sure you can appreciate."

"Yes. I'm sorry if I offended you." Katya glanced away through the open gates of the carnival.

The band members moseyed past, wiping sweat off their foreheads as they traded jokes and observations about the night.

They turned and followed the sidewalk toward the streetcar stop.

Katya waited until most of them walked past the carriage to continue her conversation with Mr. Davies. "I'm not trying to meddle," she explained. "You're just one of the few people here who treats me with an ounce of respect. To most of them, even Irina, I'm a lazy whore and nothing more."

Mr. Davies said nothing.

Katya thought back to her infamous interview with Mr. Warden. She could have walked away from his office and the promise of a job at the carnival, her reputation still intact. Sitting in the driver's seat of the carnival carriage, Katya knew she would make the same decision again. "It's my own fault, I suppose," she said.

Mr. Davies' voice rose to life. "You're much more, Miss Romanova. Although my dealings with Mrs. Irina Solomon have been few and brief, I would say you're the more caring of the two. You're more interested in the world around you."

Katya did not feel any better. "Let me know when caring and paying attention amount to anything."

"They do. It might not seem like it, but they do."

"Did you ever meet a woman you wanted to marry, Mr. Davies?"

Mr. Davies shifted uncomfortably. "Of course. Most men have."

"Did she live here or back home in Cornwall?"

"Cornwall, but that was a long time ago."

Katya let the subject rest. "Thank you for your time, Mr. Davies." She turned to step down from the driver's seat.

"Miss Romanova, I don't want you to think I don't appreciate you coming to talk to me," Mr. Davies said.

Katya turned back to him and remained beside him.

"I have such a small connection to the carnival. I rarely speak to anyone who works here except for you and Mr. Warden to pick up my salary."

"I didn't know our conversations meant that much to you."

"Let me be honest. Not everyone here is welcoming, and I'm not just talking about Mr. Lieber."

Katya understood completely. Heinz was often short with her. The English cook barely acknowledged her. Before she had gotten to know Brady, she would have counted him as standoffish or worse. Mr. Warden's security seemed downright creepy. "Why do you want to be a bigger part of the carnival? It must be nice to serve the city in some other capacity."

"The carnival's the best opportunity in the city. Between the railroad strikes and long hours at the factories, the carnival is anybody's best choice. It's not going anywhere."

"That's true, but look what happened to the other charwoman we had. Agna cried to Mr. Warden, which is understandable, but within days, that other woman was out of a job. The carnival's secure, but Mr. Warden's impossible to predict."

"That's true. Do you worry about your job?"

"No. Mr. Warden could replace me, but I know he'd rather spend his time making money than finding new staff."

"At least someone around here knows something about him. He's a bit of a mystery, isn't he?"

"Indeed." Katya realized that knowing Mr. Warden's criminal past still told her very little about him. She did not know where he came from or how long he intended to run the carnival himself. He must not anticipate being caught, or he would have left the city months ago.

The maintenance crew ambled through the gates, laughing as one voice. They noticed Katya up in the driver's seat and tipped their hats on cue. They muted their amusement as men always did when they shared jokes not meant for mixed company.

"Good evening," Katya greeted them stiffly. She did not mind the band members seeing her talking to Mr. Davies, but she did not feel comfortable having a group of rowdy workmen finding her there.

Maddox filed past at the end of the line. He tipped his hat with a respectful nod and walked on with the others toward the streetcar. Katya thought about asking Mr. Davies if he knew anything about Maddox but decided against it.

"Thank you, Mr. Davies." Katya slipped down from the driver's seat.

"Any time, Miss Romanova," Mr. Davies said. "I've got nowhere else to go."

Katya wandered back into the carnival grounds. With the band and maintenance men gone, only a handful of workers remained amongst the still machines. The security, expectantly, lingered nowhere to be seen.

Katya began one final story featuring Agna and Mr. Davies. Agna approached the carriage where Mr. Davies sat high in his usual seat. She did not glance up at him, and he did not notice anything particular about her. She climbed into the carriage, and he waited for the other women to climb in behind her.

It was the one true story she had told herself all day.

Chapter Twenty-Two

Agna labored like a constantly driven beast. Even when Katya tried to avoid her, she glimpsed Agna no less than three or four times a night, always with buckets in her hands. She wiped sweat from her face, smeared blood off the calluses on her palms, and grimaced when her apron caught the vomit of a child who rode the Kaleidoscope too soon after eating. But none of it slowed her pace or lessened her determination.

Out of growing concern, Katya resolved to follow her. She always kept a safe distance of fifteen feet, although Katya doubted Agna would notice if Katya literally waltzed in front of her. Katya usually sought out a place to eat her supper in private, but for a few nights, she nibbled it as she walked.

Agna's taut, pained expression never lightened. She never sat to rest or paused more than five minutes to consume a meal. Agna's appearance became more and more bedraggled, her hair falling out of place at the back of her head and her complexion paling.

One night, Agna stumbled over an uneven clump of earth, the weight of the buckets slinging her toward the ground. She dropped the buckets with two messy splashes before she righted herself. A man in a pressed black suit jumped out of the way as the deluge leapt at his shoes. He snapped at Agna in a language Katya did not understand before stalking on his way. Agna gave no response Katya could see. Katya's heart thumped in sympathy from deep in her belly, but before she could ask herself if she should help, Agna pried the buckets up again. She waddled away with them, and Katya turned her head. She could barely look at Agna anymore. The woman would work herself to death if no one intervened.

Katya waited until Isolde arrived and departed for the night before she made her way to Mr. Warden's office. She wondered if she should knock first. Katya had rarely hesitated before, but she was not sure how welcome she would be. Katya pushed the door open and stepped inside.

"Mr. Warden?" she called to let him know whom it was.

Mr. Warden stood up to meet her, standing by his desk in the other room. "Katya, how are you?"

"All right."

"What brings me the pleasure of your company?"

Katya stopped in the doorway between rooms. "I wanted to talk to you about Agna Lieber."

Mr. Warden lowered himself into his desk chair. His pleasantness soured. "What about Agna Lieber?"

"I'm not complaining, but she's working too hard."

"Maintenance tells me their tools have never been cleaner."

Katya quickly obliged him. "I'm sure it's true."

"The operators say the rides are cleaner than they've ever been."

"She's a great worker."

Mr. Warden leaned back in his chair, almost slumping his shoulders in an informal posture. "So what's the problem?"

"She's going to kill herself. Have you seen her?"

"Yes, I've seen her."

"She looks horrible. I thought the woman before her wore herself ragged, but this turns my stomach. She's never smiled once."

Mr. Warden offered a wry twist of his lips. "She's grieving, Katya."

Katya shook her head. "She might be grieving, but even Irina looks happy from time to time. I've never met any woman with a worse mood than Irina."

"What do you expect me to do about Mrs. Lieber?"

"Something. Anything. You're the one who gave her the job."

"I did."

"Can't you give her something else? Can't you tell her she doesn't have to wash the whole carnival by herself every night with Scrubb's Ammonia and a toothbrush?"

Mr. Warden's expression did not soften. "She wanted work, and I gave her work. I cleared the position for her. If I hadn't done that, she'd be giving up much more than her private carriage. She'd lose her house, and her little girl would be selling newspapers on the street."

"It can't be the only job she can do."

Mr. Warden sweetened his tone. "Who has more experience cleaning than a wife and a mother?"

"You know what I mean. She must have other skills."

"You want me to give her another job at the carnival?"

"Yes," Katya said, finally feeling like she was getting through to him.

"You want me to give Mrs. Lieber a better job with more exposure to the customers. You want me to give her a job where she'll have to pay to alter her clothes in order to work. I was thinking of Mrs. Lieber when I gave her this job. I did her a favor."

Katya wished she had not come into the office. "I'm telling you what I see. You don't have to be cruel."

"Katya." Mr. Warden held his hand out until Katya stepped forward and took it. "I've told you before to leave the running of the carnival to me. I have everyone's best interests at heart."

"But she..." Katya saw no point in repeating herself. Agna was wasting away, her cheeks sinking in between the bones. Her blue eyes, once lackluster, looked hollow now. "I thought you could do more."

"I would if I could, my dear. You know I would."

Katya humored Mr. Warden with a hint of forgiveness in the curve of her mouth.

"Is there anything else bothering you?" he asked.

"No."

"Good."

Katya slipped her hand out of Mr. Warden's. "I'd appreciate it if you wouldn't tell Mrs. Lieber I spoke up for her. She's not very fond of me."

"Give her a chance to know you. I'm sure she'll warm up to you."

Katya nodded. She realized the heady floral scent filling her nose must be the lingering perfume of Isolde Neumann. Katya had rarely smelled it before except on wealthy patrons and a few people she had passed while shopping downtown. "I hope you take your girlfriend on real dates, Mr. Warden, instead of restricting her to the confines of the carnival."

Mr. Warden lifted his dark eyebrows. "Oh?"

"I see her here almost every night. You're seeing Isolde Neumann, aren't you?"

"In a manner of speaking."

Katya decided not to press him. Mr. Warden was too practiced at evasion to give up easily. "She's lovely."

"As are you."

For once, Katya recoiled at one of Mr. Warden's compliments. She could hardly believe he would continue to be forward with her, but she could hardly admit it surprised her.

Mr. Warden flicked his eyes over Katya's dress. "It's been a while since you wore anything new," he added.

"I've been working on some designs. I haven't put anything on paper yet."

"I look forward to seeing you wear them."

Katya backed up into the doorway. "I won't take up any more of your time. I know you have a lot to manage with the carnival."

"But not overworking myself."

Katya flashed a tense smile.

"Don't you worry about Mrs. Lieber," Mr. Warden said. "She's well compensated for her efforts. Not as well as you are, but she'll be able to keep her house."

The bottom of Katya's stomach twisted. She wanted to ask Mr. Warden to lower her salary, to make it even with what the other women were making. But she could not. She had come to rely on that extra money, even revel in it. It paid for her costumes, her customized jackets, beautifully tailored dresses, and eye-catching hats.

Katya murmured a thank you as she turned and walked out of the office. She had never been so disappointed in herself. *Caring indeed, Mr. Davies,* she thought. *I'm as underhanded as Mr. Warden.*

Chapter Twenty-Three

Katya strolled past the Kaleidoscope, smiling broadly at the patrons waiting in line. "Are you doing all right?"

Half nodded.

"Do you need anything?" she asked.

The rest of the guests shook their heads. A young woman stood off to the side bouncing a baby in her arms, her wide eyes searching the crowd.

Katya walked over to her. "May I help you?"

"Oh, you're with the carnival." The young woman shifted the baby to the other side of her chest. Where the infant had been, a long shimmer of drool glistened on the front of her jacket. "My husband's on the ride, and it's our first time here. Do you know where I could clean myself up?"

"I can show you to the water closets. They all have sinks in them with a little pump right there."

"No, I can find them if you point them out to me. I'll only be a minute. Would you tell my husband, if he gets off before I'm back, that I'll meet him here?"

"Of course."

"He's rather short and wears silver, steel-framed glasses."

Katya gestured to the Cannon halfway across the carnival. "There's a line of them right in front of that coaster."

"Thank you."

The woman set off, nestling the baby securely against her chest. A well-dressed couple in finely pressed silks pushed a wicker baby stroller a few steps behind her, and Katya imagined the young mother would very much prefer to afford one for her own child.

Katya glanced up at the Kaleidoscope, whirling and gliding on its platform. She did not know when it might stop, but as long as she was serving one of the guests, she did not mind standing still to wait for it. Katya folded her hands together and turned her attention to the crowd flowing past her. Maddox stood behind the moving people, stationary under the glow of the lamplight shining above him. His eyes remained on Katya in every moment people did not pass directly between them.

Katya did not move from her spot, determined to carry out her word to the young mother. Maddox timed a gap in the shifting crowd and crossed through it, tipping his hat as he walked up to Katya.

"I'm waiting for a guest," Katya explained.

"What are you waiting for, exactly?"

"A woman with a baby or her husband on the Kaleidoscope, whoever reaches me first."

"So you're stuck here?" Maddox asked, perking up with a grin. "You won't be running off?"

Katya sighed. "Yes, Mr. O'Sullivan. I'm stuck here."

"I wanted to ask you if you'd like to go to the theater with me some afternoon."

Katya felt her cheeks fire into a blush. She wished she could slip away. She wished the ride would end or the woman would carry her baby back from the water closets, her jacket cleaned of drool. "I thought I told you to ask someone else."

"I don't want to ask anyone else."

"I don't go to the theater very much. It bores me."

"Really?"

"It's not a reflection on the actors or the playwrights," Katya informed Maddox, barely looking at him. "They're very good. It's just that nothing compares to the carnival as far as I'm concerned."

"I agree on that. I just thought you might like to do other things for entertainment."

Katya did not know how to send Maddox away without hurting his feelings. "I enjoy a stroll or a ride through the park every now and again."

Maddox adjusted his hat. "You like Mr. Davies better, is that it?"

Katya met Maddox's gaze. "Romantically? No. He's a friend. He's too old for me by several years."

"I thought someone more interested in money than fun might look past a man's age. A lot of women do."

Katya's hands fidgeted, each one pulling at the fabric on the gloved fingers of the other. "I don't care that much about money anymore."

"No?"

Katya looked away, searching out the woman with the baby. The Kaleidoscope whirred to a stop behind her, and one of the operators ushered the patrons down the iron staircase.

"Excuse me." Katya stepped away, studying the line of patrons. When a short man wearing glinting steel spectacles set foot on the ground, Katya approached him. He glanced around him at the waiting crowd. "Sir, I spoke with your wife. She'll be back in a moment."

The patron bowed his head in thanks.

When Katya turned to move on through the grounds, Maddox blocked her from taking a single step.

"You also told me," Maddox said, "I shouldn't waste my time asking someone to the theater or the parks. You told me a night at the carnival would win over any woman."

Katya swallowed hard. "Yes, I did."

"Would you ride the carnival with me, Miss Romanova?"

Katya laughed without meaning to.

"Have you ever ridden the carnival before?"

"No. Ask Mr. Warden for a night off? Do you know how impossible it would be to convince him of that?"

"Not a night off. We can ride everything while we're working." Maddox corrected himself. "*Supposed* to be working."

"I can't do that. Somebody will report us. We'll lose our jobs."

"I bet we won't." Maddox's eyes shone steadily.

Katya raised her palm to indicate the passing crowd. "Who's supposed to help the guests while I'm spinning and coasting all over the night?"

"They'll help themselves."

The woman with the baby gave Katya an appreciative nod as she walked by. The baby rested limply, sleeping, with its head on her shoulder. She fell into step with her husband as they headed to the next attraction.

Katya swept her hand toward them. "The new guests can't even find the water closets without my help." She blanched at raising her voice about such a private subject.

Maddox stepped back, tipping his hat in resignation. "Very well. I just thought you'd like to enjoy the place you love so much instead of always toiling in it."

Maddox walked away. Katya did not usually feel bad about turning down a suitor. Men had asked her on at least half a dozen dates while she performed her duties at the carnival. She had declined afternoons watching baseball, listening to opera, and less sophisticated suggestions of a few hours in a room at the Stock Yards Exchange and Hotel.

But just as Dr. Kirby had chosen Lizzy over Katya, Mr. Warden had moved on to Isolde's perfume and embraces. Even as young, high earning, and beautiful as Katya was, the men she wanted could replace her in their thoughts. Maddox did not represent the worst Katya could do, especially in the name of enjoying herself. If she did not take him up on his offer, he would stop admiring her, too.

As much as Katya appreciated the chance to champion her guests, she could not deny Maddox was right. She worshipped the carnival, but she had never once spent a night there for her own amusement.

Katya picked up her skirts, racing to catch up to Maddox. "Mr. O'Sullivan."

Maddox turned, bathed under the light of his usual lamppost. His darkened eyes watched her, waiting. He said nothing, and Katya wished he would make the first move. She reminded herself he had approached her multiple times with less than the results he sought.

Katya sucked up her gusto and superseded her pride. "I'll ride the carnival with you, Mr. O'Sullivan, if you're willing."

Maddox blinked at her, his expression blank and reserved. Slowly, he raised his elbow to her. Katya slipped her hand around his arm, and only then did his lips curve upward with pleasure.

"What attraction would you like to ride first?" he asked.

Katya tilted her head back to take in the full height of the Tower up ahead. "Let's start here."

Maddox guided Katya toward the line of guests at the base of the Tower. "Have you ever been up so high?"

"I don't think so. The cars go fifty feet in the air."

"Are you nervous?"

Katya's eyes lingered at the top of the metal structure. "Yes."

"Has there ever been an accident with it?"

"No. There were the usual concerns with some of the gears, but it never put anyone in danger."

Maddox led Katya right up to the Tower operator accepting tickets for the next group to ride toward the stars. "We need to get on," Maddox told him.

The man took another ticket from a guest, who walked past him into the fenced-off area for the ride. "Says who?"

"Mr. Warden," Katya interjected. "He wants to make sure it's running smoothly enough."

"Do you have to ride it now?"

"Why not? The car isn't full yet."

The operator grunted and jerked his thumb behind him. Katya and Maddox slipped past him to the wheel-shaped car waiting patiently around the bottom of the Tower's central post. They sat down in adjacent seats padded more luxuriantly than most hotel and restaurant chairs. A second operator walked around the car, helping the patrons buckle the safety belts across their middles. The car filled up, and the operators offered hand signals to each other. They kept everyone else clear of the ride.

Katya felt unsure about taking the ride up into the night sky, but not all of her anxiousness was unpleasant. Part of her looked forward to finally experiencing the journey for herself, and the other part of her searched Maddox's face for a hint that he felt the same. He beamed at her.

With a gentle lurch, the car rose into the air. Katya grabbed hold of the partitions between the seats, her knuckles bumping the hand of the guest on her left, who had also grabbed for it. Maddox did not reach for a stronghold. His mouth twisted in amusement, watching Katya seek security as everything that held her ascended ten, twenty, thirty feet.

The climb proved gradual and effortless. Once Katya began to relax, she realized how far she could see. The lamplights of the carnival looked beautiful and elegant below them. The slight flickering of the burning gas gleamed off the metal structures throughout the carnival. It lost itself in the velvet of patron jackets and glimmered off their silks. It flashed across buckles on top hats and shoes. It lit up gold and silver jewelry.

Katya could barely breathe. She almost forgot how nervous she had been moments before. The car reached the top of the tower and stopped there, offering its occupants a rare view at the world around them. Katya stared down at the carnival, trying to pick out the details of the band playing in the center of it all. The massive Beast behind it still intimidated, but from this height, Katya marveled in the majesty of its design.

The car shuddered and lowered itself, detaching from its part of the sky. The other occupants chattered to each other excitedly, but Katya could barely form thoughts in her head.

"What do you think?" Maddox asked her.

Katya recited the first thing that came to mind. "The ride lasts for three cycles." She admonished herself for relying on the only words she knew about the carnival and gave in to sharing Maddox's enthusiasm. "It's thrilling."

The car paused briefly at the bottom before lifting again. Each time it rose, Katya focused on a different part of the carnival. She looked across to the other side, where the Kaleidoscope competed against the game stalls and the Cannon for popularity. It really did shift like a kaleidoscope from this height, the colors of the booths smearing in her vision as they rotated. She looked past Maddox to the El and the food stall beyond it. Magdalene would be handing out cinnamon-sugar desserts and sausages on buns, but Katya was riding the carnival they had staked their lives on. She was riding the dream Brady had worked on years ago. She doubted even he had been able to enjoy it.

The car rested on the ground and stayed there. The operator made his rounds again, helping the patrons get unbuckled and return to their feet. He directed them to an exit gate in the fence. Katya and Maddox filed out with the others to the common grounds of the carnival.

"Where to next?" Maddox prompted.

Katya's heart pounded with the possibilities. "The coaster."

"The big one?"

"No, I don't think I'll ever be brave enough for that." Katya watched the Beast's cars roar high above them. "The smaller one here."

Katya linked her hand around Maddox's arm, and they walked to the nearby El. Maddox repeated Katya's lie to the ticket taker. "Mr. Warden wants us to make sure the coaster's operating properly."

The man hurried them past, offering a more courteous front to the waiting customers. "You'll all have a turn, I assure you. Just a routine inspection."

Another operator stood a few feet inside the fence, and he motioned for Katya and Maddox to stop where they were. They watched the coaster cars slide and weave their way along the track. A minute later, they slowed into loading position on the platform. The operator stepped over to help the guests out, and once they left the platform, his flexing fingers invited Katya and

Maddox toward him. He buckled them into the front seat of the first car.

"Are you nervous now?" Maddox whispered into Katya's ear.

Katya nodded, but she felt the rush of anticipation filling her chest. "It's not too fast, is it?"

"You should know."

"I don't know. I can't think of anything except how fun this is."

The operator filled the remaining seats in the connected cars. With a signal to the ticket taker and the man Katya could not see who ran the switches, the cars jerked forward. This time, Katya and Maddox both reached for the metal grab bar in front of them. A mechanism in the track pulled the train of cars up the initial slope. The passengers behind Katya and Maddox murmured with apprehension and breathed audibly, awaiting the first of many drops.

The train rose steadily, taking its passengers up to a short plateau. Within seconds, the cars slid down, lifting Katya's stomach into the top of her chest. She let out a shriek amidst the screams and shouts behind her. The train twisted to the left, curving to parallel the outer fence of the carnival. It rose a short distance and fell again, racing its passengers lower toward the ground. A second mechanism pulled the cars even higher than before.

In one graceful motion, the cars slipped down the next slope of track, curving away from the back of the grounds. They dipped down beside the side stage, where Katya could not tell what contest was taking place. The cars sped along, turning left only to bend back to the right. The track led them down beneath the iron structure and returned them safely to the platform.

Katya barely had time to catch her breath before the ride operator unbuckled her belt. She walked with Maddox to the exit gate, where a small wooden sign bore the words *Thank You* in painted, curling letters.

Katya leaned against Maddox for support, her equilibrium struggling to right itself even though her heart soared with excitement. "Where do you want to go?"

"Let's try something a little less intense." Maddox wrapped his arm around Katya, propping her up as they walked deeper into the carnival.

"What do you suggest?"

Maddox nodded to the attraction they were headed towards. The great Warden wheel turned slowly against the sky, the stars twinkling in competition with the lamplights of the city beyond the carnival fence.

"We get three turns around the wheel, too," Katya said.

"How tall's the wheel?"

"Twice the tower. One hundred feet. You're supposed to be able to see the whole city from the top."

"From the top? About halfway up, I'd think."

"We're about to find out."

Katya and Maddox walked up to the ticket taker. "We're here to ride the wheel for Mr. Warden," Maddox said. "Routine quality control."

The ticket taker eyed him as he accepted another pair of tickets from a couple of guests. "That's hardly routine."

"It's a new routine," Katya informed him.

"Why are you two doing it?"

Maddox leaned closer. "Do you have boating experience, sir? On the ocean?"

"In the middle of this state?" The ticket taker snorted. "No."

"Well, I do, and the motion of the rides should be as smooth as a relaxing boat ride on even water. I'm more than qualified to judge."

The ticket taker turned his sharp grey eyes on Katya.

"How can I be expected to tell the guests what it's like if I don't ride it?" she asked. "Mr. Warden knows what he's doing and knows what he wants. If you're going to take up a car with Mr. O'Sullivan, you might as well send me up, too."

The ticket taker grunted. "Fine. Go on through." Under his breath, he said, "If I catch any trouble for this, it's on your heads."

Katya refused to drop her ruse. "We'll see who gets in trouble for doing their job."

Maddox guided Katya through the low iron gate to the base of the wheel. The operator on the platform let a young, well-dressed couple off the lowest car in front of him. He motioned Katya and Maddox to step up to replace them. Heinz swiftly buckled them in, and with a brief hand signal, the wheel rotated them slowly into the air.

Katya was accustomed to riding backwards in carriages but not backwards as well as upward. She balanced the strange sensation by looking out over the familiar sights of the carnival. Maddox tapped the back of her hand, and Katya turned her attention the other way.

The southern neighborhoods of the city stretched out beneath them in a maze of streets and houses. Plotted among them, slightly larger, spread a boxy school, a rising church, and a sprawling park. The higher Katya turned on the wheel, the more of the city presented itself. Shadows darkened and muffled most of it, making it hazy. Katya squinted to make out the taller buildings amongst the lower-lying landscape: the towers flanking the edifice of St. John's Church and the broad, impressive swath of the English Hotel and Opera House.

The wheel stopped every so often to let old patrons off and new guests on. They mostly sat quietly, but if they had been screaming their lungs out, Katya would not have noticed. She stared out over the city, its many lampposts like a vast network of earthbound stars. The wheel began to let Katya down very slowly, and even when she could not see for miles, the magic vibrated in her body.

She turned her attention to Maddox, whose persistence was the only reason she had experienced the carnival from the other side. He had gotten his date, and Katya had learned the true meaning of the carnival deep into her bones.

Maddox spoke first. "I admit it," he said.

"What?"

"I did hear things about you, about your reputation when I started here."

Katya had nowhere to hide. Even as their car neared the ground and stopped there to let a couple disembark, there was nothing to shield her from Maddox. "Is that why you asked me about Mr. Davies?"

"No. I just wanted to know if you liked him." Maddox fell silent as they glided past Heinz on another round of the wheel's gradual course. "I didn't want you to think that was the reason I was talking to you. It has nothing to do with that."

"Not even a little?" Katya teased him, hoping to cover up her embarrassment.

"Not really. How reliable are rumors like that, anyway? Do you think I'm going to believe a bunch of filthy-faced men who never saw anything for themselves?"

"What, exactly, were the rumors about?"

"You and... someone else."

"Mr. Warden?"

"Maybe."

Katya folded her hands in her lap. "I've done a lot of forward things in my life but never anything that stupid before. I didn't think it through. I panicked because I wanted to work at the carnival more than anything else, and he said there wasn't a job for me. I moved here by train to work at the carnival."

Katya paused, but Maddox continued to watch her, listening. "I asked him if he had anyone to care for his guests, anyone to answer their questions and guide them around. He said he didn't. I said I was obviously a talker and I'd be more than happy to serve them."

Katya pictured the same scene she had tumbled over in her head since it happened, but now she saw it for what it was: ill advised and reckless. She summarized it modestly. "We did have a romantic moment, you might call it, and I got the job. I'm not proud of it. Maybe I was for a while, but I didn't realize how truly scheming Mr. Warden is. I may have gotten what I wanted, but he always gets what he wants, too."

Katya waited for Maddox to answer. The silence made her worry he thought the worst of her. The car rocked gently as it stopped, and Katya spoke up again. "Mr. Warden must've told Mr. Lieber, and Mr. Lieber probably told some of the other security. I'm sure it was only a matter of time until it reached most of the men who work here."

The car rose into motion once more.

Maddox laid his hand over Katya's. "I don't care. I didn't care when I heard the rumors, and I don't care now. Mr. Warden might have all the power at the carnival, but you have the most passion for it. You glow. You don't walk here. You float. You know so much, and I know so little."

"That can't be true. You've lived in places I've only heard of and probably places I haven't. If you're good enough to fix the rides, you know more than you give yourself credit for."

Maddox's eyes sparkled. "If you lived on the coast, Miss Romanova, you'd be the kind of woman men name their boats after."

The compliment warmed Katya from the inside, imagining him working on the beaches of the ocean. "What was it like on the coast?"

Maddox shrugged. "Fresh ocean air. Smell of fresh and rotting fish."

"Did you take a lot of relaxing boat rides out there?"

A sly smirk stole across Maddox's lips. "That was a lie to get us on board. There's a lot to be done during fishing season, even on the shore. I came to America in a boat, although I barely remember it. I guess I've had my share of them."

Katya hesitated in case her inquiry was too personal. "Your accent," she mentioned. "It's Irish but softer."

Maddox paused, his roguishness easing into appreciation and honest pleasure. "My mother was born in England. My father met her when he moved there after the famine in Ireland. He always meant to come here, but he didn't think he'd have a wife and kid with him when he came over. If I don't sound exactly like him, it's because I grew up listening to her."

Katya searched Maddox's smooth features, finding evidence of his family's journeys and hardships. The same twinkle of determination glowing in his eyes might have fueled his father's moves across two water-separated borders. Despite Maddox's youth and high spirits, his eyes studied her with worldly observation. He set his jaw firmly for whatever came his way. Katya realized how much she wanted to hear him compliment her again. "Would you name a boat after me, Mr. O'Sullivan?"

"I would buy a boat to name it after you."

The car carried Katya and Maddox up over the top of the wheel. It stopped with the southern neighborhoods laid out far beneath them. Katya leaned over and kissed him. The back of the car stood high enough to block the view from the couple riding behind them. They loomed too high above the ground for Heinz to see.

Maddox set his bare hand against Katya's neck. Any fear she had suffered that Maddox would rebuff her fell away. His mouth felt natural against hers. His breath tasted like the stinging spice of strong liquor, the smooth coolness of cigarettes, and the warm saltiness of popped corn. The brims of their hats bumped against one other as they bent closer together in the middle of the car.

Katya did not want the moment to end, hanging eighty to ninety feet in the air with Maddox's arms pressing reassuringly around her. As the wheel lowered them toward the rest of the world, she pulled away and simply gazed back at him, her golden-gloved hand holding his face. She lowered it into her lap before the car glided past Heinz and the line of customers waiting beyond the short fence.

Neither of them spoke until the wheel had returned them to the greatest heights of its structure.

"Do I have permission to see you again?" Maddox asked, his voice warmed by hope.

"Yes, Mr. O'Sullivan, you do."

"May I call on you at home and talk to you properly?"

Katya hesitated. Lizzie was famous for hiding around corners and listening in on any conversation held in the shared rooms of the house. Katya decided she would rather brave Lizzie's sharp ears and big mouth than let Maddox think she was too ashamed to invite him there. "Yes. I have a room at the Weekly Boarder on Plum Street."

"Where's that?"

"West of the river and the center of town. There's a streetcar route not far from there."

Maddox squeezed her hand. "I'll find you."

The wheel lowered the car on its third and last revolution of their ride. Katya tried to fit in her final thoughts. "One of my housemates may try to steal you away."

Maddox burst out with guffaws.

"I'm serious. She's already taken one man from me, although according to your doctrine of fun, he wasn't the greatest catch a woman could have."

Maddox scrunched his nose up in sympathy. "One of those stuffy lawyers?"

"A stuffy doctor, but who else can afford to take their dates to the restaurant at Bates House? They say President Lincoln stayed there once."

"Is that what you want? An expensive dinner?"

Katya relaxed beside him. "No. I think tea or coffee with you would be just fine."

Maddox kissed Katya gently, and the wheel turned until their car rested above the platform. Heinz unbuckled them, and they walked out of the Warden wheel's fenced area.

Maddox lingered close to her side. "What do you want to do next?" he asked.

Katya straightened her hat and tried to force her smile to a more professional brightness. "I think we've done more than enough for one night. I don't know that I could survive any more fun today."

"You don't want to try the Kaleidoscope?"

"No."

"Until I call on you, then." Maddox bent over in a surprisingly graceful, steady bow, lifting his hat off his head in perfect timing.

Katya pulled her shoulders back into a more proper posture. "Yes, until then."

Katya touched Maddox's hand briefly as he straightened up and put his hat back on. It tore her heart to walk away when she was just beginning to like him, but they had returned to the ground. The earth followed different rules than the air.

Chapter Twenty-Four

Katya hurried down the steps of the Weekly Boarder into the basement. She steered into the kitchen, almost colliding with Magdalene on the way in. "Is the curling iron ready?"

Mrs. Weeks stood at the stove. She lifted the curling iron away from the fire of the gas burner. "Maybe another minute or two. It hasn't been on long." Mrs. Weeks replaced it over the burner.

Katya heard a gentle splashing sound and found Mary cleaning a corner of the floor. "Did something spill?" Katya asked.

Mary glanced over her shoulder. "I dropped a jar of jam, and it broke."

Mrs. Weeks faced Katya and Magdalene directly. She set a loose fist on her hip. "Why in such a hurry today, Katya? Do you have a date?"

"No, but my curls are falling out, and I want to look my best for work." Katya unbraided her long, dark hair. She was determined not to mention a word about Maddox to anyone except Magdalene until he showed up at the house for tea.

Magdalene spoke up for the first time since Katya arrived in the room, barely raising her eyes from their thoughtful place on the stove. "No one's going to outshine you, Kat."

Katya did not doubt the genuineness of the compliment, but she caught the serious, preoccupied undertone of Magdalene's words. Katya kept to the subject at hand. "Isolde Neumann shows me up every night," she grumbled.

Mrs. Weeks turned back to the stove. "Who's that?"

"Mr. Warden's rich girlfriend. Her father owns an ornament factory."

"They're getting so popular these days. When I was a girl, everyone made their own decorations with whatever we could find." Mrs. Weeks turned off the gas burner and lifted the curling iron by one of its wooden handles. "Who's going first? Katya?"

Magdalene gestured Katya ahead of her. Katya took the spare handle, warm despite the wood, and stepped in front of the mirror hung in the kitchen for this very purpose. She squeezed the handles together, letting the spring separate the two lengths of ten-inch metal. She wound a section of her bangs around the round rod and let the other piece relax to pin it in place.

"Don't you worry, dear," Mrs. Weeks told Katya. "I've seen a lot of women in my time. Few of them were as lovely as you. Even fewer of them remain comely as the years get on."

Katya swelled with adoration at her mother away from the one who raised her. "Thank you, Mrs. Weeks."

Mary erupted into a coughing fit in the corner. Katya swiveled away from the mirror to watch Mary hack pitifully into her sleeve.

Mrs. Weeks rushed to her daughter's side. "Are you all right, Mary?"

Mary nodded, brushing her mother aside with her free arm. "It's a little dusty back here."

"Let me clean it up for you."

"No, it's all right. I'm almost done."

Katya returned to the mirror, concentrating on the loosest curls and flattest sections of her hair. The heat left her locks with the frizziness most women's hair suffered, the flyaway curls Katya expected for her look. "You need to visit the carnival, Mary. I never see you there. Even Lizzie shows up on occasion to flaunt whom she's seeing."

"I might," Mary agreed.

Katya went on as if Mary had protested. "You really should. It's incredibly fun. There are men everywhere if you're looking for a husband. The food is delicious. There are games and contests. I bet you could win a dancing contest if you found the right partner."

In the mirror's reflection, Mary stood up on the other side of the room. "Perhaps one evening, when the dinner dishes are done, I'll stop by."

"Please do. It'd be so nice to see you. It's always the same people there. Miss Neumann goes to see Mr. Warden, and another woman used to come for the same reason. I haven't seen her in ages." Katya looked to Magdalene to back her up and keep the conversation flowing.

Magdalene stared off at the counter in the center of the kitchen. She glanced up, her blonde eyebrows raised in a question.

Katya filled her in. "I said we never see Mr. Warden's old girlfriend anymore, whoever she was."

Magdalene nodded.

"Mrs. Weeks," Katya piped up.

"Yes, dear?" The old woman moved to stand behind her.

"You know, I forgot to bring down a single pin. I'd love to pin my hair back when I get finished."

Mrs. Weeks patted Katya's shoulder. "I'll bring them for you." She left the kitchen, and the short heels of her boots sounded in a retreating series on the front staircase.

Mary lifted the bucket of cleaning water off the floor with a wheezing breath. "I have to dump this outside." She ambled out the same doorway, turning right toward the back of the house.

Katya lowered the curling tongs from her face and whirled to face her friend. "What's going on, Mags? I can tell when you need to talk to me."

Magdalene stepped closer, setting her hands on the spotless surface of the large counter. "I feel scrutinized when I'm working."

"That still bothers you?"

"Yes."

"Do you think you're being watched outside the carnival, too?"

"No, it's only there. It's always security, or at least, that's who I think they are. They aren't dressed in the steampunk style, but it's always the same people, the same men."

"And they never speak to you?"

"Never. They never even get in line to order food. I think they're going to the other stall or bringing their own."

"Do you think they were given orders not to speak to you?"

"I don't know."

If it were true, Katya realized only one person could give those orders.

"Mr. Warden's onto us," Magdalene said.

Katya shook her head. It was not improbable, but they had tried so hard to be careful. "If he were, why would he have security watching you instead of me? I've only had one security guard speak to me since Mr. Lieber died. I rarely see them. You see them all the time."

"I don't know."

"Do you want to stop meeting with Mr. Kelly?"

"No," Magdalene said with certainty.

"I want to help him, too," Katya assured her. "I want to see Mr. Warden dethroned, but how can we do that when we don't know how much he knows?"

"You could try to find out."

"He won't let me. He won't tell me anything. Isolde Neumann visits him four or five nights a week. When I asked him about it, he acted cool and aloof. Then he made another pass at me. I don't want to deal with him anymore."

"We should tell Mr. Kelly we need a new plan."

Katya agreed with her, but she heard shoes thumping on the front staircase. She whispered to Magdalene. "We'll talk to Mr. Kelly. We'll work it out."

By the time Mrs. Weeks carried a handful of pins into the kitchen, Katya had rededicated herself to curling her long, thick hair. She shone a sweet smile on Mrs. Weeks and the pins in her wrinkled hands. "Thank you. You're a gem." To Magdalene, she promised, "I just need another minute with the iron."

Chapter Twenty-Five

Katya sat in the back of St. John's Church, realizing the smells there were not so different from those pervading the carnival. When she passed close by a maintenance worker or ride operator, she could smell the sweat and grease on them. The fresh air of summer tried to wash away the oil, soot, and earth, but they remained.

Those were the stenches hanging in the stale air of the sanctuary. The homeless that gathered there for rest and safety carried in dirt and sweat and wet animal funk. Their shoes smeared horse dung across the floor from the streets, where it dried and stunk less oppressively for having lost its moisture. They smelled like kerosene, singed hair, warm skin, and dry cotton.

The longer Katya shifted against the unyielding wood beneath her waiting for Brady, the sorrier she felt for the people stretched out across the pews. As usual, she could not see them. They seemed to spend the early morning hours making up for any sitting, standing, or walking they did during the day. Katya wondered how they did spend their days, if they worked or spent exhausting hours searching for work. She questioned if they had once owned houses and lost them, like Mrs. Lieber had fallen into the danger of doing. They might have had families once. Maybe they had passed away, like Brady's, or separated through some other tragedy.

Katya dove deeper into her thoughts, adrift in her dark daydreams when Magdalene patted her arm. Looking up, Katya saw that Brady had come in and was sitting down next to Magdalene.

"Do you have news?" he asked, his voice straining, hoping.

"We need a new plan," Magdalene explained. "Katya isn't comfortable trying to press Mr. Warden for more information, and I don't blame her. He's too smart to let something slip. There has to be another way."

"I've been thinking," Brady admitted. He lowered his far-off gaze to the floor, his thumbs flipping at the brim of his hat. "What place is more public to expose Warden's dishonesty than the carnival itself?"

"No," Katya said, speaking from her gut before her mind could react.

Brady lifted his eyes. "If he's there every night, it might be our best chance. He can't hide from us. We could expose him in front of the guests, the workers, even the press if we tipped them off ahead of time."

"No," Katya repeated, shaking her head. "The carnival has its problems, but it means so much to everybody. I don't want it to be destroyed like that. Who could enjoy being there after we defame it by calling Mr. Warden out on its grounds?"

Brady hid his hurt well, but it lingered like pleading shadows in his every feature. "Do you really think it makes that big a difference, Miss Romanova, if we call him out in the city or at the carnival?"

"Yes, I do. It could sabotage everything we've worked for if the carnival can't shake its memory of him. If we expose him in town, people will say, 'The Steampunk Carnival used to be run by that crook, William Warden.' But if we do it there, they'll sneer, 'The Steampunk Carnival. That's where they caught William Warden.' I don't want it affiliated with such a thing."

"You don't think the city will forgive us?"

Katya mulled it over. She wanted to fight taking that risk, but she did not want to tell Brady to give up on everything he had striven for.

"Please, Miss Romanova." Brady's eyes shimmered, and his brogue laid itself low. "You've come with me this far. If there's another way, I promise you, we'll take it. But we have to consider this one."

Katya made herself nod in agreement.

"The carnival's bigger than Warden," Brady said. "It's bigger than any travesty that happens there."

"Because Mr. Warden covers them up," Katya murmured.

"There's one other thing I wanted to talk to you about." Brady paused, which made Katya's nerves tighten like fiddle strings. "If it's too personal, I'll understand if you don't want to talk about it. But who's the young man I've seen you with around the carnival? The one who works there?"

Katya adjusted the fit of her gloves minutely, not sure if her discomfort was rooted in embarrassment, fear, or indignation. If Brady had noticed her with Maddox, Mr. Warden's spies certainly had. "Mr. O'Sullivan replaced one of the maintenance workers Mr. Warden deemed incompetent."

"How well do you know him?"

"Well enough to call him a friend."

"Do you remember when he came to work for the carnival?"

"It was around the same time we met you, after you fixed the Beast."

"It was before Lieber was murdered," Brady reminded her, tilting his forehead at her.

Katya licked her lips. She wished she had a glass of water for her suddenly dry throat. Her voice rose although she tried to control it. "Are you saying Mr. O'Sullivan could've murdered Mr. Lieber?"

"I'm only saying it's possible. I'm not accusing him."

"What motive would he have had? It must have been only a week or two before Mr. Lieber was killed. What could Mr. Lieber have done to him in that short a time that would force such a strong reaction? I don't think Mr. O'Sullivan has that kind of a temper."

"He's Irish," Brady joked in an extra-thick brogue, his expression light to dampen his dark insinuation.

"I'm serious, Mr. Kelly," Katya told him. "If Mr. Warden's bent on continuing to manipulate me, Mr. O'Sullivan might be in danger, too. His lot is in with ours, not part of the danger working against us."

"My apologies, miss. And at the risk of offending you again, I'm afraid I must ask if you've told him anything about what we're planning to do."

"I haven't, and I won't. I wouldn't betray your trust like that."

"One last question," Brady said. "When can I see it? My journal?"

Magdalene cleared her throat. "We can bring it to you at the carnival if you like. It's not ideal, but it might be a good idea to keep it close at hand in case we have the opportunity to use it as proof against Mr. Warden."

Brady nodded, slowly at first. His movements picked up speed as he gained a confidence that smoothed his furrowed brow. "I could hide it in the game stall. Behind the stuffed toys and prizes, perhaps."

"You don't think security will find it?" Magdalene asked.

"No. As far as Warden knows, the journal and his dirty little secret are long buried. The guards have no reason to tear apart my stall or any of the others."

"We'll bring it for you soon."

"Thank you." Brady's hands shook where they rested his hat on his legs. "And no one where you live knows about it?"

"No, Mr. Kelly." Magdalene watched him for a moment. Her voice treaded gently. "Will you be able to hide it at the carnival and leave it there? I know how badly you must want to take it home and search through it."

"I do, but I can't risk that. It must be in a place where we can use it if we get the chance. I can't jeopardize our plans and our lives for my selfish obsession."

Magdalene laid her hand over Brady's, her white glove making his pale skin look tanned. "You're not a selfish man. Your reasons for dreaming this carnival are more noble and honorable than most people's reasons for doing anything. I promise you we'll act as soon as we can."

Katya could think of even more urgent reasons to speed up the process. "Tell Mr. Kelly about the security men."

Magdalene turned her face toward Katya, raising her blonde brows above sharp, warning blue eyes.

Brady leaned forward where Katya could see him better. "Tell me what?"

"There's no need to worry anyone," Magdalene insisted.

Katya answered Brady's question. "Security's watching her closely."

Brady sounded serious again. "Do you think Warden suspects something?"

"He can't," Magdalene said, offering her lifted palms in defeat. "I haven't done anything I don't normally do. I haven't met with you any more than Katya has. She's spoken to you more than I have."

"What does Warden know about you?"

"Nothing he could use against me. He knows I was born in the city. He knows where I used to work as a cook. My family's very quiet. We work hard, and we stay out of trouble. Usually."

Brady clasped his hands around Magdalene's gloved fingers. "If there is trouble, send for me if you can. I'll be there. I can't let either of you get hurt because I couldn't do this alone."

"We're glad to help you, Mr. Kelly," Magdalene assured him, only a slight wavering of her voice giving away her apprehension.

"How can I repay you?"

Katya jumped in with the easy answer. "By keeping us on at the carnival when you take it over."

"Do you really think anyone will want to elevate me – the Mick – to running the entire carnival?"

"Why not? You designed it. You know how all the machines work. This city depends on the carnival. It loves it too much to let it crumble and die. You're the person best qualified to keep it with us."

Brady retrieved his hands from Magdalene's and glanced away. "Thank you for your vote of confidence." His voice shook with gratitude.

Chapter Twenty-Six

Katya did not dare speak to Maddox at the carnival. She was not so focused on keeping him out of danger that she would refuse to return a smile or nod of the head. Maddox crossed her path from time to time as he walked from one ride's mechanical workings to another. His eyes twinkled as they fell on her, and he always found time to slow his stride for a few steps, tip his cap, and greet her. "Good evening, Miss Romanova."

Katya would bow her head, finding it impossible to stop the corners of her mouth from lifting up. "The same to you, Mr. O'Sullivan."

Katya never stopped moving, determined to keep herself so busy, not even Maddox could find the opportunity to waylay her. The less Mr. Warden suspected about her – personally or where Brady's plans were concerned – the better.

Katya tried to stay near the front of the carnival to avoid running into Maddox around the maintenance building. She was assuring a family of five that they could indeed see half the city from the top of the Warden wheel when she recognized a familiar face twenty feet behind them. Mary wandered past the ticket booth, her face raised to take in the enormity of the Beast thundering and racing above the band.

"It's a magnificent view," Katya informed the family. "If you'll excuse me."

Katya hurried over to Mary before she could lose her in the crowd. She met Mary with an impetuous hug, her unexpected joy making it tighter than she meant to. "It's so good to see you. I didn't think you'd really come."

Mary glanced around, her mouth caught between excitement and trepidation. "It's overwhelming, isn't it?"

"It's marvelous. Did you just get in?"

Mary nodded.

"Let me show you around." Katya linked her arm around Mary's.

Mary slipped her arm away. "I'm not sure I want to stay long. It's so late already."

"Is it? I almost never know what time it is here."

"It was after ten when I left the house."

Katya looked from one fantastic attraction to the next, the Tower, the El vibrating beside it, and the Kaleidoscope whirring to her right. "Are you sure I can't show you around a bit? Mr. Warden hasn't given in to my suggestion that we print off maps yet. He says that's what he's paying me for."

"All right."

"You sound so tired, Mary."

The two women began to walk together. Katya did not reach for Mary's arm a second time.

"I was up about dawn," Mary pointed out, stifling a yawn behind her plain black glove. "I suppose I'm as tired as you are when you get home so late on your really late nights."

Katya's breathing shallowed. She forced deeper breaths into her lungs. "The late nights?"

"Yes. Sometimes I hear you and Magdalene come in an hour or two later than usual."

"I'm sorry if we wake you, Mary. We try to be quiet."

"It's all right. It isn't very often. Sometimes I can't sleep well, and I read a magazine for a while."

Katya had never noticed a light under Mary's door or any other door in the house after the meetings with Brady, but then again, she realized she might not have looked.

"So this is where you work," Mary mused. Her brown eyes roamed over every metal column, every wooden plank.

"Is it what you thought it would be?"

"I don't know. I remember the pictures in the papers when it opened last year. They didn't do it justice. The coasters look so much bigger in person."

"This is the side stage here." Katya gestured to another of the increasingly popular dance contests. "We used to have more eating contests and sewing demonstrations, but this has become a great way for people to meet each other."

"Love at the famous Steampunk Carnival," Mary quipped.

Katya thought of Maddox, her most enjoyable secret. "Yes. How about you, Mary? Don't you ever have any adventures? I can't remember the last time you talked about having a date."

Mary shrugged under her thin cotton jacket. "I don't have time for such things. Ever since Dad died, I've worried about helping Mom keep up the Boarder."

"I'm sure she could spare you a few hours every week or so."

"I entertain myself at the Boarder. Did you ever thumb through Mom's copy of *Miss Beecher's*? It's a few years old, but the advice is solid. Mom still cooks out of it. Miss Beecher has a very sharp wit."

"I've always preferred magazines to books. There's more pictures in them."

Katya led Mary closer to the food stall. Magdalene was too busy with customers to notice them coming.

"This is where Mags is stuck night after night," Katya said. "She's not free to roam like I am."

"Should we get in line?"

"Not if we just want to talk."

Katya reached the corner of the stand, giving the customers a reassuring smile. "Hey, Mags. Look who's here."

Magdalene glanced down, then glanced again. "Oh, hello, Mary. I didn't expect to see you. You didn't have to make the trip just because Katya keeps insisting."

"I should see it," Mary replied good-naturedly. "I'm glad I came. It's not the kind of thing you can describe in words or pictures. It's too unusual for that."

Magdalene took a few silver coins from a customer and traded them for a white paper bag of popcorn. "Are you hungry, Mary? Do you need something to drink?"

Katya encouraged Mary with shining eyes. "Live a little, Mary. We never have root beer at the house. It doesn't cost much."

"Maybe I will."

Katya turned and peered across the carnival. She was hoping to avoid Brady's game stall, too, not just the maintenance building beyond it. The journal had returned to his possession, as it should have, but Katya felt the bittersweet pull of it. She had spent as much of the afternoon as possible reading it, touching the pages Brady had once labored over before they packed it up. Magdalene had wrapped it in fresh newspaper and hidden it in the bottom of a sack she topped with several of Mrs. Weeks' still-warm blueberry muffins. Katya could not stomach watching Magdalene deliver the sack to Brady, and it would have been dangerous for her to try. She knew Magdalene had done a sincere, convincing job.

"I brought you some baked goods, sir, for your family," Magdalene would have said, or maybe, "Here are the muffins you ordered from my landlady."

Magdalene would craft the most inconspicuous wording. Katya could only yearn to explore the journal again. Perhaps one day, after they had driven Mr. Warden from his stolen property, Katya would have the chance to flip through it at her leisure.

"I should get back to the guests," Katya decided, returning her attention to Magdalene and Mary.

"I should get in line," Mary said.

"I'll probably see you sooner than you think," Katya told her. "The rides are huge, but the carnival itself isn't that big. Seek me out before you leave, won't you? Just look for the hat." Katya adjusted her navy-blue top hat, bedecked with white flowers, gears, and delicate lace.

"I will." Mary walked along the single file of patrons to the end.

Katya retraced her steps to the front of the carnival. She staked out an area not far from the ticket booth where she could greet the incoming guests and offer her help. She was glad to miss Isolde that night. The most Katya felt sure she could have managed under the gaze of the celebrated blonde beauty was a terse, suspicious grimace.

As often happened, Katya lost track of the exact time she spent there. She only measured it as *too long* when keeping to the same spot dragged her cheery disposition down with increasing boredom. At first, Katya let herself move closer to the Kaleidoscope. Meandering further, she made her way to the blasting Cannon and the line of water closets, but no one seemed to need her help there. She told a joke to herself, a resolve never to mention to Mr. Warden that the guests were slowly gaining knowledgeable independence.

Katya kept an eye peeled for Mary, expecting to see her at any moment. In her practical bonnet and plain clothes, Mary was harder to spot than Isolde Neumann or most others who visited the carnival. Even Magdalene stood out in her bold reds, wines, and crimsons.

Katya walked as far past the water closets as she was willing to go, glancing down the length of the carnival's back stretch toward the far food stall. Mary's pale skin and curly brown hair were nowhere to be seen. Katya turned, wondering for a split second if Mary had left without telling her. Mary always kept her word, Katya felt certain. She was as dependable and honest as they came.

Katya saw brief movement behind the water closets, in the narrow space between their back walls and the Cannon's support system. She assumed it must be Agna, chasing down some rubbish blown there by the wind. But Katya recognized the silhouette of Mary's bonnet and rail-thin form. Katya slipped into the slender passageway.

"I looked for you everywhere," Katya said. "Did you try the root beer? Isn't it sweet and refreshing?"

Mary coughed into her glove and nodded.

The cars of the Cannon zoomed overhead, shaking down dust, dirt, and sawdust. The image of Mary coughing before the particles tickled their noses bothered Katya.

"Are you all right?" she asked. She reached for Mary's free arm.

Mary jerked away, moving farther into the space no patron was meant to occupy. "I'm fine," she called out as the firing of the Cannon died from their ears.

Katya swept her hand out, swiping her pale ivory glove across the palm of Mary's black one. A smear of bright blood stained Katya's fabric like a sounding alarm.

"Go away," Mary pleaded, waving her back the way she came.

"Mary." Katya's voice stuck in her throat, disbelieving, her foundations rocked. "You've got–"

Mary glared at her with the strictest warning she had ever seen in a woman's eyes. Mary shamed her into silence, and Katya wished she had not pursued her.

"I need to get home," Mary insisted, maintaining her distance.

"How bad is it?" Katya hissed, feeling betrayed and protective. She had always liked Mary, but now that Mary was ill, her respect and admiration intensified.

"I can't talk about it now. I have to go." Mary looked the other way, down the other half of the chute to the main carnival grounds.

"Will you be all right? I can go with you. I can hail you a carriage for hire. I can wait with you until the streetcar comes."

Mary shook her head. She covered her mouth with her telltale glove, choking gruffly into the fabric. She walked away, past the last water closet in the line and disappearing behind it.

Katya stayed where she was, blinking to keep tears out of her eyes. The secrets she felt forced to hold onto kept piling up, threatening to crush her. She wanted to sit down behind the water closets, hidden from the prying eyes of the carnival, and cry into her soiled satin gloves.

Instead, Katya hiked her chin up and strutted out from behind the water closets. There must be patrons at the carnival who needed her, and she promised herself solemnly to find them.

Chapter Twenty-Seven

Why did Mary have to be dying?

Katya rode in the carriage along its insufferable route, dropping Agna off first in the southern neighborhoods of the city, then Irina closer to the Weekly Boarder. Katya could not wait to reach home, but she also dreaded it, which was the true mark of having to perform serious work.

Magdalene chatted infrequently whether Katya responded or not. "It was nice to see Mary at the carnival."

Katya bobbed her head slowly.

"Did she say when the last time she went out was?"

Katya swiveled her head from side to side. Her eyes focused on the scuffed floor boards past the squared toes of her narrow boots.

"I like to see Mary happy. It's so rare sometimes. She perked up tonight, though, when she tried the root beer. I only pretended to take her money in case anyone was watching. I didn't want anything that Mary's earned to go to Mr. Warden."

The carriage finally pulled up in front of the Weekly Boarder. Magdalene, seated closest to the door, stood up at what Katya deemed to be a snail's pace or slower. She eased the door open and gradually descended to the sidewalk. Katya followed close behind her.

"Good night, Mr. Davies," Magdalene bid him quietly.

Mr. Davies leaned into view and tipped his black hat. "Good night, ladies."

Katya managed a hasty but passable curtsy before rivaling Magdalene for the stairs to the porch. Katya pulled her key out of her bag and let them into the hall. She locked up impatiently, now stuck behind Magdalene's slow footsteps up the circular staircase.

In the upstairs hall, Magdalene pattered to her door. "Good night," she whispered.

"It's good morning," Katya corrected her. "Sleep well."

Katya hid in her room long enough to hear Magdalene's door click shut. Katya did not even bother removing her hat. She slipped back into the hallway and tried the handle of the room on her right. Mary's door swung open.

Mary was not sitting up reading this morning. She stretched out in bed, her eyes blinking in the dim light from the hallway that Mrs. Weeks left on for her more nocturnal boarders. Mary gazed at the wall, giving no indication she knew Katya was there. Her braided hair fell back from her face, the white cotton sleeve of her nightgown illuminated on her shoulder.

"I know you're awake," Katya accused under her breath.

Silence dominated the room. Katya would wait all night for a reply if she had to. Determination always gave her energy.

At last, Mary whispered, "Go away."

"Tell me what's going on, or I'll tell everyone first thing at lunch."

Mary pushed herself up sideways, twisted in the bed sheets to challenge Katya. "You wouldn't."

"Yes, I would. I've done worse things in my life."

Mary straightened her back and sat up in bed. "Come in before you wake someone."

"Where are the matches?"

"There by the door."

Katya felt amidst the shadows on top of the small table beside her. She closed her fingers around a box of matches and singled one out. She struck the head against the side of the box and lit the gas lamp on the wall. She blew the match out as she closed the door to the hallway. Katya left the box and the spent match on the table. She positioned herself in the center of the room and folded her arms.

"My mother needs me," Mary appealed to her.

"She wants you well. We all do." Except maybe Lizzie, who would immediately realize there would be an extra slice of pie available at dinner. Katya ignored this and focused on Mary. "How long have you been coughing up blood?"

"A few months, I suppose. Maybe half a year. I haven't been keeping track."

"You sound better now."

"It's not that serious."

"What do you have? Do you know? Have you sent for a doctor?"

"No. I think it's consumption."

Katya thought of Brady watching his wife cough herself into oblivion. "People die from that, you know. You should see a doctor. We don't want to bury you, Mary."

"I'm fine, really." A cough bubbled up through Mary's lips, and she sipped water from a glass by her bedside.

"You weren't sitting up reading all those nights because you wanted to, were you?" Katya asked, a new realization dawning on her. "You were trying to stop the coughing."

Mary nodded, draining half the water in her glass.

Katya wanted to step toward Mary and reassure her with a gentle touch, but she remembered she should keep her distance. "You should tell your mother. She'll feel awful if anything happens to you and she didn't know you were sick."

Mary nodded again.

Katya watched Mary take small sips of water over and over. Mary's insistence she was not critically ill had comforted Katya, but a sinking feeling sucked her down into the muck of reality. "You want to cough, don't you, Mary? That's why you're not saying anything."

Mary held onto the glass with relaxed fingers. "I can–" She barely threw her arm over her mouth in time to block the forceful hacks of air.

Katya lurched back a step.

Mary extended the glass toward the bedside table until it clinked steadily on its surface. She pulled a dark rag from under her pillow and coughed into it, holding it tightly over her mouth to muffle the sound.

"Mary, are you sure you're not dying?" Katya whispered. She thought of Mrs. Weeks, sound asleep at the other end of the hall. "Please, let me get your mother."

Mary shook her head vehemently. She opened the top drawer in the bedside table. A row of bottles played against each other with various high-pitched rings. Katya eased closer to look at them, staying a few feet away from Mary.

The bottles, maybe a dozen in all, lay on their sides with varying amounts of liquid sloshing inside of them. Katya recognized the glowing burgundy of Mrs. Week's favorite, Ayer's Cherry Pectoral. Some of the syrups were so dark, they gleamed almost black, while others shone amber, rosewood, and ginger.

Mary lifted out the bottle of Ayer's and took a small swig. She eased a few breaths in and out as her coughing subsided.

"How long have you been sick, Mary? Don't lie," Katya pressed her. Fury constricted her chest, and she thought about dragging Mary out of bed, straight down to City Hospital.

"I don't know."

"Why haven't you been to the hospital? This is ridiculous."

"I don't have time for the hospital. My mother needs me."

"Why don't you rest for a few weeks so you don't die and leave her to manage the house by herself for the rest of her life?"

Mary pushed the stopper into the mouth of the rectangular bottle and set it back in the drawer. "Mother would never let me help her around the house again if she found out I'd been sick."

"It's not worth your life, Mary." Katya looked away from the collection of bottles.

"They do help. They help a lot."

"You're still dying." Katya tapped her gloved fingers against her arm, trying to find a solution or at least a way to talk Mary into being reasonable.

Mary reclined against her crushed pillow. "You have to promise me you won't tell anyone. Please, Katya. It's very important to me. I'm all that Mom has left."

Katya pointed to the open drawer. "I think she's going to know you were sick when she discovers those bottles. Do you expect me to clear them out of here after you're dead?"

Mary swung her face towards the wall. "Please, go to bed. It isn't your problem."

"It's all of our problem. We could all get it from you. Do you want to kill us all?"

"No."

"Then go to the hospital."

"Only if Mother doesn't find out."

"Then I'll find you an alibi. I'll find a way to get the help you need."

Mary said nothing.

"Is there a stronger medicine I can get for you?"

"Don't use your money on me."

Katya rocked an inch toward her. "Don't tell me what to do with my money. I earned it. I fought for this job, and I didn't care that it took Mr. Warden's wandering hands to secure it for me." Mary raised her eyebrows, and Katya cut in. "Don't bother to fake surprise. I'm sure you knew."

"It's none of my business, just as my sickness is little concern of yours."

"I'll keep your secret, Mary, but I warn you. If I ever find you passed out on the floor, I'll have you admitted to City Hospital whether your mother is there to see it or not."

"That's fair." Mary dotted the dark cloth across her forehead. She shoved the covers away, only to shiver in a great, uncontrollable spasm. She rolled the covers up to her chest.

Katya backed up toward the door.

"It's just night sweats," Mary explained, her voice hushed by discomfort and exhaustion.

"Get some sleep if you can."

Katya let herself out of the room and eased the door closed. Her gaze fell over the other bedroom doors in the hallway, Lizzie's, Mrs. Weeks', and Magdalene's. Katya slipped into her room.

She was going to do something for Mary. She could not live with herself if she did not.

Chapter Twenty-Eight

Katya heard knocking at the front door. She sat at the back of the house, where several pieces of comfortable furniture filled out the living room. As Mrs. Weeks often said, the front parlor was prettier, but the living room was better suited to just that, living. Katya lowered the borrowed copy of *Mrs. Beecher's Homekeeper and Healthkeeper* from her face, listening in case the caller turned out to be for her.

Heeled boots sounded in the hallway, and the door creaked open. Mrs. Weeks' voice traveled weakly from the opposite end of the corridor. "May I help you?"

Katya caught the undertones of Maddox's Irish-tinged voice. "Good afternoon, ma'am. I was told I might call on Miss Romanova at this address."

Mrs. Weeks responded warmly but cautiously. "Please come in. I'll see if she's receiving visitors."

Katya set *Mrs. Beecher's* on a one-drawer side table and crept to the doorway at the back of the hall.

"Whom should I say is calling, sir?" Mrs. Weeks asked.

Katya rounded the corner, sweeping down the hallway towards them. "Mrs. Weeks," she called, as if her landlady should know. "This is Mr. Maddox O'Sullivan of Warden's infamous Steampunk Carnival."

Mrs. Weeks turned to look at Katya, but Katya barely noticed the trim grey eyebrows cocked in surprise. Maddox held his hat in his hands as he glanced Katya over, making her flush with pride and affection.

"Did you know he was coming?" Mrs. Weeks asked Katya.

"I knew he was coming one of these days," Katya admitted, her attention still focused on Maddox. She had never seen him in one of his own suits, a pale grey that made his mottled blue eyes irresistible.

Mrs. Weeks chattered on. "I wish you would've told me. I could've had tea ready. Would you like some coffee or some tea, Mr. O'Sullivan? I have Darjeeling. If you're staying, that is."

Katya answered without pause. "Yes, he's staying."

Maddox's gaze remained entangled in Katya's. "Tea, please, ma'am. Thank you."

Mrs. Weeks chirped on, formal but excited. "Have a seat in the parlor. I'll bring up the Darjeeling within fifteen minutes."

Katya led Maddox into the parlor while Mrs. Weeks closed the front door. She disappeared down the staircase.

"You look spectacular in the daylight," Maddox praised Katya.

Katya almost blushed as she turned to admire him, the afternoon sunlight flooding in at them through the large bay window. His medium-dark brown hair shone in highlights of blondish red. "You do, too." She noticed the hat still propped in his hands. "Let me hang that up for you."

Maddox offered his hat to her. Katya reached for it, and he snatched her hand instead. He kissed the back of it at length. "Don't walk out yet. I'm not done wondering at you."

Katya took a half-step back to give Maddox a better view. She knew exactly how she looked, as she had every afternoon since Maddox promised to stop by and see her. She had pulled her dark hair back in perfect, messy curls. Her black and white dress had been designed in the latest fashion, its bright blue jacket tailored with notched lapels in the menswear style.

"This old thing," Katya teased. She purloined Maddox's hat and drifted into the hallway. She hung it on a metal flourish of the wooden coat rack by the door.

Lizzie tossed her voice down the spiral staircase. "Was it a visitor for me? Did Mrs. Weeks tell them I'm not seeing anybody?"

Katya searched the stairwell but could not glimpse Lizzie. "Why not?"

"On account of my hair."

"What happened to it?"

"Is anybody down there?"

Katya glanced at Maddox, holding her index finger up across her lips. "Nobody's here, Lizzie. Come down and show me."

Lizzie's boots landed on each step of the staircase as she wound her way down. "I tried to dye it red. I heard the horror stories. It's worse than they say it is. Just look at what that stupid potion did to my hair."

Lizzie dropped into view, brushing stray waves back from her face. Every last strand of them wilted a sickly, muted green. As Katya's mouth gaped open at how far from henna red Lizzie's hair was, Lizzie's jaw dropped at the sight of Maddox occupying the parlor.

"You said–" Lizzie gasped in accusation.

"There's no one here for you," Katya replied coolly.

Lizzie raised an eyebrow – still mercifully chestnut brown – and strolled toward Maddox. "Elizabeth Huffman. How do you do?"

Maddox straightened out the smirk on his lips. "Maddox O'Sullivan. Very well, thank you."

"Do you think I'd look good with red hair, Mr. O'Sullivan?" Lizzie posed with her hands behind her head, her elbows pointing outward. In a golden-yellow dress, with her waist tightly cinched and her bustle even larger than Katya's, Lizzie would have looked stunning, were it not for her faded green locks.

"I'm sure you would," Maddox afforded her.

"Perhaps you should return in a few weeks, when I've restored my hair to its proper glory."

"I'm sure I will, but it'll be to see Miss Romanova again, I'm afraid."

Lizzie cast a disapproving leer over her shoulder at Katya.

"She warned me about you," Maddox added. "I'm sorry to disappoint."

Turning her nose up, Lizzie strutted the length of the hall to the far staircase and swished her sizeable bustle up the stairs.

Katya moved into the parlor. "Mrs. Weeks should only be a few more minutes."

"I can wait for tea. I couldn't wait to see you."

Katya settled onto the edge of the low, black walnut settee. "I'm glad to see you. I know the house seems quiet, but it can be as busy as the carnival sometimes."

Maddox sat down in a matching, armless side chair. "Everyone's come to see your poorest suitor, have they?"

Katya leaned forward, wishing she could say it was not true. "Who cares if you are? You look like you belong here, not like the others. They sit there with insincere praises falling out of their mouths while they eye the furniture suspiciously because it wasn't imported from France."

"Who could praise you insincerely?"

Katya knew whom: the kind of man who did not mind trading a fraction of his fortune to secure a woman to bear him a few heirs to inherit it. She appreciated Maddox's genuine incredulity and avoided the more negative subject. "That's very kind of you to say."

"I hope you don't think I'm misleading you."

"Of course not."

Mary appeared in the doorway, lingering by its dark frame. She nodded to Maddox. "Good afternoon. My mother said to tell you the tea's almost ready."

Katya frowned, but she could not really be upset with Mrs. Weeks. "Your mother told you to come check out my new suitor."

"No," Mary insisted. She looked from Maddox back to Katya. "All right, she did."

Katya lifted her hand toward Mary. "This is Mary Weeks. I like *her*."

Mary offered a shallow curtsy to Maddox. "Did Lizzie show her head?"

"Yes, her very green head." Katya's eyes sparkled to picture it.

Mrs. Weeks carried a tray in past Mary. "Now, I brought plenty of Darjeeling. It's piping hot. And I brought you some crackers and raspberry jam." Mrs. Weeks set the tray on the wooden tea cart inside the doorway. She wheeled it to the middle of the room between Katya and Maddox. "Do you read the papers, Mr. O'Sullivan?"

Maddox took a moment to answer. "On occasion."

"I've been so fascinated by the plights of our new president and the late president's murderer."

"So have I."

Mrs. Weeks released an excited coo, relaxing the matronly tightening of her muscles. "They're going to hang him, you know. Soon."

"I know. I told Miss Romanova weeks ago I thought they would."

Mrs. Weeks patted the braided bun of silver hair at the nape of her neck. "Katya's not as interested, but I can tell you I know the young Mrs. Cleveland would rather have her husband back than watch his murderer say his final prayers."

"I'm sure she would."

"And I have such sympathy for President Bayard, not that he'll mind going down in the history books as one of our presidents. But I'm sure it was quite a shock to be elevated to such a high office."

"I'm sure it was."

Satisfied with Maddox's answers, or perhaps only the opportunity to express her opinions, Mrs. Weeks retreated toward the hall. "If you want anything else, just call down the stairs. I'll be straightening the kitchen. Come along, Mary."

The two Weeks women excused themselves from the room. Mrs. Weeks sashayed with obvious approval of Katya's most recent choice in men.

Katya stood up and raised the tea pot by its handle. She wished Mrs. Weeks could be more subtle with her judgments. "May I pour you some tea?"

"Please."

Katya eased some of the honey-colored Darjeeling into a flowered white tea cup. She glanced at Maddox. Now that her housemates had stopped besieging his visit, she remembered exactly what she wanted to say but could not. *Don't talk to me at the carnival. It's too risky.* Once she had raised an alarm, Maddox would never be satisfied until he knew what the precise danger was, and she refused to betray Brady's trust in her.

Katya handed Maddox the portioned Darjeeling and spouted tea into the second cup for herself.

"What're you thinking?" Maddox asked.

Katya returned to happier thoughts. "I appreciate how nice it is to have you here. It's always refreshing to have a visitor and not talk to the same couple of people all the time." Katya replaced the tea pot and carried her cup a few steps back to the settee. "Did you have trouble finding the house?"

"No."

"I hope you didn't have to come too far."

Maddox revealed a mischievous grin above his tea cup. "Most the way across the city."

Katya lowered her cup in protest. "No."

"Yes. Do you think crossing state lines would've stopped me from seeing you? If you caught gold rush fever and ran off to the western territory, do you think I'd stay in my pitiful excuse for a boarding house? No."

Katya sipped her tea, which emitted wispy ghost-strands of steam past her face. "No, I suppose you wouldn't."

"Would you welcome my company? Amidst all the ruffians and entrepreneurs and their saloons and brothels."

"Undoubtedly, but it isn't polite to talk about saloons and... such other establishments." Katya's eyes sparkled to show such talk did not truly offend her. She favored any subject that made her appear more civilized and ladylike by comparison.

The front door creaked open, and seconds later, the lock clicked shut.

Katya ran through a mental list of her housemates. Lizzie sulked upstairs in her room or stood picking at her hair in the bathroom mirror. Mary and Mrs. Weeks huddled gossiping in the kitchen. Only Magdalene was missing. Katya had not seen her since lunch.

"Mags?" Katya called to the hallway. "Is that you?"

Magdalene stepped into the doorway, unbuttoning her jacket. She stopped when she caught sight of Maddox. "I'm sorry. I didn't realize you had company."

"Have you met Mr. O'Sullivan?"

Maddox stood up and bowed, careful not to spill his tea. "We met briefly. I sometimes help myself to roasted peanuts and root beer."

"Where have you been?" Katya asked her friend.

Magdalene's wandering gaze gave her the preoccupied look she often had these days. "I took a short ride downtown, that's all."

Katya backed off, resolving to ask Magdalene more about it in private. "Mr. O'Sullivan was kind enough to rescue me from the boredom of the afternoon. Lizzie's already set her sights on him, the poor man."

Magdalene swept her hand in a slow arc in front of her face. "Abandon all hope of eluding Lizzie Huffman, all men who enter here."

Katya stifled a snicker.

Magdalene offered a short curtsy to Maddox. "It was nice to see you, Mr. O'Sullivan." She swept out of the room toward the front staircase.

Maddox lowered himself into his chair. "She's always in a hurry, isn't she?"

Katya nodded and sipped her tea. "That's Magdalene for you. She never does anything without a purpose."

"And what about you?"

Katya thought for a moment. "I'm finding that not having a purpose is a freeing feeling I like very much."

Mrs. Weeks poked her head in unexpectedly. "Do you need more tea or crackers? How's the jam?"

"It's fine, Mrs. Weeks," Katya assured her.

"It's wonderful, thank you," Maddox added.

Mrs. Weeks nodded definitively, a cheerful glow illuminating her face. She hummed as she retreated down the hall.

Katya drank more of her tea. "It's like I told you, Mr. O'Sullivan. Watch the carnival tonight. It'll seem emptier than it has in ages."

Chapter Twenty-Nine

Magdalene had gone to the newspapers. She visited the offices of the *Mirror*, the *Journal*, the *News*, the *Sentinel*, and the *Sun*, behaving as inconspicuously as possible. In her day clothes, there was nothing to give her away as working for the Steampunk Carnival. She merely mentioned to secretaries, reporters between stories, and a few hyper-minded editors that they might want to keep a closer eye on the carnival. If they wanted to get the real story of it, they should not dress too well or flash their cameras where everyone could see them. The reporters might reap new headlines out of the establishment in the coming weeks.

Magdalene refused to give her name, simply stating she had intimate knowledge of the carnival and knew that something big was brewing. The newspapers would do well to prepare themselves.

Katya walked the grounds that night, mulling this over. No one seemed to be who she thought they were. Magdalene snuck around downtown, feeding information to the papers. Mary hid her worsening disease, doctoring herself behind closed doors and hoping she could beat the overwhelming odds stacked against her getting well.

Even Katya was changing. She had thought herself grown up before, seeing the world the way it was and willing to call it by its name. She had sunk her claws into every successful businessman she could find, trying to dazzle her way toward financial security for life.

I'm too young to think so old, Katya admonished herself. She looked around at the spinning wheels and charging coaster cars. How could she be anything but young here? How could she wander this trampled ground and think only of numbers, only of money?

A hand gripped Katya's elbow. She assumed it belonged to Maddox, that he wanted to reiterate what a lovely afternoon he had passed at the Boarder. Katya turned toward him, a worried pause creeping through her chest. Mr. Warden greeted her silently, his dark eyebrows set in expectation.

"Mr. Warden," Katya breathed, barely able to keep herself from backing away. She felt caught in the act, as if he could read her treacherous thoughts. "What can I do for you?"

"What did you want to talk to me about?"

Katya searched his face, her muscles tensing around her eyes. "I didn't need to talk to you, Mr. Warden."

"Mrs. Lieber just came into my office and said you wanted to see me."

Katya shook her head. She felt clawing, mounting dread, as if something horrible had already happened. "Did you leave her alone in your office?"

"Yes. She said it was urgent."

Katya bolted toward the back of the carnival without explaining why. Every twelve steps or so, she quickened her pace. She ran past the Beast and Brady's game stall by the time she heard a muffled sound like a wet handclap. Only then did Mr. Warden speed past her, reaching the door to his office before she could.

"Stay outside," Mr. Warden barked.

Katya was not prepared to listen. Mr. Warden opened the door, and without bothering to steel herself, Katya peered past him into the office.

In the far room, on the floor two feet from where her husband passed away, rested the finally motionless body of Agna Lieber. Katya stared at the gun by her hand. The only thought repeating itself in her head cried accusingly, *I told her. I told her where her husband died.*

Mr. Warden started forward but hung back again. Mrs. Lieber was not moving. Blood seeped across the muddy tone of her jacket.

"Where's Mr. Weis?" Mr. Warden asked, for once sounding unsure of himself.

Katya felt just as ungrounded. "I don't know Mr. Weis."

"The new head of security."

"I don't know where he is."

"Will you stay with the body, or should I?"

"I'll stay with her," Katya volunteered softly, her head swimming with the decision.

Mr. Warden strode away toward the maintenance office, and Katya moved slowly into the outer room. She pulled the door closed behind her, muting the sounds of the carnival. She looked at Agna's body for a few moments, testing her limits as her breath thinned in her throat.

What about Agna's little girl? What would happen to her? Relatives? An orphanage?

Katya stepped forward and closed the door to the inner room. She sat down on Mr. Warden's gold silk settee to wait for him and Mr. Weis.

What drove Agna to such a violent, irreversible action? Did she miss her husband, or was it too hard to support herself without his salary from the carnival?

Tears tumbled down Katya's cheeks. Missing a handkerchief, she patted the fingers of her gloves to her face.

Katya called herself a fool. She worried that Brady's plan to expose Mr. Warden to his numerous carnival guests would tarnish its reputation so badly, it could never recover. Yet under Mr. Warden's leadership, one couple lay dead. The most the public knew, the most press Mr. Lieber's murder had garnered, was a short, innocent obituary:

Mr. Ernst Lieber, a valuable employee of William H. Warden's wonderful Steampunk Carnival, passed away last night due to sudden illness.

The sudden illness of a letter opener spilling the blood from his neck.

The outer door sprang open, and a man stormed in ahead of Mr. Warden. Katya recognized him immediately as the man who had named Agna for her weeks before. Katya stared at him. He had stood right beside her and given her no indication Mr. Warden had named him as Mr. Lieber's replacement.

Mr. Weis stood taller than Mr. Warden. His soft features and bushy facial hair made him look docile and trustworthy. It was not until Katya saw his eyes that she shrank back. The mousy brown orbs swiveled unexpectedly and observantly, piercing everything they took in.

"Who's this?" Mr. Weis commanded. Katya still could not place his accent, sort of a slow, lilting affect between German and Swedish.

"Miss Romanova. She works for me."

Mr. Weis flicked his eyes over Katya. "Yes, I recognize her now. Where's the body?"

Katya cringed. That *body* was Agna Lieber, until five minutes ago, a fellow employee to Mr. Weis. She had thrown herself into work at the carnival none of the others would touch.

Mr. Warden gestured to the closed door. "In there."

Mr. Weis tossed a hand at Katya. "Get her out of here." He opened the door to the office and disappeared inside. He shut the door, but what he needed privacy for, Katya could not guess.

Mr. Warden spoke to her more civilly. "Katya, you should go. I'm sorry you had to see this. I had no idea she was planning to do it."

Katya rose to her feet, making sure she maintained a steady balance. "She's been upset for weeks."

Mr. Warden's voice sharpened. "Are you blaming this on me?"

"No, sir."

"You told me I could do better." Mr. Warden took his hat off and smoothed his straight hair with the flat of his hand. "Maybe I should've tried."

Sympathy pulled Katya toward Mr. Warden. "It might not have helped. It's not your fault, whatever you did or didn't do. She was obviously stricken with grief in one way or another."

Mr. Warden nodded, considering this. He lowered his head, easing his lips toward Katya's. She leaned back, creating an undeniable space in the smoothest motion she could manage. Mr. Warden stopped, his eyes darkening as he searched her face, looking for the reasons she was suddenly denying him.

Katya worked to keep her face a blank page. Her mind drifted to Mr. Weis' suit, a plain brown that had blended him into the crowd the past few weeks, obscuring his duties from her. Now Magdalene's newspaper reporters would be roaming the grounds, equally incognito and indistinguishable from the other guests. Katya tried to hide the pride she took in trying to beat Mr. Warden at his own game. By the deepening creases in Mr. Warden's forehead, he might or might not have noticed it.

"I don't want to be in the way, Mr. Warden," Katya explained. "Is there anything else you need from me?"

Suspicion strained his monotonous voice. "No. That's all. Thank you for your help."

Katya let herself out of the building. She moved toward the nearest food stall, seeking out Magdalene's reassuring red clothes. Her burgundy hat, star charms flashing like mirrors among the ostrich feathers, sat precisely in place atop her blonde hair. Her red sleeves moved as quickly and rhythmically as ever, down to the customers and over to Irina. Katya watched her, jealous for the first time of the certainty in Magdalene's life. Magdalene had one place at the carnival: the eastern stall. Katya might find herself on any inch of the property at any given moment. Magdalene seemed content to let rare suitors seek her out and pay visits to the house of their own accord. She performed no rush for the altar. Katya, on the other hand, had always been forward. She had always pushed for more, employing more tactics in grabbing a man's attention than most women knew to forget. She could fake a fainting spell and drop a well-timed handkerchief better than any actress adored on the stage.

Magdalene had not gotten herself into trouble with Mr. Warden, and Katya had. She decided to stop arguing with herself over whether she should have started anything with Mr. Warden or whether she should have enjoyed his illicit company so much. It was time to figure out how soon she could react and what she could possibly do to move Brady's plan forward.

Chapter Thirty

Katya was not so enthralled with the predictability of Magdalene's life that she forgot to appreciate her many freedoms. With her family seven-hundred miles away, Katya felt free to travel the city alone as she needed. Mrs. Weeks had neither the time nor the beginnings of an inclination to chaperone any of her unrelated boarders through the city streets.

Making her way along the sidewalk downtown, Katya glanced at the other young women her age. Not one of them walked alone. Some of them held the hand of a younger brother or sister. Some of them were elbowed by hawk-eyed mothers spying an acceptable suitor, and others were guided briskly away from potential suitors by more protective matrons.

Katya crossed Pennsylvania Street and reached the two-story building marked with a wide sign running between two rows of windows: *Holloway Brothers Pharmacy*. She strolled in, nodding politely to the other patrons. Even in her everyday clothes, Katya did not see the need to ignore those around her. She walked along the row of glass shelves, reading the labels on bottles even more varied than Mary's home collection. Advertisements hung on the wall above them, adding to the overwhelming display.

Little's Oriental Balm cures all aches and pains.

Veno's Lightning Cough Cure.

Mellin's Cod Liver Oil Emulsion for all chest ailments.

Katya selected a few bottles she did not recognize from Mary's drawer, a deep amber one and a mossy green vessel the color of Lizzie's fragile hair. She added a cobalt blue vial to her hands and approached the pharmacist's counter.

"Good afternoon," he greeted her, taking the bottles.

"Good afternoon, Dr. Holloway." Katya watched him pick up a pencil and start to write the costs of the cure-alls on a pad of receipts. She leaned toward him and dropped her voice low. "I also need something from the back room."

Dr. Holloway grunted discreetly. He finished adding up the cost of the medicines and set them inside a brown paper bag. "Three dollars, please."

Katya pulled the bills from her little bag and handed them across the counter. Dr. Holloway secured the money inside his register drawer. "Right this way."

Katya kept in step with Dr. Holloway on her side of the long counter. He led her to a closed door at the rear of the shop. A neatly centered sign read *Pharmacists Only*. Dr. Holloway unlocked the door, and Katya followed him inside.

The room was little more than a stock room. Expansive wooden shelves held extra bottles, jars, and boxes. Dr. Holloway closed the door and continued deeper into the room. "What were you interested in?"

"What do you have available?"

"Goodyear rubbers, of course. Those new, natural skins from New York. Diaphragms. Spermicides. Douches."

"I want..." Katya struggled to explain her thoughts without embarrassing herself. She wished Dr. Holloway had a female assistant, but talking to a woman about it would not have made her request much more comfortable. "I want something I don't have to carry with me."

"You're traveling around?"

"In a manner of speaking."

"You won't want the skins, then."

"It'll be easier to take care of at home before I leave the house than... afterward."

Dr. Holloway reached for a cluster of paper bags and looked through the boxes inside them. "Do you know how to insert a diaphragm?"

Katya's face flushed hot. "No."

"Spermicidal tablets are easier. They dissolve in the body. You can put them in beforehand."

"I'll take some of those."

Dr. Holloway slipped a small, rectangular box from one of the bags. He murmured the price to her, and Katya paid him quickly. She stuffed the box into her purse.

"Have a good day," Dr. Holloway said.

"You, too. Thank you."

Katya hurried out of the cramped, stuffy room. She crossed the pharmacy with the bag of cure-alls in her hand, relieved to reach the sidewalk.

Katya thought about taking the streetcar home but decided to walk the three miles to the boarding house. The outdoor air felt good in her lungs, even if it did reek of burning coal and horse manure.

By the time Katya reached the Weekly Boarder, her feet ached from the sidewalks, less forgiving than the open ground she walked at the carnival. She entered the house as soundlessly as she could, listening to where the others were in the structure. She could hear Mary and Mrs. Weeks talking at the back.

"Mary?" Katya called.

Mary appeared from the living room with a feather duster in her hand.

"Will you come up and help me get ready for tonight?"

"Of course." Mary left the duster on the nearest table.

Katya climbed the front stairs and waited for Mary in the hall. Katya did not open the door to her room. She motioned Mary to the other end of the hall, to Mary's room. Mary said nothing and led her inside.

Only behind the closed door did Katya hand Mary the paper bag.

Mary opened it, and as soon as she saw the bottles, she extended it to Katya. "I won't take this."

Katya folded her hands against her skirt. "You can, and you just did. I'll pay for your trip to the hospital if they don't work."

Mary's eyes burned but not as furiously as before. "If you can find a good enough alibi for my mother."

"I will. I'm working on it."

"Thank you." Mary turned and arranged the bottles in the drawer with the others. "I'm not like Lizzie. I don't care what happened between you and Mr. Warden. I don't feel good about spending your money."

"You might as well take it. I was saving it up to have a jacket made with a working clock on the back of it, but I don't want it now." It would only attract more of Mr. Warden's attention than Katya wanted.

"You're a good person, Katya." Mary wiped at her eyes and folded the paper bag along its seams with a crinkle.

Mr. Davies had told Katya the same thing. She still did not believe it.

"You're the better person, Mary," Katya said. "You don't get yourself into messes so you have to relieve your conscience by helping other people. You help because you want to."

"Do you really need my assistance getting ready for the carnival?"

"No. I'll do it myself."

Katya went into her room and stood in front of the dresser. It was easy to see where most of her money had gone. A wooden jewelry box sat on the dresser, lined in green velvet and stocked full of jewelry. In the mirror's reflection, the armoire door rested closed, but Katya did not need to see her wardrobe to know how much fuller it was than anyone else's she knew. She kept more knickknacks by her bed than Magdalene and Mary added together, and her bedding was nicer.

Irina was right. Katya was lazy and spoiled, but she was not stupid. Nothing could clear her conscience more thoroughly than exposing Mr. Warden for the fraud he was and making sure Brady took his place. Supposing the carnival did recover from such an upheaval, it would be the idyllic place to work like it had been in the beginning. No fear, no uncertainty, no lying and dodging.

They needed the perfect opportunity. They needed the press to be there in their innocuous-looking suits, ready to pull their cameras out of concealment. They needed Mr. Warden trapped in front of his patrons with nowhere to hide.

It would happen. Katya just did not know when.

Chapter Thirty-One

The carnival seemed busier and more active than usual. Katya could not tell whether it was the effects of successful advertising, Mr. Warden's added security, or the patronage of Magdalene's tipped-off journalists.

Katya needed them busy. She needed the maintenance workers focused on their machines, their fingers and faces coated in coal dust and grease. She needed the game stalls buzzing with customers trying to beat the crooked rigs. She needed the food stalls swarmed by curious, starving guests. Security needed to look the other way, and Mr. Warden needed to shut himself inside his office, his nose buried in his record books.

There was only one person Katya wanted to catch between jobs, and it took her half the night to find Maddox. He meandered her way in front of the Warden wheel, wiping his hands with a soiled rag. Katya swept up to him by the exit gate and dropped into a springing curtsy.

Maddox brightened and used his cleaner hand to tip his hat. "Miss Romanova. A pleasure to see you."

Katya gestured one of her spotless gloves to the dirty rag. "Did one of the rides break down?"

"No, it just needed a little adjusting."

"While it was still running?"

"Aye."

"How do you work on it when it's running?"

"As carefully as I can. I don't want to burn or smash my hands."

Katya did not doubt Mr. Warden condoned such dangerous tactics, but she did not like the sound of it. Brady would not make his workers risk disfigurement if he were in charge. Katya was sure Mr. Warden encouraged maintenance during operating hours under the guise of not keeping them extra late in the morning. Brady could easily find a safer solution.

Maddox pulled at each finger with the cloth. "How are Mrs. Weeks and your housemates?"

"They're well. Thank you."

"Has Lizzie repaired her hair yet to, what'd she call it? Its proper glory?"

Katya smirked. "Not yet. She damaged it too severely. She has to treat it before she can dye it. She's been wearing hats all the time, even at lunch."

"Sounds to me like justice, eh?"

Katya did not want to seem too bitter about her rivalry with Lizzie but found it impossible to be completely civil. "Perhaps."

Maddox rubbed the cloth across his palms a few times. They were mostly clean except for dark particles forming lines in the deeper creases of his hands.

"Are you terribly busy, Mr. O'Sullivan?" Katya asked. She licked her lips nervously.

Maddox grinned, his eyes shining. "Am I busy, or are there things for me to do? They're two very different questions."

"Are you busy?"

"I can always make time for a break."

"Is there a place we can be alone?" Katya could hear the scrape of desperation in her voice. She did not want to get caught, and she did not want Maddox to say no.

Maddox remained casual and upbeat. "We might be able to find one. With this many people at the carnival, it's almost as busy as your house."

Katya eased half a step toward Maddox. "I'm not talking about a conversation, Mr. O'Sullivan. I was thinking of something a little more personal." Katya slid her hand out of its purple velvet glove and touched the back of Maddox's hand, still slick and moist with oil. She traced her fingers down between his thumb and index finger, rubbing the tips of them back and forth over the skin of his palm.

Maddox shuddered and pulled his hands away. He glanced at the thick crowd passing by in both directions. "I'm sure we can find something. Let's try this way. The storage building might be empty."

Maddox guided Katya behind the western food stall to the maintenance building. He pushed the door open for her, and she stepped in ahead of him. He paused for a moment, listening to the vacant, silent rooms before pulling the door closed.

As soon as the latch clicked, Katya threw her arms around Maddox's neck. His arms pressed against her back, and his lips found her mouth. She pushed her body against his, leaving the problems of the carnival outside where she could not see them. She lost herself in Maddox, the pungent oil smell of his hands and the spicy sausage taste of his tongue.

A conversation picked up a few feet outside the door, and Katya tore herself away from Maddox. His top hat tilted back on his head, knocked there by the brim of her hat. "Is there a lock?" she asked, trying to catch her breath. Her eyes searched the door handle.

"No. This way."

Maddox took her bare hand and led her into the sitting room. Cigarette cards littered the table in sepia tones and faded hues. Maddox lifted a chair from around the table and closed the door. He wedged the chair's back under the cast iron door knob and tested it for strength.

Katya peeled off her other glove. She did not have time to find a place to lay them before Maddox scooped her into his arms. She dropped them to the floor, much more intent on finishing what she had started with Maddox before someone discovered them.

Maddox's fingers worked to unfasten the buttons on the front of Katya's jacket. She wiggled free of it, content to let it fall on the floor as well. She stripped off Maddox's jacket, dropping it as he pulled her up against him. His mouth covered hers hungrily, insistent and impatient. He inched her toward the table, her bustle bumping it and nudging her lower back. Maddox gripped her sides and plucked her up to sit on the table. He positioned himself between her legs, the fabric of her dress and undergarments keeping him from pressing directly against her body.

In her eagerness, Katya fumbled over the buttons on Maddox's shirt. He skipped ahead, unfastening his trousers before helping Katya open the front of his shirt. His suspender straps held the material against his chest on either side while it draped open to reveal the rich red of his flannel union suit. It offered its own vertical row of buttons, which Katya started on immediately.

Maddox tossed his hat onto a nearby chair. He unbuttoned Katya's bodice with nimble execution, still three layers away from her flesh. Maddox pried at the cotton corset cover, the gold silk corset, and the white chemise beneath it. He lowered his head to Katya's chest, his impassioned lips sucking at the exposed curves of her breasts.

Katya slid her hand down the front of Maddox's union suit, his length stiffening at her touch. Maddox sorted through the layers of skirt and underskirt, reaching his hands up to the band of her pantalettes. He swept them gently off her legs and over the wide, one-inch heels of her boots. He slid Katya toward him to the edge of the table.

Katya unpinned her hat and placed it beside her where cigarette cards peeked out from beneath her skirt. She took a deep breath as Maddox entered her, squeezing her fingers around his arms. Maddox held her closer, the bare parts of their chests touching as he found a rhythm with his thrusts. Katya bit her lip to keep from crying out, leaning her temple against his and making quiet moans over Maddox's shoulder. She had never felt anything so good.

With every heartbeat, the pleasure spread through Katya's body. She wrapped her legs around Maddox as best she could, pressing them tighter together. Her eyes drifted shut, her sighs and half-whines warming the top of his ear. As Maddox entered deeper, Katya's moans grew to fill the quiet room. Maddox lifted one hand off her waist and placed it over her mouth. Katya stopped trying to hold back anymore, moaning and murmuring into Maddox's dirty palm.

Maddox pressed his lips against Katya's neck. He moaned into her skin through a dozen hard, separate thrusts. Katya held him against her, her legs quivering around him as her own body released its incredible tension.

As her breathing slowed, Katya became aware of the room once again. She could hear the unending sounds of the carnival beyond the front of the building, calling voices and churning machines.

Maddox kissed her neck, her jaw, her cheek. He peeled his hand off her mouth and kissed her lips. He leaned back and wiped his sleeve across his mouth. "I got your face dirty. I'm sorry."

"It's okay."

Maddox glanced around the room, his hips still in line with Katya's. "There has to be something to clean you up with."

"I'll go down to the sinks in a minute." Katya rested her head on Maddox's shoulder, her breathing picking up as she thought back over what they had done.

"I wish we had more time," Maddox sighed.

Katya nodded, her temple swiveling against his collar bone.

"Did you..." Maddox paused, the only time he had ever hesitated in speaking to her.

Katya raised her head off his shoulder to look into his eyes.

"Did you speak with a pharmacist before you came here?"

"Yes. It's taken care of."

Maddox pressed his lips to Katya's forehead. He leaned his hips away and started buttoning up his red union suit.

Katya slipped carefully to her feet, pulling her pantalettes on. "There isn't a mirror in here, is there?" she asked doubtfully.

"No."

"You'll have to tell me when I've got my hat on straight."

Maddox chuckled. "Nothing's going to be straight about us the rest of the night." He buttoned his pants and his shirt.

Katya tugged her camisole and corset into place, neatly arranging the corset cover over it. On quick inspection, the layers seemed to have done their job and kept her sweat from staining the fabric of her dress. She reached for her hat and set it on top of the hair piled on her head.

Maddox adjusted his suspenders. "Your hat looks straight to me."

Katya stuck the pin through it, making sure to miss her scalp, and Maddox retrieved their jackets from the floor. He held out Katya's, the embroidery hazy through a sheen of dust, hair, and fibers. She took it and brushed it off before she put it on. She picked up her gloves and looked over the room, surprised she had finally put herself back together. The cigarette cards, however, had migrated to every available surface around.

Maddox pulled his jacket on and buttoned it. "It's a good thing I'm a working man. Otherwise, we would've had a vest to wrestle with, too."

Katya laughed, admiring Maddox with twinkling eyes. She pulled her gloves on without glancing at them.

Maddox kissed her again before he reached for his hat and set it on his head. "My hat doesn't need to be perfect. I'm expected to be a bit of a mess."

Katya straightened it for him anyway, already missing the feel of his naked skin against hers.

Maddox touched her face. "Don't be sad. Come on. Work's only a couple more hours. Then we can see each other again if you want."

Katya perked up at the thought.

"I do have a bed, but it isn't much. It's all right if you don't mind being close to me."

"I don't mind being close to you."

Maddox held onto his hat and kissed Katya one last time. He took the chair out from under the door handle and replaced it at the table. Maddox hastily picked up some of the cigarette cards and flung them onto its surface. He opened the door for Katya. "You should go out first. I'll leave in a minute."

Katya nodded and walked through the storage room. She slipped out the door onto the crowded grounds, the great patches of shadow and light the exact opposite of the straight-forward lighting of the maintenance building. She tried to act natural, even though for once, she did not want to be at the carnival. She did not want to wander its premises, sharing the facts of its astounding machines with the wonder-eyed patrons. Katya avoided Brady's line of sight, passing by the dark, empty side of the nearest food stall. She ambled toward the water closets, wishing she was wrapped up in Maddox's arms in his tiny bed, fighting him for space just to touch him while he enjoyed the fact there was none to spare.

Katya shut herself in one of the compact water closets. Her legs felt shaky and weak from sitting on the edge of the table, but walking had helped them regain some of their sturdiness. Katya took a clean towel off the rack on the wall and washed her face with soap, careful not to wet her clothes or her hair. She patted herself dry and left the dirty towel in the collection basket.

As she left the water closet, she spotted the new charwoman on her way to check them. She did not share the once-attractive weariness of Agna Lieber. She reminded Katya more of Irina, brusque mannered, her hefty form wedged into her uniform. Irina got on with the charwoman beautifully, chattering animatedly during every carriage ride about President Bayard's latest decision and the new sweet shop's exorbitant prices.

The charwoman barely acknowledged Katya. She offered a firm bob of her round head and swept through the water closet's open door.

Katya moved on, ready to put extra distance between herself and the soiled towel reeking of oil. She could taste it, faint but oddly sweet. She resolved to continue on her rounds through the carnival, making a wide circle to Magdalene's food stall in the back. More than anyone, Katya wanted to avoid Brady. She knew he was watching her to keep her safe, but she could not stand to have him comment about her personal life again. It was Mr. Warden and Mr. Weis she feared. They were the problem, the ones who could harm her, not Maddox. He could only hurt her heart, and if he wanted, her reputation. She did not dare think of the things Mr. Warden and Mr. Weis might prove capable of.

Katya reached the food stall and waited for Magdalene to spare her a tenth of her attention. "Can I have a small taste of the root beer, please? I'm so thirsty."

"Root beer," Magdalene repeated over her right shoulder to Irina and the Englishman.

"Anything going on tonight I should know about?" Katya asked, trying to sound lighthearted and interested.

"What do you mean?"

"Have you talked to anybody? Mr. Warden. Mr. Kelly."

"No." Magdalene accepted a mug from Irina and passed it to Katya.

Katya slurped the root beer gratefully, letting its strong, biting taste beat back the oil from Maddox's hand. She had not checked the back of her dress for stains. She hoped her jacket covered them all.

"Have you spoken to anyone?" Magdalene asked.

"No," Katya said automatically, still thinking of Mr. Warden and Mr. Kelly. She bit her lip, remembering that the lapses in her conversation with Maddox had not exactly harbored silence.

Magdalene's voice broke into Katya's reverie. "How's the root beer?"

"It's good. Thank you."

Katya walked away, sipping her root beer and using the white mug to steer patrons toward the food stall. "Have you tried the root beer? It's delicious." Even after she drained the mug empty, she sold patrons on the idea of it for half an hour. Katya left the mug in one of the collection bins to be washed and reused.

When she glimpsed Maddox again, it was only for a second. He lingered fifty feet away on the other side of the band stage. The blaring flute solo alone would have made it impossible to hear him if he had spoken. He simply smiled, bright and knowing, and Katya returned the expression, content and happy.

Chapter Thirty-Two

Katya waited in the back of St. John the Episcopal, listening to the early morning rustling of the slumbering homeless. Magdalene sat beside her, patient and still. Katya turned her head to catch the different sounds running over the room. A snore erupted in the sanctuary's front corner. A murmur of dream words sounded from the other side, cut off by a whistle of breath.

At last, even Magdalene swung her head when the front door of the church opened in the hall. Brady stepped quietly into the sanctuary and slid himself onto the bench next to Magdalene. He lowered his hat into his lap.

"Where do we begin?" Magdalene asked.

"What do you know about the death of Agna Lieber? I only know she was replaced."

Katya could not stop the answer from pouring out of her. "She killed herself. Mr. Warden kept it quiet. I saw her obituary in the *News*." Katya held up her thumb and index finger, spaced an inch apart. "That much room for her. Unknown causes, it said, following the death of her husband. Possibly died of grief."

Brady's eyes were as serious and skeptical as Katya's voice. "What form, exactly, did Mrs. Lieber's grief take when it killed her?"

"It was a small gun. A pistol? A revolver?"

"Are you sure it was suicide?"

"Quite sure. She distracted Mr. Warden, told him I needed to see him about something. He came out of his office to talk to me, and by the time we got there, she'd shot herself. No one else was in the building."

Brady's lips twisted into a wry smirk. "What did Warden say to that?"

Katya hesitated. She wanted to tell the truth, that Mr. Warden had seemed regretful and wounded by it. She did not know if Brady or Magdalene would appreciate her continuing to share that side of him. Mr. Warden had also tried to kiss her, which Katya definitely wanted to leave out. "Mr. Warden brought in Mr. Weis, the new head of security. He started taking care of the body or doing something with it. I couldn't see. I left soon after that. That's all I saw."

"Was Warden rattled?" Brady asked, relishing the thought.

"Yes." Under his cool facade, Mr. Warden had been sweating bullets.

Magdalene spoke up between Katya and Brady. "Who's Mr. Weis? What does he look like?"

"I don't know anything about him," Katya said. "I wish I did. He gives me the creeps, just like Mr. Lieber did. Mr. Weis looks like a nice man. Soft cheeks. Small nose. But his eyes devour everything. There's nothing he can't see, I'm sure of it." Katya's heart sank as she realized that might include witnessing her remove her glove and touch her bare hand to Maddox's.

Magdalene turned to Brady. "Have you heard anything about him, Mr. Kelly?"

"No, I'm sorry," Brady said. "I'm more likely to be talked about than spoken to."

"I don't know if I've seen Mr. Weis," Magdalene went on. "But I'm still being scrutinized. Even if I do everything the same way I always have, I feel I'm giving something away."

Katya laid her gloved hand over Magdalene's. "Have you ever thought about leaving the carnival? Quitting your job?"

"No. I won't do it. It's too suspicious, and I'm not leaving either of you to deal with Mr. Warden alone. Even with three of us, Mr. Warden could make us disappear and cover the whole thing up."

Brady nodded sharply. "We should act soon."

"The reporters are there almost every night," Magdalene informed him with satisfaction. "If we can get the band to stop playing, more people will be able to hear Mr. Warden's confession."

Katya agreed but did not think it would be as easy as saying it. "How will we do that? They haven't stopped playing since we opened except when the Beast blew something."

Magdalene answered without hesitation. "Use the only name that works around here. Tell them Mr. Warden wants them to stop until further notice."

Katya could not argue with that suggestion. She knew Mr. Warden's name worked. She had ridden half the carnival on that name.

Brady stroked his chin and tangled beard. "If only we could get Mr. Warden onto the band stage or the other stage, somewhere people could see him."

Katya's spirits surged upward. "Getting Mr. Warden to a place where people can see him? He'll love that. It would be the easiest part."

"So what's stopping us? What's keeping us from blowing the truth wide open the very next night the reporters are there?"

Katya could not put words to the answer, but she felt her stomach tighten. They were missing something, and they needed every last piece to fit to get it right.

Magdalene spoke up quietly. "They think we did it. They must think we had something to do with Mr. Lieber's murder."

"How could we possibly?" Katya whispered.

"Don't they always look for motive? They could say you killed him for spreading rumors about your reputation. They could say I killed him to protect you or because I thought no one would suspect me. Either one of us could have killed him because we spited him. Mr. Warden has to know nobody liked Mr. Lieber."

Brady's deeper, gruffer voice interjected. "Why should that stop us? We should act fast. We can't let them pin a murder on you."

"They'll say the journal is a cover-up to get Mr. Warden out of the way and keep him from finding out the truth about Mr. Lieber."

"It's in my handwriting," Brady insisted.

"I know," Magdalene said gently. "But Mr. Warden is worth millions, and we're nobodies. He could discredit us in an instant."

"So what do you suggest?"

Magdalene could barely push the words out. "That we wait."

Brady jerked forward in his seat. "For what? For Mr. Lieber's murderer to reveal himself and publicly apologize for any trouble he might've caused?" Brady ducked his head and ran his hands over his hair. His shoulders drooped. "Forgive me."

"I understand your frustration, Mr. Kelly. But you know as well as I do that rushing into a confrontation with Mr. Warden can only end badly."

Brady nodded, squeezing his eyes shut.

"Mr. Warden could destroy you. He's probably bribed the police and the newspapers. Nothing would stop him from creating new evidence and sending you to prison as Mr. Lieber's murderer. We'd never see you again, and you'd never see that journal. Mr. Warden wouldn't throw it in the trash this time. He'd burn it."

Brady nodded as he sat up straight and picked his head up. "What are we waiting for? We can't possibly find out who killed Lieber."

"We just need to find the right time when the newspapers are there and there are so many people to hear his confession that not even Mr. Warden can worm his way out." Magdalene laid her hand on Brady's arm. "You know what I'm talking about, Mr. Kelly. There are so many nights when the carnival runs smoothly and everything goes Mr. Warden's way. But there are the nights when the unexpected happens and strange guests show up around every corner."

"Yes, I know the times."

They flashed through Katya's mind. The frazzled woman in bulky green. The tall, stately Isolde. Agna Lieber's fists pounding Mr. Warden's chest before Katya knew who she was.

Magdalene patted Brady's sleeve. "That's the kind of night we're waiting for. We need the tide to turn in our favor. Then there's nothing to stop us from succeeding."

Chapter Thirty-Three

Katya could not help glancing the length of the dining table at Lizzie's hair. Even after a few weeks of it, the sickly green hue amused and mesmerized Katya. Lizzie's bonnet hid most of it, and Katya knew by the hat's conservative, frumpy style, just paying for it had bruised Lizzie's self-worth. To wear it for days on end must be eating her alive.

"I see you looking at me, Katya Romanova," Lizzie informed her, too proud and bitter to return the stares. She sliced the piece of chicken on her plate into tiny pieces and dabbed each one in tomato-garlic sauce before she ate it.

"I'm just saddened, Lizzie," Katya said, a hint of her devious nature rolling under her forced concern.

"Why's that?"

"You missed your big chance. At the carnival."

Lizzie finally rewarded Katya with a frustrated glare. "What are you talking about?"

"We had an opening recently for a charwoman. You should've filled it. Then you could've worn any bonnet that suited you and covered up every last curl of your hair."

Lizzie picked up one of her peas and flicked it at Katya. Katya giggled as it bounced off her shoulder.

"When are you going to dye it again?" Katya pressed. "Even Mr. O'Sullivan asked me that. If you don't dye it soon, I'm going to recommend Mrs. Weeks redecorate the dining room. Your hair clashes with the drapes."

Lizzie narrowed her eyes to furious slits and aimed another pea at Katya.

"Do it," Katya baited her. "Then we'll match."

Lizzie let the pea fall onto her plate.

Mrs. Weeks lowered her newspaper, appearing over it where the rest of the table could see her. "Now, Katya, Lizzie's hair is getting better. A few more weeks, and she'll be down at the beauty salon. You'll see."

Lizzie stuck her tongue out at Katya. "I never see you getting your hair done at the salon."

"I don't need to. I can do it perfectly fine myself, and besides, men like to do more than just look at me."

Lizzie sat up taller in her chair, relaxing her tense eyelids. "Yes, is it possible you can't afford the salon? Did Mr. Warden not think you were worth quite that much?"

Katya lunged to jump out of her chair at Lizzie but restrained herself. She remained seated, delicately lifting her water glass and taking a civilized sip from it. "How's your doctor suitor, Lizzie? I can't even remember his name, it was so long ago he courted me."

Lizzie's thick eyelids drew together again. "Dr. Kirby."

"Has he come around recently?"

"No."

Katya feigned surprise, laying a limp hand over her chest. "No? I thought you were growing so close. Can it be that he rejected you?"

"He was a toad, anyway," Lizzie scoffed. Her voice cut off, and she covered her mouth with her hand, coughing several times. "I could have Mr. Warden if I wanted him. I just don't want any part of that stinky old carnival."

"You and Mr. Warden would deserve each other. That's for sure."

Lizzie coughed harder, suppressing it with a long drink of water.

Katya watched her more closely as the coughing went on. She snuck a glance at Mary. Mary's expression hung blank, her cheeks pale and her eyes staring straight across the table at Lizzie.

"Are you all right?" Mrs. Weeks spoke up helpfully. "Mary, get the bottle of Ayer's I keep by my bed."

Lizzie shook her head, coughing harder and soon recovering from her fit. "I'm all right."

"Do you have a cold, dear?"

"I think so."

Katya asked another question. "Have you been coughing a lot, Lizzie?"

Lizzie batted a hand at her through the air. "Like you care."

"I care. Have you been sick long? Maybe you should see a doctor."

"It's a little cough. I'll be fine."

Mary spoke up, her voice tentative and shaky. "Maybe you should see a doctor."

Lizzie set her head at a disapproving angle. "I don't believe you, Mary, siding with her." Lizzie took another sip of water and stood up.

Mrs. Weeks folded her newspaper closed on the corner of the table. "Don't storm off to your room, Lizzie. Finish your dinner." Lizzie dropped into her seat, and Mrs. Weeks peered the length of the table at Katya. "I'll have no more of that sharp tongue tonight. I think we'd all agree you won that exchange, for what it's worth. If it's a husband you want, you might want to consider closing that mouth of yours from time to time."

Katya held her tongue for Mrs. Weeks' sake. She glanced at Mary, but Mary gazed down at her plate, pushing her chicken aimlessly through the fragrant sauce with her fork.

Magdalene spoke up for the first time in twenty minutes. "The chicken's very good, Mrs. Weeks."

Mrs. Weeks' solemn temper softened with a chuckle. "Thank you, Magdalene. I've always wondered that you could sit between those two while they quibble."

Magdalene sat quietly, but Mrs. Weeks watched her, awaiting an answer. "Patience, I suppose," Magdalene offered.

"Ah," Mrs. Weeks said, nodding as if she had suspected that same virtue. "Patience."

"Katya really isn't that spoiled, Mrs. Weeks," Magdalene insisted. "I wish you could see her in action at the carnival. Her outgoing nature is in its best element there."

Mrs. Weeks helped herself to another spoonful of green beans. "You finally succeeded in drawing Mary to the carnival, and now you're after me. Is that it? I don't have time for that kind of foolery, especially at that hour, but I envy you girls. I really do. If I were younger – and I won't say how much younger, but a few years at least – I'd be there in a heartbeat. I promise you."

"Do you have friends who haven't been there yet?"

"I'm sure I do."

"You should send them. Maybe if enough women want to go to the carnival by themselves, Mr. Warden will buy a streetcar of his own and send it all through the city to collect them."

"You're really something, you girls. I don't know where you get such ideas, but I suppose the carnival wasn't built on small dreams, was it?"

Magdalene answered more seriously. "No, it wasn't."

"I suppose I could recommend my friends pay a visit to the carnival. I think they'd like it."

"How about your friends, Lizzie? Have you told them about your visits there?"

Lizzie took a few moments to answer, twirling the cube of chicken on her fork in a puddle of red sauce. "Yes, I told them."

"Did you enjoy it at all? Do you think they would?"

"Are you Mr. Warden's advertising department now?" Lizzie laid her fork down on her plate. "I think they'd enjoy it more than I did."

"You should tell them to come. The side stage gets better sponsors all the time. Everyone loves the dance contests. And don't worry about your hair, Lizzie. Nobody will remember the short time it was less than perfect when you dye it back the way it was."

Lizzie wiggled her shoulders, a pucker of conceit shaping her lips. "I think you're right." She treated herself to the waiting piece of chicken, biting it off her fork with a taunting smirk at Katya.

Katya let Lizzie bounce back to her self-entitled attitude. She had tried to help Lizzie, and Lizzie did not want it. Only Katya's loyalty to Mary kept her mouth shut. She would have relished the horror on Lizzie's face when she announced "You've got consumption" from the head of the table.

Katya snuck a glance at Magdalene, demurely nibbling her dinner. She would never expose Magdalene for the cunning mind she was, but Katya did stew in the vast difference between the reputations of their personalities. Even if Katya saved the carnival singlehandedly from Mr. Warden's illegitimate rule, she would be labeled a busybody. Meanwhile, Magdalene could walk naked through the carnival, and people would call her revolutionary. Nude models would spring up in all public places, advertising the openings of banks and possibly a few churches.

Magdalene finished her dinner and placed her cloth napkin on the table. She looked at Katya's plate, still scattered with vegetables and a few bites of chicken. "I'll be upstairs getting ready."

"I'll be right there."

Magdalene strolled out of the dining room, and Katya reminded herself why Magdalene's reputation was so much better than hers. Magdalene would never think such judgmental thoughts about Katya or anyone else. No one needed to hear their thoughts to know this. It was evident in the way they spoke and the way they carried themselves. Katya had only herself to blame, something she had either accepted with a sneer or tried fiercely to dispute.

Maybe Magdalene was right. Maybe there was one place in the world Katya could inhabit better than anyone else, where her big mouth did not get her into deep trouble. Maybe, eventually, it could save them.

Chapter Thirty-Four

Maddox swept the backs of his fingers over Katya's naked skin, tracing a slow, ever-changing pattern over her body. They crowded together in Maddox's narrow bed, the only light a dimness seeping through the small room from the lamp turned low by the door. Katya lay with her back to Maddox. His fingers trailed from her shoulder down her collar bone, between her breasts, over the softness of her stomach, and up the climb of her hip. Katya felt every swipe and glide of his hand, her mind alert but troubled. She could not form her situation into words, but it haunted her. As her body glowed and reawakened to every inch of skin that Maddox rested against her back and the backs of her legs, Katya could not shake the rumble of doom.

Maddox nestled his face into the hollow between Katya's jaw and shoulder. He kissed her neck, his fingers blazing a new route down her side to the top of her thigh and up her pelvis.

Katya reached for Maddox's hand. "Hold me," she whispered. She could hear the tension binding her voice.

Maddox slipped his arm around her, letting his hand rest on her opposite arm. He kissed the back of her neck, the unforgiving bone behind her ear, and the softer padding of her cheek.

"Do you think there's something wrong at the carnival?" Katya asked. She could not tell Maddox the whole truth, but she could warn him. She had to warn him.

Maddox chuckled in her ear. "How can you think about the carnival? We finally got out of there for the night."

"Something's not right."

"Of course not," Maddox murmured, moving his lips against Katya's shoulder. "Two people died, am I right? I was talking to one of the game stall men. Did you know the games are rigged?"

Katya's muscles tightened, thinking of Mr. Kelly. "Which one?"

"All of them."

"Not the games. Which game runner were you talking to?"

"He didn't give me his name. He runs the one in the front where you throw the baseballs. Have you tried it?"

"No." Katya's restless fingers stroked Maddox's arm.

Maddox adjusted his position behind her, shifting his other arm up under his head and brushing it past her hair. "There's a mechanism under the bottles that holds them in place and makes them harder to knock down, if not impossible. One step on the foot pedal, and the game runner can make a winner out of anybody."

"Mr. Warden's behind all that."

"How do you know? Did he tell you?"

Katya found herself shaking her head, which was not a lie. Mr. Warden had never admitted to it. Brady had told her the first night they talked at his game stall. She fibbed to the first question to cover up her conversation with Brady. "It's just a guess. He decides everything."

Maddox pinned his arm closer against her stomach. "He doesn't know everything."

Katya's insistent *yes* caught in her throat. She kept it there, making her eyes water. *Mr. Warden knows too much.* She blinked the wetness out of her eyes and turned over on her back to look at Maddox.

His expression greeted her gently, confident but not arrogant. The lamplight glinted in the stubble covering his chin and jaw. His eyes shone with appreciation rather than the preoccupation weighing on Katya's mind.

"Promise me," Katya whispered, "that you'll be safe there."

Maddox breathed with good humor. "Be safe with what? Fixing the machines?"

Katya could imagine Mr. Warden rigging one of the devices to hurt Maddox, maybe even mangle his hands for life so he could never work again. "Yes, that too."

"What else, then? I don't understand why you're so afraid."

Katya tried to find the best answer that did not involve Brady and his journal or Mr. Lieber's unknown murderer. "Mr. Warden's jealous."

"Of me?"

"He's a possessive man. If he finds out that we rode the carnival together or were seen slipping into the maintenance office together–"

Maddox gave a wide grin.

Katya took a deep breath to keep herself on track. "It'd explain to him why I didn't want to kiss him."

Maddox's amusement faded as quickly as it had brightened into being. His jaw tightened, and his eyebrows furrowed over sharpened eyes. "He tried to kiss you? When?"

"After Mrs. Lieber killed herself."

"What did you say?"

"I excused myself from his office."

Maddox's tone darkened. "What did he say?"

"Nothing. He thanked me for my help, and I left."

"If he's so envious, he can clear off the side stage. I'll gladly stand toe to toe with him and fight for you. I wouldn't mind taking a few swings at William Warden." Maddox's eyes flashed in a different light as he pictured it. "I bet he's never been in a fight before."

Katya remembered Mr. Warden's more humble, thieving roots. "I'm sure he has."

"You seem to know a lot about Mr. Warden."

"Rumors. I don't think he's always had this much privilege. He started the carnival from nothing. Investors paid for it, not family fortune."

"Why didn't you tell him you were interested in me? How come nobody seems to know that we've been getting acquainted? Are you ashamed of me?"

"No." Maddox's insult pierced Katya's heart. "I'd tell anybody. I don't care. Do you honestly think it matters? Do you know what people think of me? If they saw us in the street, they wouldn't think, 'The Romanova girl's throwing herself away.' They'd say, 'He's still too good for her.'"

Maddox said nothing, and Katya rambled on, the wetness coming back into her eyes. "I'm sorry I told you money and station mattered, and I'm sorry that was the shallow, simple person I was. I don't know what you want me to say to take that back. I can't make excuses for it. I can only tell you that I like being with you, and if that's not good enough, there's no way I can make this right."

Maddox pulled Katya closer to him, his arm sturdy around her waist, and kissed her. "No, that's more than good enough." He rested his forehead against hers.

Even as Maddox's temper cooled into the reliable stillness and comfort she knew him for, Brady's words picked at Katya. *"How well do you know him?"* First Brady's gnawing questions, then the joke. *"He's Irish."* Brady's purposefully thickened accent made anger flare inside Katya like a newly struck matchstick. Maddox's indirect rivalry with Mr. Warden was justified. Katya could no more picture Maddox stabbing a letter opener into Mr. Lieber's thick German neck than she could imagine Magdalene or Mary doing it. Katya resented Brady for making her doubt Maddox, even for a second, but she understood Brady's reasons. Agna Lieber having taken her own life did not make her death any less affecting. The carnival reeked of loss and sorrow and bad fortune.

Maddox held Katya for a long time before he spoke. "There must be a better way you can come here. I don't like you riding the streetcar alone at this time of the morning."

Katya did not care for it, either, surprised at the difference between riding it home with Magdalene from St. John's Church and riding it alone across the southern part of the city. "If there is, I don't know it. The only options are to hire Mr. Davies for a few hours or purchase my own carriage."

Maddox returned to his breathy, joking responses, his face pressed close to hers. "I think Mr. Davies would rather get some sleep than wait out in the street for us to be done. As for owning your own carriage, I'm not sure your reputation could handle the extra pressure. It might be simpler for me to find another boarding house closer to where you live."

"I'd like that," Katya said, smiling although she knew she had offered the more selfish of the two possible answers. "That is," she added, "I hope it's not too much trouble."

Maddox shrugged. "I don't have much to move. Not like you would."

Katya turned under the easy weight of his arm, looking over the shapes and shadows of clothing strewn across the room. The great mass of her dress took over the back of a chair. Buckles and buttons glimmered from pants, jackets, and undergarments on the floor. "I do have a lot of things. But I only have one of you."

Maddox took advantage of Katya's twisted, vulnerable position. He kissed her neck, sweeping his hand up her stomach to her breasts. Katya shivered at the familiar sensations trickling through her body.

Katya's mind flitted past the advancing hour of the morning, which she could not read on the alarm clock out of view on the bedside table. She tried fleetingly to calculate it, how long it might have taken her to ride Mr. Davies' carriage home, slip out of the boarding house after Magdalene drifted to sleep, and ride streetcars to the southeast corner of the city. She must have been at Maddox's boarding house for at least an hour.

Maddox's lips and fingers lured her out of her practical mind, and Katya left the time of day in the hands of the clock. "I'll sleep until supper time," she murmured, but it did not seem to matter. Her body snaked and curled under Maddox's explorations, tracing borders and territories across her skin. His tongue marked cities and monuments. His hot breath drew rivers and mountains. Katya followed him down every trail, the two of them plastered close together to keep from falling out of the bed. Maddox shifted Katya's hips to the middle of the mattress, rising above her and taking his place between her legs. Katya breathed him into her, aware of all the warm places their bodies touched. Maddox lowered his chest against hers, and as one, they moved toward the discovery of a new and distant shore.

In her ear, Maddox whispered, "Yes. I'll be careful."

Chapter Thirty-Five

It was one of those nights. Magdalene worked the food stall as surely as ever, collecting coins and paper bills from the customers. She handed down the bags of popcorn and plates of sausages on buns.

Behind the customers ran the real show. Magdalene watched it play out over their heads. The stately figure of Isolde Neumann arrived and passed behind the line of hungry customers. She was not easy to miss, one of the beyond-fashionable three-story hats on her head. A black velvet bow adorned the front of the band. Golden silk covered the rest of the form, its heavy appearance lightened by matching ostrich feathers. Perched atop her gleaming hair, any carnival guest could have scaled the monstrous structure and sat as high as the top seats of the Warden wheel. Isolde barely looked around her before she passed the corner of the food stall and let herself into Mr. Warden's office. Magdalene caught her familiarity, the lack of a courteous knock to announce her arrival. She ushered herself inside as if passing from room to room inside her own house.

Magdalene was not sure how long Isolde stayed inside. Perhaps a half hour, perhaps longer. Magdalene wondered if they might be discussing business, but she could not reasonably explain what the daughter of a glass-ornament manufacturer could offer the Steampunk Carnival. Either she was making a deal to outfit the carnival over the winter holidays or their only business with each other involved no words at all.

Isolde reappeared, closing the door behind her, her face and hat as fresh as when she had arrived. Magdalene wondered how long it had taken to straighten her hat and jacket. How long had Isolde waited, checking her reflection in a sterling silver pocket mirror slipped from her purse, until the swelling of her kissing lips went down? Isolde traipsed back the way she had come, her spine straight and tall behind the line of chirping customers. With as much confidence as Mr. Warden himself, she did not glance left or right but continued on toward the front of the carnival. She rarely stayed to take in anything, save whatever awaited her in Mr. Warden's office.

Magdalene asked Irina to cover the front counter while she took a break at the water closets. She had stopped asking the Englishman to do it, which did not matter to him. Irina accepted the temporary post with a satisfied twist to her lips, knowing Mr. Warden was too busy elsewhere to keep her from working the front line of carnival employees.

Magdalene crossed the back of the carnival, passing Brady's game stall. His only acknowledgement was a gaze held longer than a casual meeting. He hid their acquaintanceship well, a great part of the reason Magdalene trusted him. He knew what he stood to lose and what he stood to gain, and he never took too big of a risk. He did not wave or wink or stare too long. He merely looked over, recognized her, and motioned the next customer to the counter to play.

A man brushed past Magdalene, a few inches closer than most guests walked by her, and she shivered. She barely recognized him, but she had seen him dozens of times over the past few months. His nondescript suit allowed him to merge in and out of the crowd, but Magdalene had learned to pick him out. She could spot Mr. Warden's security more easily every week. They surveyed her, their eyes darting away when she noticed or intensifying their stares, almost daring her to react. Her heart would race, but her hands remained calm and professional. There was always another cup of coffee to hand out, another napkin needed.

Magdalene reached the first water closet in the row and shut herself inside. It remained the only place on the carnival grounds she felt security could not peek at her. She felt their eyes on her as she nibbled snacks to keep her strength up through the night.

Mr. Warden allowed it, but she sensed their brains working, calculating how much she ate in dollars and cents. She felt watched as she walked to the front of the carnival every morning to climb into the carriage. She felt them inspecting every conversation she held with Katya and Irina.

Magdalene used the toilet and washed her hands in the sink, letting the cool water refresh her skin. She patted some cold droplets along her hairline under her hat brim, trying to ease the tension in her body. Regretfully, she dried her hands and started back across the carnival to the eastern food stall.

Irina, despite her gruffness, dealt surprisingly well with the customers. Magdalene had never heard Irina be short or annoyed with them. Irina stepped aside as Magdalene reentered the stall, and Magdalene swept back into her role, asking the first person in line, "What can I serve you tonight?"

The evening settled into a busy but predictable pace. Magdalene had almost forgotten about her close run-in with the security guard until she saw several of them leave Mr. Warden's office. They spread out with a few feet between them, combing the crowd as they stalked toward the front gates.

Magdalene patted sweat off her forehead with the sleeve of her jacket. She tried to keep up with the customers' orders, but several times, Irina had to correct her. Irina studied Magdalene's weary face but said nothing. Magdalene offered the strongest smile she could manage and only ever replied with, "Thank you. My mistake."

Magdalene felt hardly shocked – but hardly pleased – when a man reached the front of the line and stood silently instead of giving an order. His chocolate-brown top hat read slightly darker than his mud-colored suit. His sharp eyes pried information from her face from a gentle, trustworthy expression.

"Mr. Weis," Magdalene guessed, her voice trembling with certainty and uncertainty. "What can I do for you?"

"I'd like you to take a little walk with me, Miss Harvey."

Mr. Weis' unexpected accent filled his words with understated threat, making Magdalene work to keep her cool. "I'm sorry, sir, but I'm needed here."

"It's urgent. I'm sure Mr. Warden and your fellow workers would understand."

Swallowing hard, Magdalene asked Irina to cover the counter. She walked to the back of the stall and stepped out, meeting Mr. Weis at the front. He led her at a meandering, easy pace toward the entrance to the carnival.

"Are we leaving?" Magdalene asked, terrified to be alone with him.

"No."

They passed the Beast and the bandstand before curving to the right to stay within the carnival gates.

Magdalene wondered if running through the gates and screaming for help might be her best option. So far, Mr. Weis had not acted overtly menacing, and Magdalene did not want to make the situation worse in case he meant well. She continued on past the game stalls at the front of the carnival. She hated Mr. Weis' silence, the way it dug its claws into her, extracting scared blood and angry bile.

"Mr. Weis," she said at last. "If you don't intend to speak with me, I really do need to get back to the food stall. Irina hasn't been trained to deal with the customers. Mr. Warden wouldn't approve."

Mr. Weis paused with a sidelong glance. "Miss Harvey, forgive me for pointing this out, but that is not something you have previously concerned yourself about."

Magdalene rebuked herself for trying to bluff him. Of course Mr. Weis knew she put Irina to work at the counter against Mr. Warden's wishes. Meekly, she replied, "I try not to do it so much in one night."

"That's a little closer to the truth."

They reached the southwest corner of the Beast, making their way in a loop past the water closets.

"What are you and Katya up to these days?" Mr. Weis asked.

At the mention of Katya's name, Magdalene searched for her through the crowd. She found it impossible to believe she had walked almost three-quarters of the grounds without seeing the outrageously adorned hat or blue, embroidered jacket. Magdalene winced at the stabbing intuition in her gut. "You wouldn't be interested in us, Mr. Weis. The everyday affairs of women can't seem very fascinating to men with high-risk careers such as yourself."

"What do you mean, high risk?" Mr. Weis' brown eyes peeled her apart.

"Nothing."

Mr. Weis cracked a grimace meant to soothe her. "I ask because I'm interested. Please. Tell me what the two of you have been planning."

"Planning?" Magdalene's hands fidgeted in front of her. She pulled them apart and pinned them to her sides. "What would we have been devising except perhaps a lovely roast dinner to repay the kindness of our landlady?"

"Do you expect me to believe that?"

"Why not? She's been widowed these past few years, and she's been very kind to us."

Mr. Weis led Magdalene past the western food stall. He stopped outside the door to the maintenance office. "Miss Harvey, I've heard you're good at a great many things, but lying is not one of them." Mr. Weis pushed the door open and ushered Magdalene inside.

The door to the inner room stood closed. Magdalene stepped slowly into the empty storage room, her muscles tightening as Mr. Weis joined her and closed the door. She thought she heard muffled breathing or shuffling in the other room. Before she could identify it, Mr. Weis spoke, covering it over.

"You really have nothing to say to me?"

Magdalene shook her head. It sounded like sighs, like sobs in the other room.

Mr. Weis exhaled, resigning. "They told me you wouldn't talk. That's why we started without you." He turned the knob on the inner door and swung it open.

Magdalene barely kept herself from running in. Katya slumped on the floor, her arms held up by two of Mr. Warden's inconspicuous security. One of them held a hand over her mouth, dampening her groans. As he pulled the hand away, Magdalene could see the full damage to Katya's face. One eye swelled, turning purple and green. Her nose trickled blood to her lips, where the man's fingers had smudged it across her fair skin. Katya's dark hair lumped in a mess of curls and frizz, her hat discarded somewhere Magdalene could not see.

Katya hung her head for a minute, huffing each shaky exhale as she caught her breath.

One of the security men curled his upper lip. "Even the brave ones cry eventually."

Katya snapped her head up, focusing more on Magdalene than Mr. Weis. Her eyes were not pleading but defiant and pained.

Magdalene plotted her words carefully, hoping they would emerge as casually and evenly as she needed them to. "Mr. Weis, I suggest you stop this at once. There's nothing to keep me from running out of this room and notifying Mr. Warden what you're doing."

Mr. Weis scanned her face. "Who do you think gave the order? Any means necessary, Miss Harvey. Those were Mr. Warden's exact words."

"Necessary for what?"

Mr. Weis stomped his boot on the floor, and Magdalene looked at him sharply. "Do you value this woman's life?" He jabbed a finger at Katya in the next room.

"Yes."

"Then stop fooling around."

"Go ahead, Mr. Weis. Slap me as hard as you like. I have nothing to tell you."

Mr. Weis' lips pursed in taunting. "That's just it, Miss Harvey. We're not going to lay a finger on you. I'm going to ask you questions, and if you don't answer, it's not you who suffers, at least, not physically."

Magdalene heard a slight metal sound behind her and turned to the exit. A fourth man she had not noticed before, probably hidden in the corner, had moved forward. He gripped the handle tightly to the outside door.

"So I ask you again," Mr. Weis said. "What are you up to? What are you planning?"

Magdalene studied Katya before she answered. Katya, like Brady, proved too smart to signal in any obvious way. Katya held Magdalene's gaze, the same as Brady had. Magdalene steadied her breathing, forcing herself to remain calm. "Mr. Weis, I don't understand what we've done to give you the impression we're conspirators of any kind. Do women huddling together always have to be planning something, or are we allowed to talk about mundane things like hair and clothes and men?"

Mr. Weis nodded to the two men holding Katya's arms. One of them, his bold blue eyes flashing with menace, lifted her arm even higher. He adjusted his grip on it so one palm met hers and his other hand cradled her elbow.

Magdalene maintained her crafted composure. "Mr. Weis, I can't help you if you don't answer me."

"I'm not on trial here. We've been watching both of you. Every time I ask Mr. Warden or one of the security guards if you're doing something you normally do, they assure me you're not."

"May I have an example, please?"

"All of your conversations at the food stall. I hear they used to be lighter, more enjoyable for you. Now every time you're seen together, you look like you're facing the gallows."

"Work has been stressful lately."

"Why?"

"We're being watched by numerous security guards, for one thing."

Mr. Weis leaned closer to Magdalene, his brown eyes purposeful. "People who have nothing to hide don't get nervous." Mr. Weis raised his hand from his side and squeezed the fingers together into a gloved fist.

The blue-eyed man snapped Katya's wrist back. He held her upper arm firmly in place and twisted her forearm as he shoved it down into her elbow. Katya cried out, and the other man slapped his hand over her mouth. She stared at Magdalene, pleading her.

Not to tell.

"I don't know what they could've said about us," Magdalene insisted. She could feel sweat beading and itching along the top of her forehead. She dabbed it away with her glove as casually as she could.

"Don't be dense," Mr. Weis ordered, abrupt and condescending. "Everybody knows how close you are. You live together. You're always talking."

Katya stopped struggling until the man lifted his hand off her mouth. She shot a cruel smirk at Magdalene. "Please, Mr. Weis," she begged with icy sarcasm. "If I were planning anything, do you think I'd share it with her? Everyone we know is about to have her sainted."

Mr. Weis glanced Katya over, her beauty losing out to discoloration and pain. "I don't want your opinions, Miss Romanova. This conversation is between me and Miss Harvey."

Katya spat blood on the floor. "Tell them then, *Miss Harvey*, what we've been arguing about these past few months. It's obvious they want to know. It's so *gripping*."

Magdalene shifted her shoulders, injecting a little caught-in-the-bread-box uncertainty into her voice. "I don't know what you mean."

"You know, about Maddox O'Sullivan."

Mr. Weis' head swiveled between the two women as they volleyed. It gave Magdalene all the reassurance she needed to keep going.

Magdalene brushed at the skirt of her dress, pretending Katya's words were having their intended affect. "I don't think we need to talk about that."

"No?" Katya raged, sparing a sneer at security before they could clamp a hand over her mouth. "Really? Here this man is, two seconds from breaking my arm, and you want to play innocent?"

Magdalene did not respond, not sure what Katya wanted to hear.

Katya growled in thin amusement and shook her head. She looked straight at Mr. Weis. "My friend doesn't want you to know that we've been fighting over Mr. O'Sullivan for some time. I'm sure you've heard that we've been seeing each other."

Mr. Weis paused, then afforded Katya a brief nod.

Katya returned her glare to Magdalene's guarded expression. "Miss Harvey seems to think we're mismatched. She can't decide which one of us doesn't deserve the other. Am I too good for him, or is he too good for me?"

Magdalene cleared her throat. "He's a more honest person than you are. He's polite. He's kind."

"He's a vagabond, a wanderer, something you know nothing about. You've never been outside this city. But that's what you like about him, isn't it?"

Magdalene nodded to keep an unconvincing lie from destroying their charade.

"She's shy, Mr. Weis," Katya persuaded. "She doesn't want you to think she's like me just because she fancies the same man."

Mr. Weis gestured with his hand. Magdalene relaxed, thinking the others would let Katya go. The one with blue eyes jolted Katya's forearm into her elbow again, and she gasped, her mouth gaping in shock. Magdalene had to use all her restraint to keep from racing to Katya's side. Katya squeezed her eyes shut in agony, and Magdalene's heart thundered for both their safety.

"I still don't want your side of the story, Miss Romanova," Mr. Weis interrupted. He turned to Magdalene, his eyes daring her to make a mistake.

Magdalene let all of her true emotions run through her words, the fear, the helplessness, the anger. Her hands shook in front of her. "Mr. Weis, is it so inconceivable that two friends would fight over their feelings for the same man?"

"No," Mr. Weis acknowledged, waiting for more.

"Is it unbelievable that two women as different as we are could both show interest in the same person?"

Mr. Weis answered with a question. "Who else is Miss Romanova interested in?"

"What?" Magdalene's voice resonated with genuine confusion. "I don't know. She hasn't mentioned anybody else to me."

"She seems to have her delicate little fingers in everybody's pockets. Mr. O'Sullivan. Mr. Davies."

"Mr. Davies?"

"You know the carriage driver. What else would Miss Romanova possibly want to speak to him about? I've checked his background. He's a single man."

Magdalene turned her palms up in defeat. "I don't know anything about that."

"What about the Mick?"

"Who?" Magdalene could have kicked herself for playing dumb. She was letting Mr. Weis' fast pace get to her.

Mr. Weis pounced before Magdalene could recover. "The Mick. He runs the game stall fifty feet from this building. You know who he is. You've both been seen talking to him."

"Is that a crime?"

"Nobody talks to him. Ever. Nobody's heard him speak except to say 'thank you' to Mr. Warden for his salary. What business do you have with him?"

Magdalene continued to offer her upturned palms in deflection.

Katya's forced and humored breathing carried their attention back to her. Beneath her lighthearted joking, she sounded exhausted. "Are we trying to marry him, too, Mr. Weis? My goodness, your imagination is better than mine."

Magdalene composed herself while Katya's disbelief distracted Mr. Weis. "It was carnival business," she assured him, her voice warm as if remembering. "Sometimes guests leave plates and mugs on the counters of the stalls. I was merely checking to see if I could pick any up."

"And Miss Romanova?"

"She helps everybody. It's what she gets paid for. I tell you, everyone thinks she's so lazy, but when she does her job, people don't like that, either. It's suddenly suspicious."

Mr. Weis' eyebrows tensed askance, but the fire in his eyes seemed to waver. "What do you have against Mr. Warden? Either of you?"

Magdalene timed her response perfectly, trying to sound diplomatic and sincere. "What does anyone have against him? He works us hard, but that's to be expected. He pays us fairly. We respect him, and we're grateful for our jobs. We don't have any major complaints against Mr. Warden."

Katya spoke up with new energy. "Did he tell you this was about Mags and me, Mr. Weis? Because it seems like Mr. Warden's looking for an excuse to force us out of the carnival. He didn't tell you I spurned him, did he?"

Mr. Weis took so long to answer, Magdalene gave up on hearing one.

"He wasn't very pleased," Katya added. "This was his suggestion, too, wasn't it? Pitting us against each other? He knew I'd take the blows like a champ. Mags can't stand to see me hurt. He knew she'd spill everything, and here we are. We've aired our dirty laundry in front of everyone. I hope you're satisfied."

Mr. Weis looked hard at Katya and harder at Magdalene. Magdalene simply blinked at him, trying not to squirm and ruin everything.

"You turned down Mr. Warden?" Mr. Weis threw the question at Katya, his eyes searching Magdalene.

"Yes," Katya piped up. "He hasn't been happy about it, but I already stole Mr. O'Sullivan from Mags. What kind of girl would I be if I went around kissing everybody?"

Mr. Weis shoved his hand down through the air. The two men in the other room let go of Katya's arms. She draped forward, catching herself on her good arm. Her tortured limb hung uselessly beside her. Mr. Weis strode over to her and sank down on his haunches in front of her. He clenched his fingers around her chin and raised her face into view.

"Breathe a word about this to anyone," Mr. Weis warned her, "and we'll break all of your limbs."

Katya nodded, her eyes showing crisp, clean fear.

Mr. Weis stood up and walked back to Magdalene waiting on the other side of the doorway. He did not need to repeat himself.

Magdalene nodded. "I understand."

Mr. Weis gestured for the men to follow him, and he marched them out of the building. The door clicked shut, and Katya let loose the longest string of Russian curse words Magdalene had ever heard.

In seconds, Magdalene crouched at her side. "Are you all right? How's your arm?"

"Forget about my arm." Katya met Magdalene's gaze with blazing eyes. "Remember how you said to wait for a strange night to confront Mr. Warden?" Katya spat at his name, splattering the floorboards with more blood-tinged saliva. "It doesn't get any worse than this."

Chapter Thirty-Six

Katya picked herself up off the floor, wincing at every minute movement of her left arm. She held it against her side with her right hand, unable to control it below the shoulder. She eyed the dust and dirt clinging to her dress, wishing she had the strength to brush it off. It could have kept her mind off the stinging in her face, although she could not ignore the closing of her eye. "I won't protect Mr. Warden anymore."

"What do we do?" Magdalene asked.

"Tell Brady to get the journal out. We're going to confront Mr. Warden with it."

"Where?"

"The Warden wheel, if he can manage it. It's the tallest point in the carnival. His voice should carry very well."

"There's still a lot of noise to take care of."

"I'll find the water boys. They can carry a message to all the ride operators to shut down for a while." Katya twisted her mouth wryly. "Mr. Warden's orders, of course."

"What about your face?" Magdalene raised her hand to touch Katya but lowered it again. "Someone should send for a doctor. You should lie down until he gets here."

"Never. I'll sit when the police drag Mr. Warden away in handcuffs." Katya glanced around for her hat. The once-lovely accessory sat squished in the corner. She picked it up and blew dust off the crinkled crown, as if that were all it needed. "How's my hair?"

"Awful, but not as bad as your eye."

"I'll heal, Mags." Katya studied her friend with a newfound respect. "Nice lying, by the way. I hoped you had it in you."

Magdalene started for the other room. "I think we both gave a stellar performance. If we make it out of this with all our limbs intact, we should make a new career on the stage."

Katya followed Magdalene to the front door. "Wouldn't that make Lizzie crazy? She'd go to the theater to get away from us, and there we'd be, right smack in front of her."

Magdalene opened the door, and they stepped out into the sparse grass. "Good luck," Magdalene said.

"I don't need it. Send it to Mr. Warden."

Magdalene walked away toward Brady's game stall, and Katya looked around her for the boys who carried the water buckets. A pair of them hobbled away along the side of the Beast, too far away for her to call to them. A few other boys ambled toward her, swinging their buckets with ease. Katya waved them toward her. They stared and squinted at her, her face bruised and her crushed hat in her hand. She tossed it aside like the irreparable thing that it was.

"Boys," she said, raising serious eyebrows. "I need you to do a favor for me. Mr. Warden wants you to leave your buckets here and deliver a message for him. Will you tell all the ride operators to stop their rides until further notice?"

The boys bobbed their heads up and down.

"I'll take care of the Warden wheel, but you must tell all the other operators."

The boys abandoned their buckets and jogged off through the crowd. Katya opened the door to the storage room and snatched up the buckets. She stowed them away out of sight and closed the door.

Katya tried to spot Magdalene and Brady through the crowd, but she could not. She fought her way across the current of guests to the game stall. Magdalene was not there, but Brady was. He turned his customers away, apologizing that rats had gotten into the prizes and eaten holes in them.

Brady swore under his breath when he saw Katya's face. "Those bastards."

"What's going on? Where's Mags?"

"She got Mr. O'Sullivan to lure Warden out of his office. He'll get him over to the wheel, and I'll approach him with the journal. Is this noise going to stop soon?"

"Yes." Katya realized she had forgotten about the band. She looked for more boys or even the charwoman, but she could not spot anyone who worked at the carnival. She stopped a young couple walking past with their children. Katya crouched down to eye level with the kids. "Would you like to do me a favor and help out the carnival?"

The kids nodded politely, almost eagerly.

"Would you please tell the band leader that the band can leave early tonight? Mr. Warden said they could all go home right away and get a good night's rest."

"Yes, ma'am," the children chimed.

Katya smiled at the parents, who eyed her face with concern. She waved to encourage them on their way.

Brady leaned closer to Katya. "Are you all right?"

"I'm fine," Katya said, regaining her right hand's support of her useless left arm. Her satisfaction eased her grimace. "I'll be better when Mr. Warden's name is painted over on the carnival signs."

"It won't be much longer." Brady rubbed his hands together.

Katya laid her hand on Brady's arm. "Don't be nervous, Mr. Kelly." She glanced at a few customers who stopped by the counter. "The game isn't running right now. I'm sorry."

They drifted on, and Katya peered desperately through the crowd for a sign of Maddox or Mr. Warden. "He doesn't have a limb to stand on, not with the evidence you've got."

The Beast sputtered into silence behind the game stall. Katya's lips perked up at the lack of rattling and roaring.

Magdalene rushed up to her side. "Mr. Warden's out now. Mr. O'Sullivan has him by the wheel. He's going to get Mr. Warden to ride it."

Brady grabbed the journal from a box under the counter and strode around it. "He'll ride it, all right."

Brady headed straight for the Warden wheel. Katya and Magdalene followed at a distance, hoping to stay out of Mr. Warden's sight until he was in no position to come after them. The band finished its song, and for once, another march did not follow. An eerie emptiness crept through the carnival as rides shut down. Katya glanced over her shoulder. Several people were stealing prizes from the game stall, but that was the least of the carnival's problems.

Katya and Magdalene reached the edge of the crowd and stopped. Brady strode up to the ride operators, who were arguing with Maddox and Mr. Warden. Brady pulled a small handgun from under his jacket and aimed it at Mr. Warden's stomach.

In the increasing silence, over the murmur of the crowd, Katya could hear Brady's commands. "Leave the people in their seats. They'll want to hear every word of this. Warden, back up toward the wheel."

Katya's heart skipped a beat to see the great William Warden herded toward the giant wheel like an animal. The operator had already stopped it, and Brady backed Mr. Warden all the way up onto the loading platform. Instead of clearing the bottom-hanging seat of its guests, Brady lingered with Mr. Warden in front of it. When Brady stepped back, Mr. Warden remained leaned against it.

Brady waved the operator toward the controls with his gun. "Start it up. Stop him at the top."

The operator pushed a lever, and as the wheel slowly began to shift in its circle, it lifted Mr. Warden with it. He kicked his feet at the air, then suddenly stopped, his face white and pinched.

Maddox bolted out of the fenced area, half watching Mr. Warden's rise into the night and half searching the staring crowd. Katya raised her hand in a low wave, not proud to show him her swelling face. Maddox ran to her, grabbing her upper arms in his hands.

Katya sucked in a breath at the shooting pains numbing her left arm. "My elbow hurts, but I'm all right."

"I'll kill him," Maddox swore. "Tell me who did this."

"The man who ordered it is twenty feet in the air. He might fall to his death before you can get to him."

Maddox glanced up at Mr. Warden, riding higher and higher along the wheel's path. "Have you asked for a doctor?"

Magdalene shook her head. "She won't take the time. She wants to see this through first."

Katya watched Mr. Warden reach the full height of the wheel. It shuddered to a halt. Mr. Warden twitched every once in a while, no doubt uncomfortable hanging there by his clothes. He always stopped himself from moving too much to tear them.

"I'll kill him," Maddox repeated, squeezing himself into the crowd next to Katya. He slipped his arm carefully around her.

Katya winced as he brushed against her throbbing forearm.

The band leader stormed through the crowd, emerging into the wide berth around the wheel's waist-high fence. "Where's Mr. Warden?" he demanded. "Some kids said we had the rest of the night off."

Half the crowd pointed skyward to Mr. Warden dangling from the wheel.

Brady stepped back to the gate leading to the ride, partway between Mr. Warden and the anxious crowd. He kept the gun in one hand and raised the journal in the other. "Do you know what this is, Warden?" he shouted, a wild, excited look in his eyes.

Mr. Warden tugged his shoulders against whatever held him. When it made his body swing to and fro, he stiffened his limbs against the momentum. "I don't know," he called down. "It's hard to see it from up here."

"It's a journal you threw away several months ago after you started getting death threats."

Gasps and whispers ran through the crowd. Katya nestled closer to Maddox to keep his reassuring presence beside her.

"You kept those death threats from the public," Brady went on. "Why?"

"There was no need to worry anyone," Mr. Warden insisted. "As you can all see, I'm healthy and very much alive."

A few people applauded, but most people stood motionless, staring and inhaling raspy breaths.

"That's not why," Brady challenged, holding the journal higher. "You knew that someone from your past would be looking for you. Why else would you try to get rid of this?"

Mr. Warden kicked a shiny, black shoe. His body swayed out from the wheel, and he promptly straightened his leg back under him. "Let me down. We can discuss this in my office."

Brady shook his head. "Oh, no. I've dreamed of this moment for three long years. Do you have any idea what you took from me, from the ghosts of my dead family? Do you have any idea who I am?"

Mr. Warden sneered. "You're a man without a job tomorrow."

Brady tore the hat from his head with a few fingers spared from holding the journal. His other hand pointed his gun at the ground. "Does my name mean anything to you? Brady Kelly?"

"No," Mr. Warden retorted.

"Would you tell me, then, why a man who got rich off a creation such as this carnival would try to destroy the original notes for it?"

Mr. Warden pumped his arms as if he could snatch the journal from where the wheel held him. His body rocked from side to side. The unsteadiness widened his eyes, and he reached for the support structure above him, but his fingers could not grasp it.

"Because you stole it," Brady roared. "You stole this from me. Now you remember me, don't you?"

"You're drunk," Mr. Warden countered. "Get me down from here."

The first camera leaned out from the crowd and clicked. Katya could see several cameras emerging in the front row of onlookers. The whites of Mr. Warden's eyes grew even larger.

"Tell us, Warden," Brady beckoned, waving the journal over his head. "Tell us how you broke into my room at that cheap little boarding house and stole this from me. It's a journal, yes, but it's my ideas. It's my carnival."

Mr. Warden cracked a smile. "Your carnival? Why don't you tell us how you broke into my office and stole that from me?"

Katya burst forward into the empty space between the crowd and the fence. "That's a lie!" Her voice echoed off the metal beams, startling Katya for a moment. Its stretched, strained quality made her calm herself before she shouted again, taking care to strengthen her voice. "I found that journal in the garbage. Mr. Kelly knows everything about this carnival, more than Mr. Warden ever could, aside from the money."

Katya looked up at Mr. Warden, her fury making her puffy eye smart and her nose burn. Mr. Warden looked so small from the ground, like a miniature or a caricature of himself. She could hardly find him menacing or sympathetic now. "Say what you want, Mr. Warden. The handwriting in that journal is not yours, except a few places where you made changes. There isn't a thing in this carnival that wasn't already in that journal. It's not even laid out the same, so if this is your journal, where's the drawing for that?"

Mr. Warden jerked his shoulders, his gloved hands tightening into white fists. His jaw clenched, tightening against forming his thoughts into words.

"Go ahead," Katya challenged him. "Have your so-called security beat me again. The press is watching. Your precious crowds are watching." Katya swept her arm through the air to show them to him.

"Miss," someone called.

Katya turned toward the unfamiliar voice, furious to see one of the photographers motioning to her. She resented Mr. Warden for making her get her picture taken with her face all battered and bruised. She faced the eager cameras nonetheless, holding her injured arm motionless against her side. Gritting her teeth, Katya tilted her chin up for the lights to catch her swelling eye and the blood she was sure still stained her upper lip. The photographers fought for the best angles and positions, jostling bystanders out of their way.

Mr. Warden called down from his great height, confident and appealing. "You believe her word over mine?"

Katya craned her neck to look over her shoulder at Mr. Warden. She could not believe he had thrown her away so easily. One denied moment, and he had handed her over to Mr. Weis and his henchmen. At the same time, she would have done the same to him. "Why shouldn't they?" she shouted up at Mr. Warden. "I might be nobody, but I'm more honest than you are."

"Let me down, Katya," Mr. Warden crooned, softening his approach. "I can still save your job."

Katya balked, her mouth falling open. She turned to face Mr. Warden head on, propping the fist of her good arm on her hip. "I'll have a job at this carnival when Mr. Kelly takes it over, thank you very much."

A line of policemen broke through the crowd, using night sticks to part the people to either side of them. Brady kept his gun lowered as he turned to meet them.

The band leader pointed him out. "He's armed. He's crazy."

Several policemen hung back to keep the crowd at a distance. The others approached Brady, one of them breaking away to walk toward Katya.

"Your face, miss," he said, reaching out to it.

"Please don't touch it," Katya pleaded, cringing at the intent.

"Is this man holding you hostage?"

"No. He's not dangerous, and he's not crazy. He has evidence he created the carnival. Mr. Warden stole it from him."

"Has a doctor tended you?"

"No." Katya tried not to sound as aggravated as she felt. "I will not see a doctor until Mr. Kelly is properly heard."

The next sound that reached Katya's ears was not Brady's voice. It was a searing, ripping sound, the increasingly high pitch of rending fabric. Her eyes, along with hundreds of others, flew to the sky. Mr. Warden dangled lower than he had before, drooping like a pendant pinned to the wheel. He was not moving now, just swaying, his bulging eyes locked on the platform below.

"Will you admit it now?" Brady shouted up at him.

Mr. Warden remained silent. His clothing ripped again, plunging him several inches toward the wooden platform. He cried out in terror, and the crowd jumped, sucking in rushes of breath and raising their hands to their mouths. Many women turned their heads, squeezing their eyes shut while clutching their husbands closer.

"Yes," Mr. Warden hissed, his hands reaching vainly for any beams or spokes around him. The snug fit of his jacket around his shoulders kept him from extending his arms all the way. "Yes, I stole it. I stole it. Let me down, you fools."

Two of the police opened the gate and motioned to the ride operator. "Let this man down," they ordered.

Katya felt a hand cover her elbow – gratefully, her strong right one. Maddox filled her vision, her heart overflowing at his presence. Katya took his hand. They looked up together as the wheel stuttered and turned, slowly rotating to the left. Mr. Warden hung very still, his clothing lurching him downward a few inches more as he rounded the wheel. The passengers in the cars held their eyes almost as wide as his, all staring, all praying. Mr. Warden's shoes reached the platform, and the wheel stopped. He pulled and strained against the wheel's hold until, with a splitting rip, he lunged forward, free.

"That could've been murder," someone muttered from the crowd.

The two policemen flanked Mr. Warden, one of them producing glinting metal handcuffs from his pocket.

"Why are you looking at me with those things?" Mr. Warden asked, his tone a blend of offense and humor. He pointed a rigid finger at Brady. "This man openly admitted to sending me death threats, all of which I have in safekeeping in my office. If you're going to be matching handwriting, match that."

The policemen gave little reaction. The one with the handcuffs stepped behind Mr. Warden. "We'll be taking both of you in. You can plead your cases at the station."

"I don't have a case." Mr. Warden's eyes burned at Brady. "I have the truth."

The second officer reached for Brady's journal. Brady handed it over with the slightest hesitation, a split second of questioning trust that Katya and Magdalene might have been the only two to know the significance of. The officer pulled out another pair of shining cuffs, using them to pin Brady's wrists to his lower back.

The officers barring the crowd began to shift the onlookers, making way for the men in custody.

Katya studied Mr. Warden with renewed curiosity. She knew Brady would be all right. She believed in the strength of the evidence to prove him the carnival's rightful owner. It was Mr. Warden she had favored and disliked over the past year, Mr. Warden who had pulled her close on first meeting and thrown her to his wolves tonight. Of everyone who had ever loved or hated Mr. William Warden, Katya felt certain she had loved him harder and hated him more. If she thought he was worth it, she would have spat right at him. It was a story big and dramatic enough for all the papers, but she kept it quiet. She would not be known for this. Let her go down as the pictured beating victim, one of the women who supported Brady Kelly's good cause. But do not ever let them know the roller coaster her heart had taken once Mr. Warden started it. She would never hear the end of it, and she certainly wanted to.

Fuzzy in her vision, the other policeman guided Brady through the gate and toward the crowd. Mr. Warden's expression was hard to read as the second officer steered him across the fenced area and out the same gate. Katya squinted to make out the complex emotions hidden in Mr. Warden's face. Handsome, yes, but telling. Fear mixed with knowing, pride, and certainty. It was strange to see him worry, he so rarely showed it.

Mr. Warden turned his head and met Katya's gaze for several steps. His eyes neither accused her nor validated her. He simply watched as if he knew what she was thinking, that in all probability, if justice were served, this would be the last time they ever saw each other. He did not wink or purse his lips in hubris. He did not scowl or stare to intimidate her. He displayed the quiet air of someone realizing that an era had come to an end, no matter what happened afterward. There was no going back.

Mr. Warden peered ahead of him at the break in the crowd although Katya's eyes continued to follow him. The back of his finely tailored jacket gaped in tatters from the collar down between his shoulders to the middle.

Maddox squeezed Katya's hand. "Monster," he muttered. "I hope he gets what he deserves."

The officer guided Mr. Warden past the first row of onlookers, and Katya lost him in the sea of hats and heads.

Magdalene arrived at Katya's other side. "Who's going to run the carnival the rest of the night?" Magdalene asked.

"I don't know. I didn't think about that." Katya shifted her focus to the crowd itself, standing listless and confused in the quiet lights.

The policeman who had spoken to Katya lingered nearby. Katya addressed him as politely as possible. "Sir, you'll also want to look for the security guards Mr. Warden hired." She gestured to her face.

The policeman nodded sharply. "Yes, miss."

"Unless they ran out already." Katya glanced around for Mr. Weis and his crew.

Maddox tugged her hand as the policeman strode away toward his colleagues. "You shouldn't be worrying about this. Let's get you home and fetch a doctor."

Katya looked across the empty circle of grass at the food stall. In the elevated interior, she could clearly make out Irina and the Englishman, for the second time that summer completely still. The line of ravenous customers had turned to watch the proceedings, and there was no one clamoring to be served at the moment. Katya could smell the acid char of sausages and popcorn burning.

Maddox patted her hand. "Please, Katya. We need to get some ice on your face."

Katya gave in and nodded. She could find nothing else to double-check, nothing else to oversee. Tucked behind the Warden wheel and the food stall hunched Mr. Warden's office, which with any luck, Brady would soon take over. Katya sighed, her dwindling adrenaline leaving her mind drained and her body sore.

"Do I have to take the streetcar home?" Katya asked, dreading the thought. "I don't want everybody to see me like this."

Magdalene placed a steadying hand on Katya's back. "It's too late to worry about that now. It'll be in the papers tomorrow."

Magdalene and Maddox led Katya toward the crowd, where a space still cut a clear path through it. The journalists rushed at them, the photographers thrusting their cameras forward.

"Please, no more pictures," Magdalene said, holding up her other hand to shield her face.

"Please, miss," a reporter interjected. He held a pencil and notebook ready in his hands. "Can we have a statement for the *News*?"

Magdalene arrested her steps. "Mr. Brady Kelly has been working for months to expose Mr. Warden for the thief he is."

The reporter scratched this onto paper. "May we have your name, miss?"

"Oh, no. Mr. Kelly deserves the spotlight, not us."

Magdalene guided Katya and Maddox forward. Katya felt almost claustrophobic in the tunnel of people. Their eyes pried and pawed at her even as they held their hands back. She was glad to reach the end of it and move toward the gates of the carnival.

"Who will lock up?" Katya asked.

"The police will get it," Magdalene assured her.

"Will the carnival be open while Mr. Warden and Mr. Kelly are in jail? It could take days to question them and get it straightened out."

Maddox shook his head. His lips curved in disbelieving sympathy. "Don't worry about the carnival. It'll be fine. It's your face that's bleeding."

"My elbow hurts a lot. It feels like it's split in half." Katya secured her upper arm in place against her side, but nothing stopped the constant ache. "I can't help worrying about the carnival. Besides the two of you, it's the most important thing I have, no matter who's in charge of it."

Magdalene focused on the gate up ahead, half the carnival away. "The only thing Mr. Warden has going for him are the death threats."

Katya stopped walking. For an instant, she considered running back to the office and finding them. Mr. Warden had indicated he threw the last one out, but if he had kept any of them, Katya could destroy them before the police reached them.

"No," Magdalene said to whatever plan Katya was hatching. "Mr. Kelly will explain they were harmless threats meant to rile Mr. Warden up, which they did."

"What about our parts in all this?" Katya began to walk again.

"I think we should stay out of it as much as possible. I know the press wants the whole story, but I won't give it to them. This is Mr. Kelly's victory. Everything we did – all the late mornings we stayed out – was to get him here."

"They're not stupid," Katya said. "It doesn't matter if you don't talk now. You went to their offices and told them to be here. They'll figure out what roles we played. Someone will talk, and we'll be in the papers before you know it."

Magdalene raised a blonde eyebrow. "You don't mind that?"

Katya shrugged her good shoulder. "I've always been on the front lines here. The papers already have their pictures of me. I can't take back my involvement now."

Maddox spoke up on Katya's other side. "You're not giving them a statement this week. You're staying in bed. You're doing whatever the doctor tells you to."

"Is that what you came all the way from the east coast for? To battle dangers and ride the rails for free to keep me confined in my bed? That'll be the day."

"He's right," Magdalene agreed.

Katya exhaled, too tired and outnumbered to fight any longer. "Can I at least go down to the dinner table and hear the daily news updates about the carnival from Mrs. Weeks?"

"Yes. Of course you can."

Maddox patted Katya's shoulder. "I'll come over as much as I can to keep you company. Every day if you like."

Katya smiled through the tingling and pain of her arm. "I'd like that very much."

Chapter Thirty-Seven

Maddox and Mrs. Weeks seemed to have little better to do than to fret over Katya's every move. Mrs. Weeks snatched up pillows to support Katya's back or mending arm. Maddox dove to pour tall glasses of sweet iced tea before Katya could interject or Mrs. Weeks could do it herself.

Wherever Katya rested, they offered suggestions of where she might recline more comfortably.

"The sunlight's lovely in the parlor this time of day," Mrs. Weeks chirped in the dining room.

"You're fond of the living room, aren't you?" Maddox chimed in once Katya climbed into bed.

Frustrated heat rose in Katya's cheeks by dinnertime. "I love you both, but please don't henpeck me anymore. I'll go where I want, and I'll be all right. I have a dislocated elbow and some bruises, not a disease or a disability." Katya tugged at the beige fabric of her sling. She appreciated that it cradled her healing elbow against her side but despised its ugly color every moment she had to wear it.

Maddox settled into a chair at Katya's bedside, and Mrs. Weeks disappeared into the garden to pick tomatoes for her dinner salad. Katya chose to eat in her room, hunched over a tray with Maddox for company, enjoying a private conversation.

When Mrs. Weeks reappeared in Katya's doorway, she held up a copy of the *News*.

Katya pushed herself up straight in bed, wincing as she tried to use her aching left arm. Her eyes widened at the headline: *Police Shut Down Carnival!* "What's it say?" she insisted.

Mrs. Weeks strolled in. "It says I'm glad I found out what you were up to when you came home so early last night. I had no idea what you girls were involved in."

"And now you do," Katya replied pointedly.

Mrs. Weeks afforded her a patient upturn of her lips before reading from the front page. "Last night, police closed the popular Steampunk Carnival pending an investigation into allegations brought forth by Mr. William Warden, owner, and Mr. Brady Kelly, employee. Police arrived to find Mr. Kelly using a revolver to hold several carnival employees hostage, including its creator, William Warden. Mr. Warden hung by his clothing at the top of the Warden wheel."

"Yes, I know," Katya interrupted in a hush. "What about the investigation?"

Maddox said nothing, his eyes intense as they focused on the newspaper.

Mrs. Weeks held the paper higher to read further into the article. "Mr. Kelly has accused Mr. Warden of stealing his ideas to build the carnival. He offers as evidence a journal of drawings and plans in his own handwriting. Police anticipate hiring an expert to evaluate these claims." Mrs. Weeks lifted the newspaper another inch. "Mr. Warden is charging Mr. Kelly with mailing him several death threats earlier in the summer. These letters will also be evaluated by an expert in handwriting analysis."

Katya leaned toward Mrs. Weeks, trying to read the paper for herself. "Is there anything else?"

Mrs. Weeks handed the paper to Katya.

Katya scanned the page quickly. "Although no formal charges have been filed, a woman later identified as Miss Katya Romanova–" Katya flashed a grin at Maddox. "–alerted police that she had been recently brutalized by men Mr. Warden hired to provide security. Bruises and blood were evident on her young face. Police located and took into custody Mr. Frederik Weis, Mr. Alberto Labue, Mr. Falk Huber, and Mr. Ilya Dyakov. At least two of the men showed bruises and cuts on their hands, possible evidence of their involvement. They are being held awaiting further information."

Maddox shook his head, a serious tension maturing his features. "You should press charges," he prompted Katya.

"I am. I think they deserve to rot in jail."

"No, I mean a lawsuit. You should get some kind of compensation for what they did to you."

Katya wrinkled her nose. "I don't want their money. My arm's not broken. I'm not dying."

"I heard you scream when the doctor put your elbow back in place. Not to mention how tender your face must feel." Maddox tilted his head to look over Katya's bruises. His eyebrows loosened from the tilt of anger to the gathering of concern. He brushed his fingers across her cheek.

"I'll heal," Katya assured him, passing the newspaper to Mrs. Weeks. "I'm surprised no one came by to see me today."

Mrs. Weeks folded the newspaper loosely in half. "They did, several men. Lawyers, doctors, policemen. You were asleep. I kept their business cards for you. I didn't want to wake you."

"But I've been up for hours. You could've given them to me."

A twinkle glimmered in Mrs. Weeks' eyes. "I didn't want to disturb your visit with your gentleman friend." Mrs. Weeks swept into the hallway, taking the newspaper with her.

Maddox leaned over and kissed Katya. "I should take the streetcar home. I'll have to find some temporary work in the morning."

Katya felt sorry to see him go but understood not everyone had savings and a generous landlady to fall back on.

"I'll be back as soon as I can," Maddox promised. "Can you get by without me 'til then?"

Katya put on a gracious demeanor. "I'm sure I can."

In the morning, Katya discovered the house quiet and almost empty. She walked the halls and wandered in and out of rooms in a random pattern. Even giving herself the widest berth possible at the boarding house, its three stories could not compare to the size and spectacle of the carnival. She was used to walking, and walking she did. But the closest sound to the band was the tap of her shoes on the wooden boards like tiny drums. The only laughter came from Mrs. Weeks enjoying the jokes in the previous night's *News*, and the only screams issued forth from Lizzie's throat when a spider dropped on her hand during lunch.

Katya soon grew tired of trying to duplicate her evenings roaming the carnival. She split the afternoon between the parlor and the living room, staving off boredom by reading books and magazines Mary brought for her.

Maddox stopped by after dinner, and Katya welcomed the distraction. She guided him back to the living room to sit down.

"What did you find for work?" she asked.

Maddox ran his fingers through his chaotic hair. "Sweeping a factory floor."

Katya pressed her lips together, imagining a dimly lit, dusty room in place of the carnival's open air. "How common," she sighed.

"I swept it in circles," Maddox admitted, a sly tilt lifting his features. "The man paid me an honest day's salary for a very dishonest day of work. But as I left, a small but ferocious stray dog chased me for blocks. I learned my lesson, I suppose."

Katya tittered into her glove, imagining every step of Maddox's day. Only when the front door clicked shut did Katya remember what she had spent her hours anticipating, the arrival of Mrs. Weeks with a hot copy of the *News*.

Katya leapt off the settee and scrambled for the hall with Maddox on her heels. "Really, Mrs. Weeks," she said, hurrying toward her from the other end of the corridor. "Can't we get a daytime paper this week?"

Mrs. Weeks offered a sympathetic smile. "If everybody buys the morning papers, the *News* will go out of business."

"There will be other papers. What's the news of the day?"

Mrs. Weeks tapped the front page. "You're not the only one who wants some answers from Mr. Warden. Such a shame. He seemed like a nice man."

"Seemed," Katya echoed with a bitter edge. "What's the paper say about him?"

Mrs. Weeks gestured to the article. "While the carnival remains closed, several reporters gathered sentiments from the crowds which hang around the locked gate every night. The bystanders all anxiously await its reopening. Mrs. Elfriede Diederich, sister of the late Mrs. Agna Lieber, a charwoman at the carnival, also hopes for more information concerning her sister's death. Mrs. Diederich reminds the city that both her sister and her sister's husband, Mr. Ernst Lieber, died on carnival grounds."

"Neither death was Mr. Warden's fault," Katya spoke up.

Maddox glanced at her over the newspaper, unappreciative of her protecting Mr. Warden, even if it was the truth.

Mrs. Weeks continued, oblivious to their tension. "Several carnival employees, including Mr. Garrett Davies, stood present. Mr. Davies is eager to resume his duties driving a carriage for the female employees. He hopes that Mr. Warden will not return as the head of the carnival."

A supportive wryness puckered Katya's lips. "Good old Mr. Davies."

"It also mentions Mr. Warden is in the process of finding a lawyer but hasn't chosen one yet."

Maddox huffed. "What's he waiting for? They'll hang him before he hires a lawyer."

Katya tilted her head doubtfully. "They're not going to hang him for stolen property."

"The crowds might."

Mrs. Weeks nodded slowly, still reading the article. "A lot of people are angry. They want to know how Mr. Warden got a hold of the journal and why it's taken so long to find all of this out."

"Now, Mrs. Weeks," Katya reminded her in a tone too sweet to be taken seriously. "You know Mr. Warden is innocent until proven guilty."

"Innocent," Mrs. Weeks grumbled. Maddox's voice overlapped hers, saying, "Innocent until a judge hears him out." They bowed their heads at each other in approval.

Katya expected sarcasm from Maddox but studied Mrs. Weeks in wonder. "I didn't think you'd have such a strong opinion about it, especially against Mr. Warden."

Mrs. Weeks shrugged. "I've been following the details very closely. Didn't you see the pictures? Mr. Warden looks so smug in his expensive suit, and Mr. Kelly looks so hardworking and downtrodden. Honestly, how did he keep quiet all these years?"

"He didn't know what else to do. He didn't have any evidence until I found it in the garbage."

"That's something else I was glad to see put to rest. You and Magdalene's humility. How could you not want your names in the paper for this? No one ever would've known that you helped this disadvantaged man bring down the corrupt Mr. Warden if the reporters hadn't pressed for more of the story. I think you both deserve to star in every article."

"We agreed to stay out of it as much as possible. We want to let Mr. Kelly have his day."

"But the trial. You'll have to testify. You're not going to lie to the judge, are you?"

"No. I suppose the entire truth will come out eventually, but like Mags said, Mr. Kelly deserves the attention, not us. He invented the carnival. We just work there."

Mrs. Weeks' eyebrows shot up. "You still want to work at the carnival?"

"Of course. What else could I do?"

A fierce bout of coughing erupted from the second floor.

Mrs. Weeks winced, rolling her eyes toward the ceiling. "You could help me look after Lizzie. She won't send for a doctor, the stubborn girl."

Katya tried to allay her conscience. "She's well enough to go to work."

"That's true."

"So am I," Maddox sighed with regret.

Mrs. Weeks pattered up the stairs to check on Lizzie, and Katya saw Maddox to the door.

Maddox continued to drop by every day, and every day Katya waited for fresh news on the carnival. She sent letters to the doctors thanking them for their concern and assuring them she already received the best of care. She selected a lawyer with Mrs. Weeks' help, whose indispensible knowledge covered the professional and personal reputation of most of the lawyers who offered their services. Katya's final letter she mailed to the police, supplying a thorough account of the beating orchestrated by Mr. Weis. She gave the police her full cooperation and conducted herself as politely as could be when an officer arrived to verify her statement.

Within a matter of days, the slamming of the front door startled Katya almost out of her skin. Mrs. Weeks tore into the house, calling out while she rasped to catch her breath. "Mr. Warden's gone!"

"What?" Katya raced down the long hallway. She reached Mrs. Weeks' side and read the headline for herself. *William Warden Escapes!*

Mrs. Weeks trailed her thin fingers down the page alongside the words. "Mr. William Warden... escaped from his holding cell last night. He leaves... nothing but mystery in his wake."

Katya snatched the newspaper from her hands as Maddox caught up to her. "Investigations into Mr. Warden's background followed tips provided by his accuser, Mr. Brady Kelly. Police research turned up little information. Police presume Mr. Warden's name is an alias." Katya stopped to catch her own breath. "Why doesn't this surprise me?"

Mrs. Weeks waved a hand at the newspaper. "What else does it say?"

"Mr. Warden's flight does nothing to persuade police of his innocence. Handwriting analysis has proven that Mr. Brady Kelly told the truth. The journal was clearly written by him with certain drawings and schematics marked by Mr. Warden's hand."

"How did he get out?" Mrs. Weeks wondered.

"It says the police are looking into it." Katya did not share her strong intuition that Mr. Warden had not needed to plan a complicated escape complete with accomplices and scaling high walls. He had bought his way out, she felt sure of it.

"Are they looking for him?"

"Of course." Katya scanned more of the article. "The police are going to throw out Mr. Warden's case against Mr. Kelly if he doesn't return."

Maddox spoke up. "Why would he? Just to wave those death threats around?"

"Exactly. Mr. Kelly's going to go free." Katya tried to think of what that might mean.

Mrs. Weeks glanced around the front hall and up the staircase. "Where's Magdalene? I haven't seen her one evening this week."

"She's been all over town, talking to people, mostly the workers. She's been trying to find out what they really think, trying to rally support for Mr. Kelly."

Katya knew what it could mean. Victory, in the greatest sense of the word. Not simply justice against Mr. Warden but the realization of their biggest dream: Brady taking his rightful place as the owner and manager of the Steampunk Carnival.

For several days, the headlines tracked the uncertainty of the carnival's future. Despite Magdalene's best efforts, her name dotted the papers. Reporters cited her continued displays of support for Brady, leading right up to the rumor she would soon speak on his behalf at a carnival shareholders' meeting.

Katya sulked about that. She did not mind appearing in the papers only as a victim of violence and the retriever of the journal from the trash. She wished with all of her aching bones and discolored flesh that she could join Magdalene in front of those grumpy old investors. Katya walked Magdalene to the front porch, where Mr. Davies waited with his carriage to drive her to the meeting.

Katya gave her friend a warm hug. "Best of luck."

Magdalene nodded. Her long days strolling the city and longer nights visiting the carnival's perimeter showed in the shadowing of her face. At Katya's insistence, atop her normal, everyday outfit, Magdalene wore a red hat decorated with steampunk buckles and shining gears. "How do I look?"

"Perfect. They'll remember how magical the carnival is, and they'll want to side with you. I wish I could go. I could convince them."

"Not with your face all yellow and green," Magdalene said, gentle and pitying. "We want them to remember the carnival for what it was, for what Mr. Kelly would make of it. A safe place. A place to enjoy ourselves."

Katya knew this, but it did not stop her from imagining herself flinging the door to the meeting room wide open. She would strut in, dressed from head to toe in her spectacular steampunk garb, and convince them to replace Mr. Warden with Mr. Kelly through a long, impassioned speech.

Magdalene disappeared out the door, and Katya dragged herself back to the unfinished book waiting for her in the living room.

By the time Mrs. Weeks arrived with a copy of the *News* the next evening, Katya knew the story. Magdalene's earnest plea had won over the group of shareholders – half of whom, she informed Katya, were not old curmudgeons but young entrepreneurs. With the shareholders' and most of the employees' approval, Mr. Brady Kelly was named acting manager of the carnival. Over time, with his salary, he could purchase Mr. Warden's share of it and own its majority.

The next afternoon, when the door knocker sounded, Katya expected to hear Maddox's voice greeting Mrs. Weeks. Instead, from her settee in the living room, she heard Brady's much more formal, awkward entreaty.

"Good day, ma'am." There was a pause, and Katya imagined Brady tipping his hat. "My name is Brady Kelly. I work for the..."

"The carnival," Mrs. Weeks finished excitedly.

"Yes, ma'am. I wanted to thank Miss Romanova personally. I wondered if I might speak to her."

Katya set down her magazine and walked the length of the hall to the front door. Brady's thin body looked rattled and worn, but his eyes sparkled. He gripped his hat in his hands.

Mrs. Weeks glanced at Katya. "Mr. Kelly to see you, dear."

Katya nodded. She could not take her eyes off Brady. He was the first person she had seen from the carnival in over a week who was not a friend or a lover. Seeing him made her realize, made her *know* in her bones the fight against Mr. Warden was over. "Please come in, Mr. Kelly."

Brady stepped in past Mrs. Weeks, who shut the heavy door. In a motion Katya did not expect, Brady threw his arms around her back and sobbed. She held onto him, feeling the shake and heave of his chest against her body.

"Thank you," Brady said when he could speak. "Thank you so much. Not just for me. For Sarah and Nathaniel, too. If there were anything I could do to pay you back for what you've done for me, I would do it."

"All I want is my job at the carnival."

"You'll always have it. You know that." Brady stepped back and pulled a handkerchief from his pocket. He wiped his face.

"I know Magdalene will be happy to know you're out of jail."

"She knows, miss. She met me when they released me."

Katya looked down at the bell of her dress, too wide for her to see the toes of her shoes. "I'm glad. I didn't know she met you. I'm not told much these days. I'm just trying to stay out of the way until my face heals."

"Miss Romanova, I hope you won't wait that long. I'm reopening the carnival in a couple of days."

Katya looked up quickly. "You are?"

"Yes, as soon as I can. There are people waiting to go back to work. I'm told a few have quit, so I'll have some positions to fill."

Katya edged toward him, her fingers fidgeting against each other. "Mr. Kelly, I was thinking. I wanted to find a way to help the homeless who sleep in the pews of St. John's Church. I thought some of them might have skills you can use."

Brady smiled, the wrinkled skin constricting around his eyes in gratitude. "Thank you. I'll check there first."

The knocker rapped at the door, and Mrs. Weeks pulled it open.

Stationed on the porch, Maddox lifted his hat. "Good afternoon."

Brady set his own hat back on his head. "I should be going. I'll be in touch about the carnival reopening. The police gave me Warden's keys, so I'll have to find the employee records in his office."

"A lot's going to change, isn't it?" Katya asked, hopeful but knowing the answer.

"All for the better, Miss Romanova."

"Good luck at the carnival."

"Thank you." Brady turned as Maddox stepped into the hallway. "Have a pleasant afternoon." Brady slipped out the door and crossed the porch to the steps.

Mrs. Weeks closed the door. "I can hardly keep track of all your visitors."

Katya beamed at Maddox. She could never help her heart from soaring when he fixed her with so much adoration. "This is the last visitor I expect today, Mrs. Weeks."

"Perhaps it's time I finally visit the carnival. Do you think it'll be running smoothly enough to give me a good experience?"

"I'm sure it will. Whatever you want to do, Mrs. Weeks."

Maddox's eyes roamed Katya's figure from the hem of her dress to the curls of her hair.

Mrs. Weeks started down the stairs, muttering to herself about where she had last left her glasses.

Maddox stepped forward, and Katya met him with a full, lingering kiss. His face was still close to hers when he spoke. "So the carnival's reopening."

"Soon. Very soon. You're staying on under the new management, aren't you?"

"Of course. That's the only way I can see you at night."

Katya laughed and pulled away from Maddox even though she wanted to remain as close as possible. She did not know when Magdalene would come home or when Mary might need to pass through the hall to clean.

"When do I get to hear the rest of the story?" Maddox asked. "The whole story, all the way from the beginning. Not the abridged versions for Mrs. Weeks and the newspapers."

"They've gotten most of it. They're only missing scraps."

"Hasn't the carnival had enough secrets?" Maddox teased her.

Katya reveled in having Maddox near her, both of them safe after so much risk. "Yes, but these are the kinds of things that can't hurt anybody. I'll tell you everything in time."

Chapter Thirty-Eight

If Mr. Warden had stayed in town and managed to win the battle facing him, the carnival reopening would have unfurled much differently. Katya imagined huge, colorful banners on every section of the fence. Mr. Warden would have doubled, if not tripled, the size of the band. He would have searched high and low for the perfect act to host on the side stage. He might have given away some sort of cheap prize or keepsake to every guest as an incentive and celebration.

Brady's reopening, like him, was marked by simplicity, humility, and honesty. He hired several of the city's homeless as security and maintenance. No special banners graced the perimeter, but a newly constructed sign welcomed visitors in place of the original bearing Mr. Warden's name: *Mr. Brady Kelly's Carnival For All Ages.* The other signs hung where Mr. Warden left them.

Brady gave a small speech to his employees before the gates opened. Katya took more interest in watching the expressions of the others than hearing Brady's actual words. They seemed to accept him as their new boss despite how unlike the dashing, charismatic Mr. Warden he conducted himself. Brady's final announcement was a reminder that all children under the age of twelve would be allowed free entrance to the carnival that night. Katya could hardly wait, outfitted in shades of blue from crown to ankle. She felt at home, and when she caught Maddox's approving gaze, she knew she looked the part.

Katya was surprised at first how effortlessly she slipped back into her routine of walking the carnival. She should not have been, she told herself. She had walked it almost every night for over a year. Brady had shown her a few sketches he had drawn in police custody, waiting to be released. They held new ideas for the carnival, new rides and games, new places for new stages.

Katya tried to picture it, Brady's vision for the carnival. It would not be Mr. Warden's ideal layout anymore, with the food stalls and final game tucked in the back, luring customers past all the more frivolous attractions. Brady trusted his guests to know what they wanted and to stay long enough to experience it.

Within a few weeks, by the time Katya's bruises faded from her fair complexion, the carnival returned to its normal, smooth operation. Katya aided guests from one side of the grounds to the other, excitedly informing them what fresh attractions they could look forward to in the coming months. She stopped by the food stall on occasion to talk to Magdalene, especially when her crimson-clad friend was cooking instead of dealing directly with customers. Brady allowed Irina to trade off regularly with Magdalene, and Katya had never seen Irina in a better mood. She carried out her duties as a strict professional, but pure joy tugged at the corners of her thick mouth from time to time.

The crowds packed in so densely, Katya could hardly believe the coincidence of running into anyone she knew. Mrs. Weeks kept her word, showing up with a small entourage of friends. Katya appointed herself their personal guide and gave them a spirited tour of the grounds designed to make them carnival guests for life.

Katya was still congratulating herself on a performance well given when she caught a flash of green amongst the black jackets and yellow dresses. She almost continued on her way before she remembered the woman in ill-fitting clothing who had frequented the carnival so long ago. Katya ducked back through the crowd, trying to find the green again in a sea of blues and purples. She might have given up hope if her curiosity had not been strong enough to drive her all night if need be.

Katya spotted the woman more clearly. She had stopped with her back to Katya, not as certain as she once was about heading to Mr. Warden's office. She hesitated by the corner of the Beast, not far from the game stall where Katya had first approached Brady. He walked the grounds himself now, seeing to guests before attending to the account books. A new man stood in the stall with only one set of rings to hand to customers. Brady had straightened out all the games when he took over.

Katya sidled up to the woman, hoping she was not approaching the wrong guest. This woman had the same shining black hair, the same lackluster bonnet. Katya patted her lightly on the shoulder. "Pardon me. Do you need some help?"

The woman twirled to face Katya. She bounced a baby in her arms, swaddled loosely in pink cotton. Her dark eyes strained wide with confusion. "I'm looking..." She sighed. "No, I'm... I wondered if somebody might know where Mr. Warden ran off to."

"No, I'm sorry. Nobody knows. We don't expect to see him again." Each of Katya's professions made the woman look more lost and disheartened. "Is there anything I can help you with?"

"I... I don't think so." The woman lowered her face to the baby, bouncing her bundle a little faster but just as smoothly.

Katya remembered too well Mr. Warden's impact on her and her life. She wanted to help, and she would not walk away unless she knew there was nothing she could do. The great Beast's metal cars rattled and careened over their heads as Katya reached out and touched the woman's shoulder. "My name is Katya. I was like an assistant to Mr. Warden, or maybe I wished I was. I saw you here a couple of times. I know you were talking to him."

The woman nodded. A thin wetness glimmered in her eyes as she raised them. "My name is Gianna. This is my daughter, Lucretia."

"Mr. Warden's daughter," Katya said. She admonished herself for saying it so bluntly, so sure of herself. She should have asked. She should not have mentioned it at all.

"Yes," Gianna admitted. "I told him she was on the way."

"He didn't believe you?" Katya stroked Lucretia's soft, supple cheek with her fingers.

"He said it could be anyone's. I told him it couldn't."

Katya recalled the calculating flash in Mr. Warden's eyes when she had pulled away and denied him the kiss he tried for. She could only imagine the expressions and coldness Gianna must have met with. "Was he mean to you?"

"A little. Not as cruel as the German."

"Mr. Lieber?" Katya's heart skipped as her mind raced to make connections she never thought she would.

Gianna looked down at her baby. "I think so."

"Were you here on the night he died?" Katya asked, choosing the least accusing of words.

"I was here much earlier," Gianna insisted. Her eyes shot up, wide and sharp with panic and pleading.

"I'm sure you were," Katya assured her.

"I was."

Katya remained determined to tease out the rest of the story. "But Mr. Warden wasn't in his office, was he?"

"No. I didn't see him at all that night, only the German. But this was hours earlier."

"Of course." Katya edged closer to Gianna. "I know what a bastard he was, pardon my French. I'm sure he wasn't pleasant for you to deal with."

Gianna's jaw quivered. "Would you mind holding my baby?"

Katya gathered Lucretia into her arms.

Gianna produced a handkerchief from her threadbare purse and patted it under her watering eyes. "I've never been spoken to like that. I've had things yelled at me. I've heard the rough way men talk to each other, but that man..."

"I'm sorry."

Gianna shook her head. "I was polite. I assumed Mr. Warden was in his office as usual, so I let myself in. When I saw it was just him – Mr. Lieber – I asked him where I could find Mr. Warden. One look at me, and he guessed the whole thing. He told me to go home and find an ignorant cuckold to take care of my child."

Gianna pressed the handkerchief to her mouth and squeezed her eyes shut. She sobbed into the wadded fabric.

Gianna's pain tore at Katya's chest. She held Lucretia against her, safe and loved.

Gianna recovered and dotted her cheeks dry. "So I left," she said hurriedly. "I was very upset, and I left Mr. Warden's office. I left the carnival as quickly as I could. I never came back until tonight."

"Gianna." Katya waited until the woman stopped stuffing the handkerchief into her purse and met her gaze. "I know what you did, and I'm glad. I'm glad, and I'm not the only one."

"Please don't send me to prison." Gianna's fingers pulled at Katya's sleeve through thin gloves.

"I won't tell a soul. You should be paraded up and down Washington Street as a hero if you ask me. Most of us hated him."

"What happened to his wife?" Gianna's fear compounded, tensing deep folds into her features.

"Don't worry about her. She can't feel pain anymore." Katya left a light kiss on Lucretia's wrinkle-free forehead and passed her to Gianna. "Do you have a decent place to stay?"

"We're rooming with my parents for now. It's not much, but it's clean."

"Do you need a job?"

"No. I clean houses over on the east side."

"If you need anything, Gianna, I'm serious. Let me help you. I know how charming Mr. Warden was." Katya wondered at how long she had savored the feeling of his hands on her body. "He was good at many things. You could be standing in a crowd of women, and if he looked at you, you believed you were special."

For the first time, Gianna nodded in relief, the tension releasing from her face. "Yes."

"I do understand. Take care of yourself and Lucretia. Don't be afraid to come to the carnival. I'll be the only one who knows who you are."

"Bless you, Katya." Gianna leaned forward and pecked Katya on both cheeks. She walked away toward the exit with Lucretia held tightly in her arms.

Katya released a long breath. She could see the scene play out, all the details Gianna had not provided. She was a slight woman in messy clothes. She would have stepped into Mr. Warden's office with a hopeful, hopeless expression that Mr. Lieber would have pounced on.

"What do you want?" he would have demanded. Katya could not decide if his tone would have been condescending or humored by Gianna's appearance.

"I'm here to see Mr. Warden," Gianna would have answered. Mr. Lieber's piercing gaze would have made her shift her limbs uncomfortably in the baggy sleeves and oversized skirts. "Do you know where I might find him?"

Mr. Lieber looked Gianna over, seeing from his angle what Katya never could from the back and through the thick crowds. Gianna attempted to hide her extending belly under unnecessary drapes of fabric. "Go home," he sneered, enjoying the opportunity to turn away one of Mr. Warden's many affairs. "Find yourself a cuckold willing to raise that little brat."

Gianna, whether more words were spoken or not, let her temper rule out over fleeing the office in broken tears. She grabbed Mr. Warden's letter opener – Katya saw it as a recently sharpened blade, perhaps with a fancy sterling silver or inlaid pearl handle – and without thinking, speared it into Mr. Lieber's neck. He never would have expected it. He would not be laughing now, realizing that the ripping pain and spurting blood were going to leave him dead on Mr. Warden's hand-chosen carpet. Gianna must have been horrified at herself. How long had she stayed? Did she reach her hands out to try to help, or did she turn and run?

No, Gianna would not have run. She would not have called that kind of attention to herself. She might have noticed she had blood splattered on her jacket and taken it off as she left the office. She would have made herself walk across the entire depth of the carnival grounds to the gate, her jacket folded neatly over her forearm. She would have gone home, washed the jacket or burned it. By that time, Katya was walking innocently into Mr. Warden's office and finding the police there.

Someone tapped Katya's arm, and she jumped. Brady stood beside her, his confidence wavering under the brim of his new black top hat.

"Are you all right?" he asked.

Katya rushed to reassure him. "Yes. I was just helping someone, and she's been taken care of. I was thinking of where I should go next."

"You can always try the entrance, but then again, you've worked here longer than I have. I won't tell you how to do your job."

"Can I tell you something, Mr. Kelly?"

Brady raised his eyebrows.

"I'd rather work for you than anyone else in the country."

Brady suppressed a smile. "I haven't been in charge long. I haven't made many alterations yet. You might change your mind."

"I don't think I will. For the first time since I started this job, I trust the person I work for."

Chapter Thirty-Nine

The brim of Katya's hat bumped the outside back wall of the maintenance building where she leaned her body. Maddox's lips pressed against hers, his hands flat across her lower back, pulling her hips closer. The chugging and whirring of engines and machines reverberated around them, never letting them forget they were stealing a moment from their jobs at the carnival.

Katya kissed him harder, knowing they could not spend much more time there. She laughed at herself as she pulled away. "It's only a few hours," she sighed.

Maddox had moved into a boarding house two streets away from the Weekly Boarder, the convenience only fueling their need to spend time together. If any of Katya's housemates noticed her slipping out in the early morning and back to her room before Mrs. Weeks served breakfast, no one mentioned it.

Maddox collected his hat from where he had laid it atop the grass. He brushed off the underside of the brim. "Only a few unending, insufferable hours." He grinned and placed the hat on his head.

"It's not insufferable. It's a good thing we work together and not on opposite sides of the city." Katya adjusted the position of her hat.

"Do you think that would keep me from seeing you? I've traveled half the country. What's a few miles between us?"

"Then you won't mind moving back across town," Katya teased, pretending to preoccupy herself with brushing lint off the sleeve of her jacket. She was glad her elbow had healed well enough to achieve this without discomfort or her sling. "You live too close. It's too much of a distraction."

Maddox grabbed her waist and tugged her up against him. "Some day I'll ask you to marry me, and we'll buy a house together. I'll never let you out of my sight. How's that for a distraction?"

Katya bit her lip, tempering her smile to make sure Maddox did not know how much she wanted that. "I look forward to hearing your proposal, Mr. O'Sullivan. I'll have to consider my answer very carefully."

"You won't think. You'll just say yes."

"You're very sure of yourself, aren't you?"

"Aye. That's what you like about me."

Katya kissed him lightly and strolled to the corner of the building.

Maddox called to her. "Miss Romanova."

Katya turned to him, striking a pose with her perfect posture.

"I like your new dress."

"Thank you, sir."

Katya wove herself into the crowd, ecstatic with the latest tailored and embroidered outfit she had put together. Part of it was Mary's doing, luring Katya to the seamstress' shop under the pretense of shopping together. The back of the luxurious velvet jacket had already been outfitted with gears and a working clock just as Katya envisioned. Mary stayed to watch Katya try the jacket on while Katya explained at length how puffy she wanted the shoulders of the sleeves constructed.

Lizzie had already been too ill to continue working in the shop. She divided her time between her bedroom and the backyard, either confining herself or sucking down copious amounts of outdoor air. Neither one helped, and the entire house erupted in a frenzy when Mrs. Weeks found Lizzie dead in her bed. The household showed up dutifully at the funeral her parents held, standing in a depressing black row in the clinging cemetery mist. Mary did not speak to Katya about it for several days afterward until she let herself into Katya's room one afternoon, so guilt stricken she could barely speak.

"It was no one's fault but her own," Katya said, hiding her guilt behind strict objectivity.

Mary grabbed Katya's arms, tears shining in streaks down her face. "I killed her, Katya. You know I did."

"Look on the bright side, Mary. Lizzie dyed her hair dark again before she gave up the ghost."

Mary tossed Katya's arms down, not completely missing the humor. "Be serious, Katya."

"Then go to the hospital so you don't kill the rest of us."

"Do you have an alibi for me?"

"Yes. I have the best one now, don't I?"

Within the week, Katya convinced Mrs. Weeks to plan a vacation. "See the east coast, Mrs. Weeks," Katya persuaded. "See the ocean. You've had far too much stress lately."

"What about Mary?" Mrs. Weeks protested.

"Don't you worry about Mary. I'll send her on vacation, too."

The day Mrs. Weeks boarded the train for Rhode Island, Mary, as President Cleveland once had, set off from Indianapolis for Terre Haute. She wrote to Katya often from her private room at St. Anthony's, and Katya hid every letter from Mary in the bottom of a drawer in her room.

Another letter, hidden in the sleeve of her glove, scratched Katya's arm. This one had come for her at the carnival from a person who, as usual, surprised and did not surprise her with his actions.

My dearest Katya, it began in generous, swooping letters as if he were not on the run from the law.

I wish you were here. The Idaho Territory has a sparse sprawl of civilization across it but tons of opportunities for a trained eye such as mine. Katya doubted he would be smart enough to stay in the territory now that he had mentioned it in writing. She expected him to reach Canada by the end of the month.

I hope you are healing well. I suspect that had certain plans played out differently than they did, things would've ended much differently for the two of us.

In a grand sign-off across the bottom, he had written, *Yours always, William Warden.*

More than the assumed name in his signature, the last full sentence haunted Katya's memory. *Yes*, she thought. If he were still a pillar of the community and a sought-after entrepreneur, he might have reeled her in even farther than he did. She imagined she might have gone so far as to marry Mr. Warden if he asked her. Given the way he played Isolde Neumann, he would have entertained a new mistress every week while Katya struggled to keep up the house. She was glad for many reasons things had not worked out any differently at all. She was happier with Maddox than any older, established man could have made her, including the talented Mr. Warden.

Katya stopped in her tracks, grabbed by an unexpected image. Isolde Neumann, the gilded peacock, glided past her in another elaborate three-story hat. One hand held a parasol over her shoulder, and her other hand rested around the arm of a man Katya did not recognize. So even Isolde could get over the mysterious Mr. Warden without batting an eye. The man's suit was perfectly pressed and clean, likely a lawyer or restaurateur. Katya was glad she did not look like a money grubber anymore, seeking out men much better off than herself to take care of her. Katya wondered, as Isolde's green velvet dress disappeared into the crowd, if Mr. Warden had sent her a letter as well. She doubted it. Mr. Warden might have been interested in Isolde's fortune, but he had demonstrated his interest in Katya time and time again. They remained tightly tangled in each other's lives. He could disappear into the western wilderness without notifying Isolde of his thoughts, but he could not flee incarceration without one last communiqué to the woman who brought him down.

A lot had happened since Mr. Warden's flight. Katya testified against Mr. Weis and the other security men. Her face might have healed, but photographs and a dozen testimonies made the men look worse than scoundrels in public opinion. Magdalene remained reluctant to testify, afraid the defense would insist she was too close of a friend to Katya to tell the absolute truth.

Katya's lawyer persisted, especially interested in Magdalene's account of seeing the security guards leave Mr. Warden's office. He included a few character witnesses for Magdalene as insurance, including Irina, who won over the courtroom with her blunt observations.

"I don't like many people," Irina famously said, quoted verbatim in all the papers. "But I've always liked Miss Harvey. She's a decent woman. She wouldn't lie."

It had given Katya little pleasure to point out Mr. Weis and the two men who had laid hands on her sitting in the courtroom. She felt a lot better once they were found guilty and almost vindicated when she read about their sentencing to jail.

"It seems like too short of a sentence," Mrs. Weeks said, shaking her head at the *News*.

Katya was just relieved she had proven her point and the men had been sent where they could not touch her in the near future. "It's all right, Mrs. Weeks."

"What if they want revenge? What if they come after you when they get out?"

Katya considered it, but she thought it unlikely. They would probably find a hard time getting a job in the city when they left jail, and Katya hoped they would join the gold rushes out west. She braved a smile for Mrs. Weeks. "With Mr. Warden gone? I doubt they'll try anything. They couldn't get to me, anyway. I'm usually surrounded by people."

Mrs. Weeks accepted Katya's logic with a series of slow nods. "I'll have someone put an extra lock on the back door, though, just in case."

Katya broke free of her heavy memories and caught someone waving to her. It took her a few moments to recognize Mary. She looked resplendent in a new white silk jacket, white satin gloves emerging from the sleeves. Katya greeted Mary with a squeeze. "You look wonderful. How do you feel?"

"Much better." Mary's blue eyes outshone her jacket for health and gratitude. "Thank you again. When's my mother coming home?"

"Soon. She's having a marvelous time. I'll have to show you the postcards she's been sending to the house. The views and the inns she's staying at are stunning."

Mary gestured to something behind Katya. "The carnival's expanding, I see."

"Yes." Katya turned. The once-perfect rectangle of the fence had been added to in the southwestern corner. "A horse-riding attraction is going in behind the Kaleidoscope." Katya pictured Mr. Davies, a few years older than she was looking for but closer to Mary's age. He was single, kind, and direct, much like Mary.

"I've never ridden a horse," Mary said, enthralled with the idea.

"Our carriage driver thought of it, Mr. Davies. Have you met Mr. Davies?"

"No."

"He's a pleasant man. I think you'd like him."

"Katya." Mary sighed. "I got out of the hospital yesterday."

"And you never looked better."

A young man walked up to Katya, his young wife on his arm. "Excuse me, miss. Do you have any more of those colored maps?"

Katya gradually remembered she had been on her way to Brady's office to pick more up when she ran into Maddox outside the maintenance office. "No, I'm sorry. I'll bring more out soon."

"That's all right. Can you point me to the Wheel of Independence?"

Katya pointed toward the band stage and the Beast's winding track. "It's at the very back of the grounds, sir. You can't miss it."

"Thank you." He led his wife away, their eyes taking in everything around them.

"I should go take care of that." Katya patted Mary's arm. "It's good to see you. You'll stay at the carnival for a while, won't you?"

Mary nodded. "Of course."

"I won't introduce you to Mr. Davies if you don't want," Katya said. She was already imagining leading Mary around the carnival while they talked, walking her close by where Mr. Davies oversaw the layout of the horse ride. She could call it a happy accident all night, and Mary would see right through it. It did not matter to Katya so long as she introduced them before Mr. Davies found a girlfriend on his own. "I'll talk to you later."

Katya walked past the band, which Brady had added two musicians to in the past month. She passed the side stage, where several people were giving cooking demonstrations on small gas burners. She reached the food stall and offered Magdalene a wave. Magdalene took the time to return it before accepting coins from a customer and passing down a bag of popcorn.

Katya was not sure how to repay Magdalene for all of her help and support. She knew it was the kind of thing a friend should simply accept with a genuine thank you and move on from, but Katya knew that nothing would have turned out right without Magdalene's sly eye and silver tongue.

Katya approached Brady's office and let herself in. She did not feel any of the rush or anxiety she had experienced when it was Mr. Warden's office. It felt homey and comfortable, like visiting a friend. Brady had even moved Mr. Warden's desk to the center of the far room where he could see and be seen as people entered.

Brady set his pen down on the record book and flexed his fingers. "What can I do for you, Miss Romanova?"

"I need more of those maps." Katya strolled up to his desk and joined him on the other side of it. "The guests really like them. I always thought they would."

Brady opened the bottom drawer and handed Katya a stack of a few dozen maps. The name *Steampunk Carnival* was printed in sturdy black letters over a curling gold banner at the top.

"We'll need new ones when the additions are opened," Brady said.

"And these will become collectibles."

Brady picked up his pen but hesitated to jump back into the facts and figures filling the columns in his book. Katya lingered over the framed photographs he kept on his desk, one of Sarah and one of Nathaniel. He had never shown them to her, but she knew who they were. Sarah stood humbly with her hands on the back of a chair, dark hair uncovered and wedding band encircling her thin finger. Nathaniel's picture had likely been taken after his death. He rested in a bed with a far-off look in his eyes. It was a fine family any man would have been proud of, but Katya did not say it. She kissed Brady gently on the cheek.

"It's going very well tonight, Mr. Kelly," she told him.

"Good."

"It should go well every night. Except for the night none of us want to mention, it was always like that. A success."

"Thank you for making it so."

Katya laughed as she stepped into the front room. She wanted to tell Brady he was wrong, that the carnival sold itself. It invited the guests, not her or anybody else. But maybe he was right and Katya did add to the magic of it, its untouchable mystery. Katya reached the outer door and opened it. Thinking of nothing else to say, she stepped out into the night and pulled the door shut behind her.

About the Author

Cassandra Leuthold's hilarious fantasy adventure, *The Corundum Conundrum,* won recognition as a New Apple Book Awards official selection. Writing hooked her at age seven, and she never really stopped.

She loves playing with ideas most people think of as opposites: the magical and the everyday, the modern and the vintage, the darkest nights and brightest lights. Even while delving into fictional worlds, she remains a tea aficionado, DIY crafter, and unapologetic music junkie.

Cassandra stretches out in front of the TV with her writer husband and their cats. She wields a Bachelor's in Liberal Studies and a Master's in English.

Find freebies and more book fun at her website, cassandraleuthold.com.